William's Angel

BY THE SAME AUTHOR

Martyrs of Science
The Angel Asrael

William's Angel
and Other Stories

by
S. Henry Berthoud

Translated, annotated and introduced by
Brian Stableford

A Black Coat Press Book

Visit our website at www.blackcoatpress.com

ISBN 978-1-61227-875-9. First Printing: July 2019. Published by Black Coat Press, an imprint of Hollywood Comics.com, LLC, P.O. Box 17270, Encino, CA 91416. All rights reserved. Except for review purposes, no part of this book may be reproduced or transmitted in any form or by any means, electronic or mechanical, including photocopying, recording, or by any information storage and retrieval system, without permission in writing from the publisher. The stories and characters depicted in this novel are entirely fictional. Printed in the United States of America.

TABLE OF CONTENTS

Introduction

"L'Ange de Williams" by S. Henry Berthoud, here translated as "William's Angel," was originally published in the *Musée des Familles*, of which the author was then the editor, in September 1838. The other stories supplementing it all appeared in *Chroniques et traditions surnaturelles de la Flandre: deuxième série*, published in Paris by Werdet in 1834, although the portmanteau entitled "Les Sept damoiselles de Béthencourt" had previously been serialized in three issues of Émile Girdardin's pioneering fashion magazine *La Mode* in 1830.

A previous Black Coat Press collection of Berthoud's early works, *The Angel Asrael and Other Legendary Tales*,[1] similarly supplemented a novella featuring characters named Asrael and Astaroth, first published independently as *Asrael et Nephta* (1832), with a series of stories, in that case drawn from *Chroniques et traditions surnaturelles de la Flandre* (1831), the collection to which the volume containing the supplementary stories translated herein was represented as a continuation. Perhaps confusingly, the cherub Asrael featured in "L'Ange de Williams" is not the same character as the repentant fallen angel of the same name featured in the earlier novella, and the stories featured in the second series of the *Chroniques et traditions surnaturelles de la Flandre* only contain two items that reproduce the quasi-folkloristic form of the majority of the items in the first

[1] ISBN 978-1-61227-613-7.

series. In fact, the work contained in that "second series" can far more readily be seen as picking up were another short story collection published in 1831, *Contes misanthropiques* (tr. as *Misanthropic Tales*; samples included in the Black Coat Press collection *Martyrs of Science and Other Victims of Devilry and Destiny* [2]), had left off—and the story series published in 1830 must, in fact, have been written immediately after, if not alongside, the stories in that collection.

The brief biography of the author included in the 1842 bibliography of *La Littérature Française Contemporaine*, edited by J.-M. Quérard, records that he was the son of a printer, born in Cambrai on 19 January 1804 and that, in 1817, he received a bursary to enter the Royal College of Douai, which he left in August 1822. He subsequently became the literary editor of a local periodical, the *Journal de l'arrondissement de Cambrai*, and, in 1828, founded *La Gazette de Cambrai*, in which he published much of his early short fiction, some of which was pirated by Parisian and other provincial periodicals, and even by periodicals in England, America and Germany. That experience led to his recruitment by the pioneering Parisian journalist Émile Girardin, who employed him on the editorial staff of *La Mode* and *La Presse*, and he also worked for *La Revue des Deux Mondes* and *La Revue de Paris*—then the two central organs of the burgeoning Romantic Movement—as well as *La Silhouette* and *L'Artiste*, before he was entrusted by Girardin, first with the sole editorship of the revamped *Mercure de France*, and then with that of the pioneering "family magazine," *Le Musée des Familles*.

---

[2] ISBN 978-1-61227-229-0.

The 1842 biography makes no mention of Berthoud ever having attended university or having lived in Paris prior to relocating there permanently in the early 1830s, but there can be no doubt that his friendship with Honoré de Balzac was initially formed some years before then, and it is probable that he spent some time as a student in Paris during the early 1820s, which he later erased from his biography because he failed to take a degree. In the late 1820s, however, he became an important person in Cambrai, working in local government, primarily in public education—he organized free courses in hygiene, anatomy, geometry, literature and the arts—and subsequently as the administrator of the local hospitals during the great cholera epidemic of 1830-31, during which, according to the biographer, the public health precautions he introduced allowed the epidemic to be attenuated more effectively in Cambrai than in any other city in France.

Berthoud was still in Cambrai—and the cholera epidemic was still raging—when he wrote the stories collected in *Contes misanthropiques* and "Les Sept damoiselles de Béthencourt," as well as *Asrael et Nephta*. The stories making up the portmanteau must have been submitted to *La Mode* from Cambrai, but the author was obviously in communication with Girardin before then, because he published a poem by the latter's wife, Delphine Girardin—the former Delphine Gay—in one of the publications he supervised in Cambrai, and might well have met her in the early 1820s. When he relocated permanently to in Paris in 1832, in the hope of making a living with his pen, Girardin became his employer, and remained his principal source of income for the next five years.

As an editor, Berthoud became one of the lynch-pins of the French Romantic Movement, and he did a great deal to stimulate its prose component, especially the imaginative fraction of that component.

In addition to *Asrael et Nepthta*, he published another book-length work of fiction in 1832, *La Soeur de lait du vicaire* [The Curate's Foster-Sister], of which the commentary in the 1842 bibliography—presumably written by Berthoud himself—observes that: "This novel was initially entitled *Bah!* By that title, the author said, he wanted to express the derisory insouciance with which the passions and their consequences are envisaged today. The author's friends assembled extraordinarily and, it appears, found *Bah!* too pretentious and too affected a title." If that is really what happened, one can hardly blame his friends for thinking that, but it is significant that Berthoud's initial impulse was so aggressively contemptuous, and it reflects the general bitterness of his attitude at that time.

Contes misanthropiques was the first collection to consist entirely of what later came to be known as *contes cruels*, and its contents certainly rage against "the derisory insouciance with which the passions and their consequences are envisaged," but the continuations of the series included in the present collection takes that rage to a further extreme, not only in many of the flamboyant inclusions in the portmanteau from *La Mode*, but also in the story that precedes them in the *Chroniques*, "Pile ou face" (tr. as "Heads or Tails"), and most of all in the remarkable novella "Le Nez rouge (tr. as "The Red Nose"), which must have been written shortly thereafter, while he was still in an extremely acerbic state of mind.

The 1842 biography, as might be expected, has little to say about the intimate details of Berthoud's early life, but it concludes with the observation that: "In addition to a certain talent that distinguishes him as a man of letters, Monsieur Berthoud possesses special qualities that render his relations precious and which have acquired him numerous friends, among whom one remarks Madame Desbordes-Valmore, whose disciple he is. Endowed with a meditative mind and a great tact as an observer, he is particularly attached to the study of the human heart, and he has obtained a noble profit from that science."

The reference to the Douai-born poet and actress Marceline Desbordes-Valmore (1786-1859), whom Berthoud presumably first encountered when he was at school in Douai, is significant in identifying the esthetic and philosophical position Berthoud took up in affiliating himself to the Romantic Movement, and it might have been her who recommended him to Émile Girardin and secured him the editorial work on which his long-term financial stability was built.

After her father, an armorial painter, was ruined by the Revolution, Marceline Desbordes had been taken by her mother to Guadeloupe, but when her mother died of yellow fever, she returned to France, still in her teens, and began a career as an actress in Douai. After a passionate liaison with the writer Henri de Latouche in 1810-12, she married her second husband, the actor Prosper Lanchantin-Valmore, in 1817, and published the first of six volumes of elegiac poetry in 1819 before retiring from the stage in 1823; her poetry became increasingly lachrymose as all her children died, one by one.

Greatly admired by Charles-Augustin Sainte-Beuve and Charles Baudelaire, Marceline Desbordes-Valmore was the only female writer included in Paul Verlaine's famous study of *Les Poètes maudits* (1884), and Lucien Descaves wrote the most exhaustive of several memoirs of her life, *La Vie douloureuse de Marceline Desbordes-Valmore* (1910). Along with Sophie Gay and her daughter Delphine, she was one of the women who played key roles at the heart of the French Romantic Movement, underestimated by history, and the fact that Berthoud knew her well before going to Paris had a considerable influence on his attitude to his work, and to life. Although his principal case-study in his philosophical analysis of the works of the human heart was his own, hers must have been the second, and much of his early fiction undoubtedly owes a good deal to his first and most dominant muse.

It is difficult, in reading Berthoud's early work, and especially the supplementary work featured in the present collection, to avoid drawing the inference that he had suffered a deep and injurious amorous disappointment, the impact of which was permanent. Exactly what that disappointment was, we cannot know, but the depth of feeling contained in "La Batelière" (tr. as "The Boatwoman"), "La Veuve" (tr. as "The Widow"), and "Le Nez rouge," certainly suggests that a woman that he loved dearly and lost might have deserted him for a soldier.

Equally significant, however, is the fact that, in Berthoud's more intensely lachrymose stories, the focal point is not the suffering of the male characters, however intense it might be, but that of the female characters, the invariably mortal victims of masculine/diabolical chicanery. That compassionate empathy, remarkable even in a writer of the Romantic school, where pride in compassion and empathy was by no means uncommon, probably owes something to his relationship with Marceline Desbordes, but it might also be worth noting that in a strange autobiographical digression in "Le Nez rouge," Berthoud reveals that he had a sister of whom he was very fond, and of whose fate history seem to have no mention.

As well as impelling him to become an important pioneer of the *conte cruel*, the impetus of Berthoud's empathic intensity led him to become one of the first writers to experiment with that would later be called "stream-of-consciousness" narration. His experiments are awkward, because they mostly consist of brief lapses, and the abrupt transitions to and from past tense to present tense and to and from a relatively distant third-person narrative voice to an extremely intimate tracking of internal monologue, seem a trifle bizarre, but they are nevertheless bold technical explorations with few, if any, literary precedents. Perhaps "Le Front sanglant" (tr. as "The Bloody Forehead") and "Le Nez rouge"—the stories in which such transitions are most flagrant—are not entirely successful, and they are certainly very odd, but the latter, in particular, is certainly not ineffective in its use of the device, and in employing it to capture something of the depth of feeling that the author was investing in his work at that time.

Whatever the source of Berthoud's psychological trauma was, its effects were long-lasting. He never married, and a biographical sketch of the author published in a newspaper in the early 1860s found him living alone in Paris, save for his dog Maître Flock and a pet lemur called Mademoiselle Mine. That disillusionment, as the note in the 1842 bibliography observes, was not merely personal, but colored his view of everything that was happening around him, having already encouraged him before writing *Bah!* to call his second story collection—without his friends intervening—*Contes misanthropiques* (although, in fact, he was not misanthropic at all, and his misandry only became intense occasionally.) It must be observed, however, that once he was settled in Paris, he got past that quasi-nihilistic phase in his writing, and contrived to import more iron into his soul. He did not find amour there, but he did find solace, as well as distraction in hard, perhaps obsessive, creative labor, and although he never achieved the *succès d'estime* that he would dearly have liked, he did manage to remain active for more than half a century—he was still working not long before his death on 26 March 1891—and to avoid poverty through some very difficult economic and political times.

Although Berthoud soon abandoned, or at least greatly modified, the love of reckless fantasy that was conspicuous in many of his early works, and is still evident here in such conspicuously Gothic horror stories as "La Nuit des noces" (tr. as "The Wedding Night") and "Le Chapelain" (tr. as "The Chaplain"), in order to concentrate on the disenchanted naturalism first exhibited to the full in the *Contes misanthropiques* and subsequently featured in almost all of his novels, it is highly probably that that development of his work was impelled by market forces. The Devil never entirely disappeared from his work, and kept cropping up occasionally, rarely but insistently, even in the 1860s, when almost all of his work was aimed at a juvenile audience and very carefully sanitized.

There are good grounds for considering *Asrael et Nephta* to be the most personal of his novels, precisely because it is the purest of his fantasies—the one that looks back at the perverse and unsatisfactory operations of the human heart from the remotest hypothetical standpoint—and it is significant that not only does the Devil plays a vital but tacit role in the deeply-felt "Le

Nez rouge," but that, in 1838, when *Le Musée des Familles* was taken out of Émile Girdardin's hands by his shareholders, and Berthoud must have known that his dismissal as its editor was imminent, he deliberately added a garish diabolical subplot to one of the last of the many long *études historiques* that he produced or that magazine, in order to make up the curious hybrid narrative "L'Ange de Williams." That story, too, is very odd, and some critics might regard it as unsuccessful, but it is certainly not lacking in enterprise or emotion. It is by no means one of the most refined products of French Romanticism, but it is certainly one of the most unrepentantly Romantic.

Berthoud was, in some ways, an atypical member of the Movement, determinedly apolitical while many of his compatriots were fervently republican, and resolutely devout while most of them were atheists; in terms of the core philosophy of the Movement, however, he was steadfast, and the passage in "Le Nez rouge" in which he summarizes the nature and effects of "the Romantic disposition" is as accurate as it is succinct. He certainly had no illusions about the value of a Romantic disposition in winning social success in a materialistic and egotistical society, but he felt as intensely as anyone the tragedy of that inutility, and he only wavered briefly in his conviction that a successful defiance the Devil is not impossible, even for the seemingly damned, and that no matter what existential problems a Romantically-disposed human being might face in world of ever-present hypocritical diabolism, the beleaguered spirit of Asrael can never be entirely defeated.

The translation of "L'Ange de Williams" was made from the 1837-38 volume of *Le Musée des Familles* reproduced on the Bibliothèque Nationale's *gallica* website, and the translations of the stories from *Chroniques et traditions surnaturelles de la Flandre: deuxième série*, from the copy of the 1834 edition reproduced on the same website.

Brian Stableford

WILLIAM'S ANGEL

Chapter One
William Longbeard

As soon as he had arrived in England and taken possession of his throne again, having been held prisoner for two years by the Emperor of Germany, King Richard the Lionheart occupied himself solely with the project of taking his revenge. It was Philippe, King of France, whose calumnies, intrigues and fraudulent machinations had not only prolonged that captivity but also troubled, by all possible means, the peace of England, that he resolved to punish first.

He therefore departed for Normandy, took away the command of that province from his brother John, and did not take long to find himself, with considerable forces, in the presence of his enemy, the king, who was advancing at the head of his troops. It was in the Saintonge, near Niort, that that encounter took place. During the night, the two armies camped facing one another, only separated by a small river, and at daybreak the following day, each prepared its arms for combat.

The cavalry were already mounting up and the infantrymen were searching for places to ford the river, when suddenly, to the great surprise of the men-at-arms, a religious hymn was heard rising up between the two camps, and a numerous procession of bishops, priests and monks of different orders were seen arriving.

They stopped on the river bank and, after erecting an altar of turf, on which they placed the Holy Sacrament, they all knelt down and began chanting psalms. After those public prayers, the bishops of Troyes and Niort gave their blessing to the soldiers, and the former went to the tent of the King of France, while the latter to the King of England, in order to beg them to defer a combat that would desolate the region and cause the death of so many brave men. They aided those supplications by proposing several arrangements that might terminate the war.

Richard welcomed these supplications and consented to make a few concessions, but Philippe remained firm and inflexible.

"I shall not quit the sword," he said, "until I have received the oath of vassalage from King Richard for the provinces of Normandy, Guyenne and Poitou, which belong to me."

He spoke thus because he believed that he had attracted the Danes to his party, by means of promises of gold, who had sworn not to commit their own troops to the encounter. But when, as they were about to come to get to grips, he saw that hope disappointed, and the Champenois putting helmets on their heads in order to march to battle, his rudeness and inflexibility were changed to fear. He had the Bishop of Niort recalled and sent him to Richard to tell him that he declared that prince acquitted of all vassalage and that he wanted to sign a peace treaty.

When the prelate and his retinue met the English monarch, the latter, with is helmet on his head and his sword in his hand, had just crossed the little river that separated the two camps, and without paying any heed to the bishop, who advanced to speak to him, he turned to his archers and gave them the order to unleash the first arrows. The prelate ran to the altar, seized the Holy Sacrament and came back to place himself in front of the king, whose passage he barred.

"In the name of the blood of Christ, shed for us on the cross," he cried, "in the name of the salvation of our soul, go no further and take pity on our tears and our anguish. The King of France declares that he had renounced any pretention to the vassalage of your provinces, and he will retire this very day to the territory of his realm."

Richard directed a bellicose gaze at his army, and full of confidence and pride, he spurred his horse to urge it forward, forgetting in his warrior ardor that the bishop was before him. The old prelate, knocked over by the charger, fell heavily to the ground, and the holy pyx that he was holding slipped from his hands and went to break against the trunk of a tree. At the sight of the sacred host lying in the mud of the river, and in the presence of the unconscious old man, Richard wanted to advance nevertheless, but the bishop got up, his face bloodied and his garments soiled with blood, and cried: "Peace, Sire, peace, in the name of Christ!"

"Peace! Peace!" repeated all the priests and monks.

A flash of rage shone in the king's hawk-like eye.

"Forward!" he cried. "Forward, men-at-arms!"

"Forward!" replied the army.

"In order to advance, then, you will trample under the feet of your horses an old ma and the body of the living God!" said the bishop, pointing at the host.

"Forward!"

But this time, to that cry of the king another clamor responded, for everyone recoiled before such a great profanation. The bishop, the priests and the monks took advantage of that hesitation to repeat: "Peace, Sire! Peace, Sire!"

The king darted a gaze of indignation and scorn at his soldiers.

"Since the men-at-arms think like the priests, since they're afraid of denting their breastplates and spoiling their helmets, so be it, peace. Let King Philippe come to find me and let the conditions of the treaty be regulated immediately."

A few moments later the King of France arrived, only followed by a few men-at-arms. He gave them a sign to stop at the entrance to the camp. Then, after dismounting, he went straight to Richard's tent, and before the latter had had time to advance to met him he said, with a grace and courtesy full of charm: "Richard, I have come to you alone, not as a king but as a brother, as befits a Christian prince who renounces any intention of war and no longer has any but one desire, that of meriting your amity."

The anger and resentment of the King of England could not resist those gilded words; they sufficed for him to forget King Philippe's treason; too honest to doubt the honesty of another, passed his arm under the arm of the King of France, and it was thus that they emerged from the tent and showed themselves to the two armies.

At that sight, cries of joy rose up from all sides, and the Bishop of Niort intoned the *Te Deum*, which the priests repeated in chorus. The two kings knelt down; everyone followed their example, and all the men who had been previously disposed to fight one another united their voices in the same prayer.

Soon, the two camps only formed one. As the majority of the knights that served under each of the princes already knew one another, they came together in order to celebrated the peace with feasting, and the next day, at dawn, as a chronicler of the times says, each of them "departed for his domains, and no longer thought about anything but hunting and the pleasures of a peaceful life."

The King of England and the King of France, with their retinues and a small number of lords, whom they summoned to accompany them, went to Niort in order to finish agreeing the terms there of the ten-year truce that they had resolved, and to make up a few hunting parties, for Philippe was justly reputed to be one of the greatest experts in venery of the day, and Richard, jealous of that renown, wanted to prove to him that he possessed a knowledge no less great of the noble science of Saint Hubert. Thus, they ran after red deer, forced wild boar and put to death more than one bear and wolf, to the great satisfaction of the King of England, to whom the wily King of France left all the honors of the hunt, more desirous of obtaining advantageous conditions of peace that directing the dogs and giving the first thrust of the dagger to the beast.

It resulted from those clever concessions that Richard took his brother of France in great amity, an amity from which he profited in consummate diplomacy to file the claws of the lion somewhat. Moreover, they never quit one another, dining at the same table, lying in the same bed and not giving any truce to joyful speech.

One morning, Richard was sounding the horn in the courtyard of the Episcopal Palace, where the two kings were lodged, greatly amused by the feigned difficulty with which Philippe imitated his fanfares, when a man of tall stature who wore a long beard, contrary to the fashion of the time, entered the royal abode, went straight to the English monarch and knelt before him.

"Sire," he said, "I have come to request peace and protection for the poor people of London."

"And since when have my people in London lacked peace and protection?" demanded Richard, whose discontentment was visible.

"Since you are no longer there, Sire, to protect them against the prevarications of the aldermen charged with collecting and distributing the taxes. They exempt from any contribution those in the best condition to pay and overwhelm the artisan who only lives on the work of his hands, and they have just decided, in order to put the cap on their pillage, that every townsman should pay the same sum regardless of the difference in fortunes. In sum, they always act in such a way that he heaviest charge falls upon the poor folk. That is why, Sire, I have quit my wife and mother and have come to lay at your feet the plaints of our faithful friends and subjects, sure that you will have compassion for them."

"Yes, by the salvation of my soul, it will be as you say, worthy man. I do not want my people to suffer and be pressured by pillagers who are thinking of filling their own coffers rather than mine. But who are you, to have undertaken such a long journey without fear of the perils to which such a courageous enterprise might have exposed you?"

"My name is William, called Longbeard.[3] I'm a Saxon. I owe to my labor a petty fortune that I acquired

---

[3] This character is based on William FitzOsbert, who led a popular uprising by the citizens of London in the spring of 1196, an account of which is contained in *Historia rerum anglicum* by William of Newburgh. Allegedly, he did visit Normandy in order to inform the King that he was not rebel-

in commerce by the sweat of my brow, and, having retired from business, I utilize my time in studying the laws of England and defending, when necessary, the rights of poor people."

"Well, William, you are a loyal and courageous subject. Depart again for London, and you will scarcely have returned than you will see that I have not forgotten the complaints that you have just laid at my feet. Go, and may God go with you."

"Here is a parchment, Sire, in which are set out all the grievances that the townsmen have against the aldermen."

"I swear by my holy patron that there will be good and prompt justice in this matter."

"May Heaven bless you Sire, as the entire city of London will bless you when I inform it of your loyal and paternal words."

"And to prove those words, you will be able to show my good city of London this gift of our munificence, which I grant you as a reward for your noble and courageous enterprise."

So saying, the king detached from his neck a rich gold chain engraved with his armories, and threw it over William's shoulders. William, moved to tears, immediately returned to the sea port, where the vessel that had brought him from England was waiting for him.

---

ling against him, but the details of their encounter given here are imaginary.

Chapter Two
The Gratitude of the People

Sometime after that, three men were walking on the sea shore, in a location appropriate for the secret disembarkation of a small ship, and seemed to be waiting anxiously.

"A month has gone by since his departure," one of them said, "and William Longbeard has not yet returned."

"Adam Bel," replied a man in the prime of life, who was holding a crossbow and was followed by two enormous greyhounds, "You were foolish to have recourse to the justice of the King. It's necessary to have recourse to your own justice, as I advised you to do. In exchange for his respectful words and his remonstration to Richard, William will have received the rope of a gallows. Praise God, it is crossbow bolts and swords that would have librated the citizens of London."

"I recognize Robin Hood in that! But comrade, the population of London, honest workmen accustomed to living peacefully on the labor of their hands, eating a head of boiled mutton on Sunday and finding shelter under a good roof from the cold and the rain, would not adapt well to your nomadic life as a hunter."

"Yes, you're right, companion! The population of London is imbecilic and cowardly, so it's not for them that I've quit my forests and my brave companions, Friar Tuck, old Seth Lockes, Muck and my four hundred intrepid hunters. It's for William Longbeard, whose courage and composure astonish me all the more because he isn't a swordsman but a man of knowledge of study."

"Listen—that's the signal that was agreed. Can't you hear, amid the din of the waves, the sound of a horn? The tune of The Ballad of Robin Hood—it's William."

And, indeed, a large Norman boat came to land in the little bay where Robin Hood and his two companions were.

"Glory to God!" cried William, leaping from the boat to the sand. "Glory to God, the heart of King Richard was moved by my words; he has sworn to me by his salvation that he will take into consideration the plaints of the good city of London; he detached this chain from his neck and put it round mine."

"And the charter? The charter by which Richard grants to the citizens of London the freedoms demanded and a sage division of tax revenues?"

"What, Robin! The word of Lionheart does not appear sufficient o you?"

"Lionheart has doubtless already forgotten the promises he made you. He's too far away from London, too busy with battles; he feels the need for money too much to remember the remonstrations of a poor fellow who came to him without gold and men-at-arms. In any case, even if he summoned the aldermen to divide the taxes differently from Normandy, they'd continue to do it as they wish. Believe me, William, in spite of the golden chain that King Richard has given you, don't expose yourself to further perils, and don't expect the accomplishment of a royal word already forgotten. I'm returning to my forests, Adieu."

"He's right," added Adam Bel. "For myself, I'm going to return home peacefully and not worry about breaking with such little chance of success the submission I've made to the king."

"Me neither," replied Clem Cloudesly, their other companion.

"Well," cried William Longbeard, "for myself, I believe in the royal word. I'm going to tell the people what promises Richard has sworn to me, and we'll see whether the aldermen will do as you say and won't believe this chain to be an irrefutable pledge of the word of Lionheart.

Clem and Adam went away silently, their heads bowed. Robin Hood remained alone with William.

"It's a foolish thing you're going to do," he said, "but no matter. It won't be said that Robin Hood has abandoned a brave companion at the moment of peril. If you go forward, I'll go forward with you; only remember that you're committing a folly."

But William, without listening, went straight to the main square of London. Scarcely had he been perceived than he populace surrounded him eagerly. Soon, an immense crowd followed his footsteps, uttering joyous exclamations. As everyone knew about William's voyage and the objective he had proposed or it, everyone was impatient to know what response King Richard had given the defender of the people. Moreover, they had taken up the small arms that citizens then had at their disposal—which is to say, iron-tipped staffs, axes and iron levers.

More than fifty thousand people, says one historian of the time, Guillelmus Neubrigenisis, assembled thus around William, who, in order to satisfy their impatience, was obliged to climb on to a butcher's stall after that improvised podium had been dragged into the middle of the square.

There, in view of everyone, he cried: "King Richard has sworn me an oath to order the aldermen to make a sage vision of taxes; this is the pledge that he gave me of that word. Come with me, then, to consecrate this golden chain to the church and to the tomb of Saint Thomas à Becket, whose holy protection has enabled me to be welcomed compassionately by the king."

He tried to descend from the butcher's stall, but the members of the crowd took in their arms the man who had just given them such good news, and it was with such popular honors that he arrived at the church. There he deposited the golden chain on the tomb where King Henry II, Richard's father, had come to weep and humiliate himself under the discipline of the English clergy. After that offering, he turned to the people and, taking for the text of the speech he was about to make a passage from the Holy Book: *Haurietis aquas cum gaudio de fontibus salvatoris*,[4] he said: "Permit me, brothers, to apply those words to myself, for I come to your as the savior of the poor. You poor people, who have experienced how hard the hand of the rich is, draw now from my well the water of a salutary doctrine, draw it with joy, because the hour of your relief has come; I will separate the waters from the waters—which is to say, men from men; I will separate he humble and sincere people from the proud and faithless people; I will separate the reproved classes, as God separated the light from the darkness; march with me, listen to my voice, and soon injustice will have ceased and everyone will obtain his right. We have for a pledge the protection of Heaven, the word of the King, and the justice of our cause."

Cries of approval and enthusiasm responded to these words, and certainly, if William Longbeard had want-

---

[4] Author's note: "You shall draw water with joy from the well of the Savior."

ed it, at that moment, it would have been all over for the aldermen and their iniquitous power. Such was the opinion of Robin Hood, who wanted to march at the head of the people against the Pharisees, he said, and avenge the citizens of London by their death. But William, far from profiting from that enthusiasm, repressed it with all his power and swore an oath that he would abandon the cause of the citizens if they committed the slightest disorder or shed a single drop of blood. It was necessary, therefore, to be content with going to see the aldermen, to inform them of the king's will and demand its execution.

The latter refrained carefully from resisting and making the slightest refusal in the face of the perils that menaced them. They responded that they would conform to the king's orders as soon as those orders had been transmitted to them, and asked for a week, a sufficient delay, according to them, for Richard to send the charter promised by him to the citizens of London.

In acting thus they only wanted to gain time, to allow the effervescence of the people to die down, and to take the measures necessary to repress any further riot, for they knew only too well how lightly Lionheart made promises and forgot them; they were only too well aware of the imperious need for money that he had to have the slightest dread of the arrival of the letters patent on the hope of which William Longbeard was relying.

Thus during the delay of a week, they put secret agents to work in order to spread out among the citizens and inspire them with distrust against William. The Archbishop of Canterbury and his justiciary convened several meetings of the better-off citizens, spoke to them about peace and order, and obtained a hearing all the more sympathetic because thirty thousand men-at-arms came to reinforce the troops that already formed the London garrison. The citizens, partly out of weakness and partly out of fear, gave hostages, who were hastily taken far from London.

Meanwhile, William, retained in his house for several days because his wife had just rendered him the father of a daughter, and who was, in any case, too honest to doubt the honesty of others, had no suspicion of the perils that menaced him, when one day, the faithful Robin Hood came to warn him that only one means of salvation remained to him, which was to flee into the forests.

"Let us depart instantly," he said to him. "Your wife and your child, confided to Tuck or another of my outlaws, will come to join you tomorrow."

"Flee, me!" cried William. "No, truly, the Archbishop of Canterbury would not dare to act against the wishes of the King, whose promise I have received to affranchise the citizens."

"Richard doesn't remember you or his promises. Flee with me, come."

"Far from it; I shall leave my house and show myself to the populace, and if kings break their word, if archbishops and aldermen are traitors, the populace is grateful and will defend their defender."

"The populace is ingrate and inconstant. Come, William, accept the refuge that I'm offering you."

But William, without listening to his friend, went immediately to the public square. Scarcely had a few people approached him than the rest ran away, in a cowardly fashion. Among the citizens who came to salute William was a man named Geoffrey, whom Longbeard had obliged on many occasions. After having chatted which his benefactor for some time, the man suddenly raised his arm and drew a dagger. At the same instant two assassins rushed upon William, but the latter, who was on the defensive, had already killed the traitor Geoffrey with a dagger thrust, and, seconded by Robin Hood, stood his ground courageously against the two cutthroats, who succumbed. Several soldiers ran then to take possession of Longbeard, who succeeded in escaping and took refuge with Robin and nine of his friends in a nearby church called Saint Mary-le-Bow.

There they prepared to defend themselves bravely until the citizens, warned of their peril, came to liberate them; but there was no movement on the part of the citizens, because there were so many men-at-arms in London, and it was feared that a movement of rebellion would case the death of the hostages. Thus, the soldiers sent to render themselves masters of William were able to surround the church and the bell-tower without the slightest resistance, and to put a large quantity of dry and green wood around it, to which they set fire immediately, and which produced such a large quantity of smoke that the besieged men were obliged to surrender, with the exception of Robin Hood, who took flight, although wounded.

At the moment when William came down from the bell-tower of Saint Mary-le-Bow, the son of Geoffrey threw himself upon him and struck him with a dagger; then the soldiers seized the wounded man and dragged him to the gibbet, where they only suspended his cadaver, for William had died during the journey.[5]

---

[5] According to William of Newburgh, William FitzOsbert was indeed stabbed by the son of the man he had earlier killed during his arrest, but he survived to be tried, convicted and sentenced to be "torn asunder" by horses before being hanged from a gibbet, along with nine accomplices who were captured

At this point in the story the author inserts a long note:

This is how Augustin Thierry[6] recounts the story of Robin Hood:

In the time when the heroes of the Anglo-Norman barony visited the forest of Sherwood, a man lived in that same forest who as the hero of the serfs, the poor and the petty—in a word, the Anglo-Saxon race. "Among the disinherited," says an ancient chronicler, "the famous brigand Robert Hode was then remarked, whom the common people love so much to celebrate in games and comedies, and whose history, sun by minstrels, interests them more than any other." To those few words are reduced all the historical data regarding the last Englishman to follow the example of Hereward;[7] in order to recover a few features of his life and his character, it is to old romances and ballads that it is necessary to have recourse. Although one cannot add faith to the bizarre and often contradictory reports of this poetry, it is at least an incontestable testimony to the ardent amity of the English people for the leader of the band that they

with him. Berthoud presumably considered that detail too gruesome for reportage in a family magazine.

[6] The Romantic historian Augustin Thierry (1795-1856), the author of *Histoire de la conquête de l'Angleterre par les Normands* (1825), from which the passage is taken verbatim. Thierry's acceptance of Robin Hood as a real person and leader of anti-Norman resistance was considered highly dubious by rival historians.

[7] Hereward the Wake as legendary eleventh century Anglo-Saxon nobleman said to have led local resistance to the Norman conquest in East Anglia. His story, derived from a twelfth-century Latin text, is probably fictitious.

celebrate, and for his companions, who, instead of laboring for masters, roamed the forest, merry and free, as the old refrains put it.

One can scarcely doubt that Robert, or more vulgarly, Robin Hood, was of Anglo-Saxon origin; his French forename proves nothing against that opinion because, as soon as the second generation after the conquest, the influence of the Norman clergy caused to fall into desuetude the ancient baptismal names, then replaced by the names of saints or others customary in Normandy. The name Hood is Saxon, and the most ancient ballads—and, in consequence those most worthy of attention—rank the ancestors of the man who bore it among the peasant class. Later, when the memory of the revolution operated by the conquest was weakened, village poets imagined embellishing their favorite character with the pomp of grandeur and wealth; they had him a nobleman, or at last the grandson of a nobleman, whose daughter, having been seduced, fled and gave birth in a wood. The last supposition gave birth to a popular romance full of interest and gracious ideas, but nothing probable authorizes it.

Whether it be true or false that Robin Hood was born, as the romance states, "in a verdant wood, in the midst of lilies in flower," it is in the woods that he spent his life, at the head of several hundred archers, redoubtable to the comtes, vicomtes, bishops and rich abbés of England, but cherished by famers, laborers, widows and poor people. He accorded peace and protection to all who were weak and oppressed, shared with those who had nothing the spoils of those who grew rich on the harvests of others, and, according to the old tradition, was good to every honest and laborious individual.

Robin Hood had the best heart and was the finest archer in the entire band; after him was cited Little John, his lieutenant and brother in arms, from whom he was inseparable in peril and in joy, and from whom he ballads and English proverbs do not separate him either. Tradition also names a few of is companions, such as Mutch, the miller's son, old Scath Locke, and a monk named Friar Tuck, who fought in his habit and contented himself with a heavy staff for his only weapon. They were all of jovial humor, not aiming to enrich themselves, but only to live on their booty, and distributing anything superfluous that they had to families expropriated during the great pillage of the conquest.

Although enemies of the rich and powerful, they did not kill those who fell into their hands, and only shed blood in their own defense. Their blows only fell upon he agents of the royal police and he governors of cities or provinces, whom the Normans called Vicomtes and the English called Sheriffs. "Bend your bows," said Robin Hood, "and try their strings; set up a gallows nearby, and a curse be on the head of any man who gives mercy to a sheriff or his sergeants."

The Sheriff of Nottingham was the man against whom Robin Hood had most frequently to battle and the man who pursued him most ardently on horseback and on foot, putting a price on his head and exciting his companions and friends to betray him. But no one betrayed him and several aided him to escape the peril into which his boldness often led him. "I would rather die," a poor woman said to him one day, "than not do everything to save you, for who has nourished and clothed me and my children? Is it not you and Little John?"

The surprising adventures of that twelfth-century bandit chief, his victories over the men of the Norman race, his stratagems and his escapes were long the sole foundation of the national history that a man of the English people transmitted to his son, after having received them from his ancestors. The popular imagination lent to Robin Hood all the qualities and all the virtues of the Middle Ages. He was reputed to have been as devoted to the Church as he was brave in combat, and it was said that, once having entered to hear mass, whatever danger arrived, he never left until the end. That scruple of devotion exposed him once to capture by the Sheriff and is men-at-arms, but he still found the means to put up resistance, and it was even him, the old history said, somewhat suspect of exaggeration, who captured the Sheriff.

On that theme, the English minstrels of the fourteenth century composed a long ballad, a few lines of which merit being quoted, if only as an example of the frank and animated color that the people give to their poetry in times when a veritably popular literature exists:

In summer, when greenery is lovely and leaves broad and long, there is pleasure in the forest to listen to the birdsong,

To see the roe deer quit the hill to retreat to the meadow and taking refuge under the greenwood.

Early one Pentecost day in the month of May, a day when the sun rose fine and the birdsong was gay,

"By the cross of Christ," said Little John, "this morning is fine, and in all Christendom there's no more joyous man than me.

Open you heart, my dear master, and think whether there's anything finer than a morning in May."

"One thing that troubles me," said Robin Hood, "and hurts my heart is not to be able, on a feast day, to heat mass and matins.

I've not seen my savior for a fortnight and more, and I want to go Nottingham with good Mary's aid."

Robin goes to Nottingham while Little John stays in Sherwood; he goes to Saint Mary's Church and kneels before the cross...[8]

Robin Hood was not simply renowned for his devotion to saints and feast days; like the saints he had his own feast day, and on that day, religiously observed in the hamlets and little villages of England, it was not permissible to be occupied with anything but games and pleasures. That custom was still current in the fifteenth century, and the descendants of the Saxons and the Normans both took part in the popular amusements, without thinking that it as a monument to the old hostility of their ancestors. On that day, the churches were as deserted as the workshops; no saint or preacher took precedence over Robin Hood, and that lasted until the Reformation had given a new impetus to religious zeal in England. This is a fact attested by an Anglican bishop of the sixteenth century, the celebrated and respectable Latimer:

"Traces of that long remembrance, in which the very memory of the Norman invasion was annihilated for the English people, still subsists today. In the county of York, at the mouth of a little river, there is a bay that bears the name of Robin Hood on all modern maps, and

---

[8] This is a paraphrase by Thierry, rendered in French, not a quotation, although he does add a few footnotes which credits the original to "Jamieson's Popular Songs" [i,e Robert Jamieson's *Popular Ballads and Songs* (1806)] I have back-translated Thierry's paraphrase rather than substituting the Medieval original, whose Chaucerian orthography makes it a trifle difficult to construe.

it is not long since, in the same county, near Pontefract, travelers were shown a lovely and clear fresh water spring known as Robin Hood's Well, where from which they were invited to drink in honor of the famous archer. Throughout the seventeenth century, the old ballads of Robin Hood, printed in Gothic letters (a species of printing for which the English common people have a singular affection) circulated in villages, where they were taken by men who sang them to a kind of chant. Several complete collections were compiled for the usage of readers in towns, and one of those collections bears the elegant title of *Guirlande de Robin Hood*. Today these books, having become rare, only interest the erudite, and the story of the heroes of Sherwood, stripped of its poetic ornaments, is only read any longer among stories for the usage of children."

None of the ballads that have been conserved for us recounts the death of Robin Hood; the vulgar tradition is that he perished in a convent of women where, feeling ill one day, he went to ask for help. It was necessary to bleed him, and the nun who knew how to perform that operation, having recognized Robin Hood, carried it out in such a way as to kill him. This story, which can neither be confirmed nor contested, is sufficiently in conformity with the mores of the twelfth century; many women in rich monasteries occupied themselves then with studying medicine and composing remedies that they offered gratuitously to the poor. Furthermore, in England, since the conquest, the superiors of abbeys and the greater number of nuns were of Norman extraction, as their statutes, written in Old French, prove. That circumstance might explain how the leader of the Saxon bandits, whom royal ordinances had put outside the law, found enemies in the convent where he went to seek assistance. After his death, the troop of which he was the leader and soul dispersed, and Little John, his faithful companion, despairing of maintaining himself in England and driven by the desire to continue the war against the Normans, went to Ireland, where he took part in the indigenous revolts.

Chapter Three
Angel and Demon

While that murder was accomplished, the young wife of William Longbeard, who had recently given birth, let herself go to the wellbeing of convalescence, and spent entire days, lying limply on a bed of repose, gazing at the cradle in which her new-born child was asleep. Jane, the daughter of a rich London merchant, loved William with an amour full of veneration. Although he was much older than her, she had preferred the courageous and disinterested defender of the citizenry to all the handsome and rich young men who had disputed her hand. William was everything to her; her heart did not lack anything and no desire presented itself to her imagination when William was sitting beside her and she could attach her gaze to the noble and masculine features of that courageous man, when she heard his voice, so powerful and so soft. In order to please him she had associated herself with her husband's patriotic devotions, but she only took the part in them befitting a woman; the poor and the sick blessed Jane with almost as many benedictions as they gave William, for Jane always had alms for their poverty and a balm for their maladies; people went to Jane when they were unfortunate, and none of those who implored her aid quit her without blessing her, for, merely in seeing her they felt that they had less to lament.

Jane was unaware of all the perils that menaced William, and the latter, taking advantage of the reclusive fashion in which his wife had lived since becoming a mother, had expressly forbidden all those who approached her to alert her in any fashion to what was happening. Thus, full of security, placid and happy in her maternity, she was waiting without any anxiety for William's return, whom she as used to seeing absent himself from the house for entire says, when she suddenly saw a poor woman come in whose child she had once cured of an illness regarded as mortal.

"Jane," cried the woman, "it's necessary to flee, for men-at-arms are coming to your house and they'll do to you and your child what they've already done to your husband: they'll kill you."

At those fatal words, Jan went as pale as a corpse. She ran to her daughter's cradle and seized her in her arms; then, half-naked, her hair scattered, she started to run at random, without any objective. It was after having wandered thus through the deserted streets, where terror had closed the doors of all the houses long before curfew, that she arrived in a solitary place unknown to her, exhausted by fatigue, with her feet bloodied. There, she collapsed at the foot of a stake that the moon soon illuminated clearly. It was the gibbet where the soldiers had suspended William's body.

But Jane gazed at the gibbet and the cadaver without any emotion appearing on her motionless features. She was no longer paying any attention to the wailing of the new-born that she was clutching in her arms mechanically. The unfortunate woman had lost her reason, and only one thought any longer remained to her, and one sensation: terror.

She remained there, leaning toward the earth, lending her ear to the sound of dry leaves rustling, listening to the breath of the wind and shuddering every time a gust uttered a more lamentable plaint.

Gradually, the wind died down, and the dry leaves became still. Then Jane set her back against the foot of the gibbet and fell into a kind of torpor produced by fatigue and cold. Meanwhile, the moon had disappeared again behind the thick clouds, through which some of its rays had escaped a little while ago. Snow began to fall from the sky in large flakes, and gradually, Jane and her child disappeared beneath an icy shroud that accumulated slowly on their almost-unclothed limbs.

A funeral silence reigned for a long time in that sinister and accursed place. The nocturnal birds, chased away by the snow, had taken refuge in the depths of the deserted ruins neighboring the gibbet. No breath of wind agitated the air, and London, buried in slumber, as if numbed by the cold, did not send the slightest murmur into that remote solitude.

Suddenly, Jane shuddered and raised her head; doubtless her reason had returned to her at the approach of death, for the unfortunate woman attempted to flee from the gibbet and tried to warm her child up against her breast; but it was in vain. The poor woman fell again on to the icy ground; two tears moistened her eyes, the child escaped her arms, and silence fell again.

Then an angel descended from the heavens in order to collect the pure and saintly soul that had just been delivered of its mortal envelope.

"My sister," he said, leaning over her with the ineffable smile that only belongs to the blessed, come and take your place among the choir of martyrs, where William—your William—is waiting for you, his head circled by an immortal aureole. The felicity that is commencing for you will have no term. Come to the feet of God for eternity."

But a terrestrial thought, if one can call by that pro-fane name an impulse of maternal love, still remained in the stainless soul ready to enter Heaven.

"My daughter!" she murmured, turning her eyes toward the earth. "My daughter!"

"A few more moments," replied the angel. "She will follow you into Paradise."

And the saint, borne by the wings of her divine guide, flew radiantly toward the celestial Jerusalem. Then the angel returned toward the child.

Imagine his surprise and consternation when he saw a demon crouched before the frail creature, prey to the convulsions of death-throes.

"What are you doing, reproved?" cried the son of Heaven. "Don't you know that this child is the daughter of two martyrs?"

"It's for that reason that Hell will find her a more precious prey, handsome cherub," sniggered the demon. "Yes, the daughter of two martyrs, the daughter of two inhabitants of Paradise, will share our eternity of desola-tion, for she has not been baptized. Thus, she belongs to Satan, my master."

"Back!" said the angel, leaning over the cadaver of the mother to pick up, at the tip of the branch that he was holding in his hand, one of the tears that was still shining on Jane's eyelids. "Back, for this tear will baptize the child."

"If I let it," replied the demon, whose fiery breath dried up the tear instantaneously.

Consternated, the angel turned his had away, and the demon enjoyed the few moments of triumph that he had just obtained.

"You're vanquished, cherub. You can resume your flight toward Haven alone, and the smiles of the other angels will welcome you with a poignant sarcasm. It's a cruel check to your pride."

"Wretch! Pride and sarcasm are unknown in Heaven."

"But not regret, at least. Now, it's a just motive for regret to lose the soul of a child, to see falling into eternal darkness one for whom the hosannas and alleluias might already have commenced among the celestial choirs. The holy soul is mine!"

The angel veiled himself with his wings in order to hide his sadness from the gaze of the evil spirit.

"Come on, don't despair thus," said the demon. "You can still redeem this soul. The child hasn't yet rendered the last sigh, and if you wish, I consent, not that it will enter Paradise immediately, but to let it live.

"Several of William's friends are searching for Jane and her child; thus far I've kept them away from this place. Accept the conditions I want to propose, and I'll return to my somber realm. Then the citizens will arrive here, find the child, baptize her, take her away and bring her up; and it's to the more adroit of us that her soul will belong. Do those arrangements suit you?"

"And what price do you put, son of Hell, on the conditions you're proposing to me?"

"Only one: that you let me take a kiss from your forehead."

"Wretch! Flee, or I'll call my brothers to strike you with their flaming swords."

"Aha! You preach charity, beautiful angel, but you don't practice it. You prefer the doom of a soul to the temporary pollution that my lips would cause you. So be it: to me the child's soul, for I'd be insensate, as a demon, to testify compassion for an angel who feels none for her."

As he spoke he reached out his clawed hands to seize his prey. The angel uttered a cry of dolor.

"Forgive me, my God, for what I'm about to do in order to redeem a soul!" he cried. "But did not your divine son die on the cross for the salvation of humans, and ought I, in cowardly fashion, to prefer my own well-being to the eternal happiness of that child? I accept, demon."

And, trembling and consternated, he presented his forehead to the filthy lips of the reproved. The latter hastened to give the fatal kiss to the angel, who shivered under the abominable contact, and whose face expressed something of the sublime dolor that Rubens put into the face of the Magdalen in his paining *The Descent from the Cross*.

"It's not everything to be charitable," the demon sniggered, when he had imprinted his infernal pollution on the cherub. "it's not everything to be charitable; it's also necessary to be prudent. Now, handsome angel, the stain with which I've stigmatized your forehead is eternal—at least, I hope so—and you'd have avoided it if you'd acted with less stupidity and learned from our brothers what you're about to learn from me. That child isn't and has never been destined to die today. Your God destines it for a long life of ordeals. You've acted with presumption, and I've told you a lie. Adieu! You'll remember Astaroth!"

He disappeared, leaving behind him long trails of flame.

The cherub, confused, with his head veiled by his wings, knelt down and extended his hands toward the skies in a sign of repentance and to implore divine mercy. Soon, he felt himself enlaced in the arms of an angel, and he heard a voice consoling him; it was Gabriel, the leader of the divine militia.

"Asrael," he said, "console yourself, for your misfortune is not without remedy and your afflictions will have a term. If you had not doubted the mercy of God your forehead would not be afflicted by that pollution, which forbids you entry to Heaven; but the Almighty, in his mercy, and because you sinned out of charity, is leaving you the hope one day coming back to take the place that you occupied among your brothers. On the day when William's family counts four martyrs worthy, by their virtues or by the expiations they have supported, to form a new choir of the celestial militia, your ordeals will be concluded and you'll return to us in Heaven."

With those words, Gabriel quit the angel and left him shedding bitter tears, and regretting having despaired of Paradise, which would remain closed to him for such a long time of trials.

Chapter Four
The Old Priest

When he had ceased to hear the voice of the arch-angel, when he found himself alone and abandoned on the earth, the cherub Asrael emerged from the profound dejection into which the sentence had thrown him, and tried to launch himself in the tracks of his brother, who was rising into the sky. He rose up rapidly to the limits of the atmosphere of our globe, but when he arrived there, an insurmountable force thwarted the effort of his wings.

He could never cross the invisible barrier that retained him captive, and neither his efforts, nor his tears, nor his imploring prayers could bend the divine will that repelled him. Overwhelmed by lassitude, his heart heavy with tears, he went back down to earth and found William's daughter and Jane surrounded by a numerous group of people who had come to render the duties of a sepulcher to William Longbeard, and had been surprised and consternated to find his dead wife and his dying daughter near his cadaver.

A woman took the little girl, wrapped her in the folds of her cloak and tried tenderly to warm her up with her breath. In the meantime, four men detached William's body from the gibbet and placed it in a shroud that they had brought. Two women rendered the same care to Jane and made use of their long veils, attached together, to wrap her.

Then, all of them loaded the two precious burdens on to their shoulders and headed silently for the church of Saint-Mary-le-Bow, where three kneeling priests were waiting for them in the choir, reciting prayers. When the footsteps of the lugubrious cortege grated as they slid over the damp flagstones of the nave, the priests stood up, and the oldest sprinkled holy water over the icy bodies of the two spouses; then he commenced he office for the dead, celebrated the mysteries of the mass, and after having concluded them he turned to the eight or ten people kneeling in the shadows, who were praying with him for the defender who had died for the exemptions of the city.

"Brothers," he said to them, "the bravest and most virtuous of the citizens of London has perished, the victim of a cowardly trap and an odious treason; three duties remain for us to fulfill for him; will you swear by the salvation of our souls, your share of Paradise, and in the name of the Father, the Son and the Holy Spirit to acquit those duties?"

""We swear it by the salvation of our souls, on our share of Paradise and in the name of the Father, the Son and the Holy Spirit!" all the voices cried, unanimously.

"Amen," said the priest. "Now, hear me and hold yourselves warned. The first of these duties is never to reveal to the Normans the sepulcher in which the remains repose of the generous and loyal defender whose body we are about to deposit in the crypt. I declare felon, traitor to his oath and excommunicate, expelled from the Holy Church, the culpable individual who, directly or indirectly, by word or by gesture, betrays the secret of that tomb and exposes such holy relics to profanation. Anathema upon him!"

"Anathema upon him!" repeated all the witnesses, with gestures of menace and malediction.

"Secondly, the grave and slow voice of the priest went on, it is necessary to swear to persevere in the work that he commenced so loyally and bravely. For that, it is necessary that one of you undertake the voyage to Normandy that William once undertook for you. The man who takes responsibility for that mission will throw himself at the knees of King Richard, inform him of William's murder and demand justice against the treason of the aldermen and the iniquity of the Archbishop of Canterbury. Which of you will depart in order to fulfill this perilous duty?"

A profound silence followed the priest's question.

"I did not believe that I would find so much ingratitude in the face of the relics, still warm, of a martyr dead for your cause!" cried the priest, indignantly. "If no one can find it in his heart to undertake this voyage to go and ask King Richard for justice, it is me, an infirm old man, who will take charge of that care. What! No one responds? Not even you, Bertrand de Gourdon, the brother-in-law of William Longbeard, who married his wife's sister?"

Bertrand de Gourdon stood up among the kneeling crowd and said: "Father, you doubtless know that I am only Saxon by virtue of my marriage to a Saxon woman, the sister of that poor Jane, who was still consoling me yesterday with her kind words for my recent widowhood. My father is a citizen of Limoges; I was born in the Château de Chalus, which depends on the same comté, so it would be inappropriate for me, not being his subject to go to King Richard to ask for justice for William. But since there is no one among all these Englishmen who is brave enough to devote himself to William's cause. I offer you all I possess to subsidize the expenses of your voyage, and what is more, I will accompany you, my crossbow on my shoulder, wherever you go. Thus, so long as a breath of life remains within me, you will not have to fear any peril, for my eye is accurate, my hand is sure and my courage proven."

"We'll depart this instant," said the priest. "God will protect us and give us the strength to accomplish our work."

Then, without anger and without reproach, he turned to those who were present and asked: "Which of you will take charge of watching over William's daughter? Which mother will become her mother? Which father will adopt her and make her his daughter?"

"It will be me, if you please, who will take William's child into my home," said a citizen named Godwin. My wife has not waited until now to take her as her child, and you can see her already nourishing the little orphan with her milk; from this moment, William's child becomes mine and will live under my roof, will take her place at my table, will be dressed like my own children and will share the heritage that I leave. May God curse me if I break my word and if I do not become her father immediately."

"And I her mother," added the citizen's wife, advancing with the little girl attached to her breast.

"God receives your oath, Master Godwin. Go in peace, my brothers."

Everyone withdrew silently. The priest remained alone with Bertrand de Gourdon.

"Are you ready, Brother?" asked the priest. "A boat that I have had prepared for any event is only waiting for its passengers to set sail for Normandy."

"Grant me a quarter of an hour and I'll come back, never to quit you again."

"What adieux have you to make in London, Bertrand, whose wife is dead and whose father resides in the comté of Limoges? You have neither wife nor child."

"I have no less need of a quarter of an hour before leaving," replied the archer, who left the church and headed for the gibbet. There he took a knife from his pocket, detached a piece of wood from the stake half as long as his palm, and placed it, carefully wrapped, in the quiver where his arrows were. Then he returned to the church.

"I have four hundred gold coins in my satchel," the archer said. "Will that suffice for the expenses of our journey?"

"My wallet contains eight hundred," the priest replied. "Let's be on our way, Brother, let's go before the Archbishop of Canterbury gets wind of our plan and puts shackles on it."

"Let's go!"

"My God, help us!" cried the old priest before leaving the church. "Give persuasion to my voice and strength to my limbs, chilled by age. It's a matter of your cause, since it's the cause of the oppressed!"

A few minutes later, a boat received them both, and took them to a ship that was anchored not far away. Commanded by a Saxon captain devoted to the cause of the citizens of London, the vessel set sail for Normandy, to which it was summoned by commercial affairs.

The following morning, the populace which had allowed its defender to be massacred tranquilly the previous day, did not fail, out of curiosity or devotion, to visit the gibbet. Their surprise as great when the disappearance of the cadaver was perceived, especially when they noticed the notch cut in the stake by Bertrand de Gourdon. Only able to explain those mysteries by means of the marvelous, they did not fail to say that the angels had carried William's mortal remains to Heaven, and they saw in the fragment cut from the stake a revelation of miraculous virtues attached to the wood, the instrument of a martyrdom.

As soon as that explanation was proposed, everyone adopted it with enthusiasm; the gibbet was felled, and the smallest pieces of it were disputed as precious relics; those who were unable to procure some parcel of the wood scraped the ground in which it had been planted, so well that in very little time a deep ditch was formed in the place formerly occupied by the gibbet.

Soon, the rumor of the death and the miracle operated by the intercession of the blessed William having spread throughout England, people came in pilgrimage to the gibbet from the various cities of the realm, and more than twenty thousand Saxons accomplished that pilgrimage to the site of the torture of Saint William. The priests of various London churches—Saxons, for the most part—preached the canonization of the martyr to the national case, and it was in vain that the Archbishop of Canterbury, conjointly with the chief justice, Hubert, employed prison, the whip and the rope in order to prevent the veneration unanimously rendered to William's memory.

For more than a century, William's name was invoked as that of one of the blessed, and several manuscripts of the time attest that even the Normans ended up adopting the English saint and having recourse to his intervention, forgetting that he had died the victim of the injustice and oppression of their forefathers.

Chapter Five
A Battle

Meanwhile, King Richard, who had forgotten William Longbeard and the promises he had made him a long time ago, was no longer thinking about anything but avenging himself on the Comte de Limoges, against whom he felt a great anger.

These were the motives that had irritated the monarch so greatly.

Rightly or wrongly, the rumor had spread that the Comte de Limoges had just discovered a treasure of immense value hidden in a place in his estates; there was talk of nothing less than a hundred thousand tons of gold found in the depths of a cave, into which a shepherd had entered by mistake, at midnight on Christmas Day. Tradition claims that at midnight on Christmas Day, all unknown treasures become visible, and the demons posted to guard them remain powerless until the moment when the priest quits the altar after having celebrated the first mass.

As soon as Richard learned about that marvelous event, he demanded his share of the tons of gold, claiming that the cave where they had remained hidden for such a long time had once belonged to his ancestor William the Conqueror. The Comte de Limoges replied that he had not found any treasure, and that if he had found one he would have kept it for himself, given that he was the sovereign lord of his comté, and owed nothing in any fashion to the King of England and the Duke of Normandy.

It required much less than that to make Lionheart take up arms, being ever ardent and prompt to seize his sword and deliver battle. He assembled his troops, therefore, gave the signal to raise the banner, and a week later, Fort Chalus, where the Comte de Limoges lived, was blockaded by an army of eight thousand men, commanded by Richard in person. He believed that he would only have to raise his hand to take the citadel, but his surprise and anger were great when he saw the comte at the head of a strong garrison and was informed that the city was well provisioned, not only with munitions but with engines of war.

In his ordinary impatience, the king wanted to attack immediately. Without giving his troops time to rest, and without waiting for several machines that might have had marvelous effects against the besieged, he sent ladders forward, which soon collapsed, broken by enormous stones dropped from the walls and thrown by machines that were brought into play. It was therefore necessary for the Anglo-Norman army to beat a retreat, erect tents and establish a camp fortified by redoubts, in order to guard against any sorties that the besieged might attempt, inspired by their initial advantage.

For the three days that the establishment of the camp required, King Richard did not want to take the slightest rest, and did not even permit his varlets to unlace his coat of mail at night. It was only after seeing his retrenchments constructed and entirely ready that he went into his tent, where he went to sleep on the lion skin that served him as a bed when he was on campaign.

Overwhelmed by fatigue, his slumber lasted no less than twelve hours, and might perhaps have been even more prolonged without a tumult that rose up near his royal tent, produced by the arrival of an archer bearing the arms of the Comte de Limoges embroidered on his cloak.

That archer was ne other than Bertrand de Gourdon, accompanied by the old priest of Saint Mary-le-Bow. At first they had penetrated the cap without difficulty, because the archer's costume had not been noticed to begin with, but it was soon remarked and he was surrounded. As he continued to march silently toward the royal tent, which has indicated to him by the red flag that surmounted it, the soldiers barred his path.

Without being intimidated, he seized his dagger, and swore that he would strike he first man who opposed him talking to King Richard. They tried to throw himself upon him to disarm him, but he defended himself vigorously, and it was that squabble and the ensuing racket that put an end to King Richard's slumber.

Woken up with a start, the monarch thought that the besieged forces had suddenly attacked the camp. He seized his weapons and launched himself out of his tent, half-naked. He only saw the brave Bertrand, who was standing up to eight or ten assailants, and the old priest, who was trying to interpose himself between the combatants in order to restore peace.

Richard uttered a cry; abruptly, everyone stopped, and the priest was able to advance freely, with his companion, toward the king, before whom the old man knelt down. The archer remained standing, and contented himself with rendering the monarch a military salute. Lionheart darted an angry gaze at him.

"Since when," he said, "does a vassal not bend his knee before his lord and master?"

"I am not the vassal of King Richard," replied Bertrand de Gourdon, calmly. "I belong to the Comte de Limoges."

"Then what are you doing in the enemy camp?"

"I have come to accomplish the oath that I swore on the altar of Saint Mary-le-Bow to bring this venerable priest of Jesus Christ to you safe and sound."

"And why has this venerable old man undertaken such a difficult journey? What obliged him to quit his church in the city of London?"

"Sire," relied the priest, "I have come to accomplish a holy duty, to enlighten your justice and the enable you to hear the plaints and laments of your faithful citizens of London."

"And what do my faithful citizens of London want of me?" cried Richard, furiously. "They only know how to complain, and if my memory serves me rightly, I have already received a visitor of your species a few months ago...yes, the memory is coming back to me clearly; it was one of those incorrigible Saxons who wear a long beard in order not to resemble my Normans. Well, have I not done right by his demands? Are there new concessions that you have come to solicit from my munificence?"

"It is justice, Sire, that I have come to request of you. William Longbeard, that faithful subject, that intrepid citizen, not only did not see the effects of your royal word realized, but for having demanded it, was put to death, treacherously slain by order of the Archbishop of Canterbury."

"This is strange news!" murmured Richard, and then went on, in a loud voice. "After all, the Archbishop of Canterbury is just, and knows what he is doing. If he has condemned this William, it is because this William was guilty."

"Sire, William as innocent, I swear it by the salvation of my soul," said the priest. "Do not refuse justice to his memory. Do not hesitate to punish those who assassinated him, for it is a fatal hour, the hour when a king dies who has not rendered each of his subjects the justice he owes him!"

"Trumpets, sound!" ordered the king. "I'm wasting precious time here, which would be more usefully employed in an assault."

"Don't refuse me, Sire. Don't send me back without having listened to me! Or I shall attach myself to your steps and you will only get rid of a poor priest by having him put to death, as has been done to the blessed William."

"The blessed William!" repeated Richard, beside himself. "Upon my soul, they're already making him a saint, like Thomas à Becket!" And one day or another, it will be necessary for me, too, to flagellate myself on the tomb of a saint. Back, old man!"

"Since the voice of justice alone cannot reach you," said he old priest, the voice of a dying father might perhaps be less impotent. Listen to me, them Richard Plantagenet. Ten years ago, to the day, a poor priest happened to be in the city of Chinon, and a woman ran to him in order to ask him to come and exhort, in his final hour, an old man who was dying. That woman took the priest into an abandoned house, where the moribund lay alone, on a disordered bed.

"The priest was afraid and wanted to flee far from that sinister place, for the dying man was only proffering words of vengeance and blasphemy. 'A curse upon my son John,' he cried, 'who has allowed himself to be corrupted and seduced by my son Richard! Anathema upon me, a feeble and culpable man, who has sacrificed my conscience and the wellbeing of my people to vain thoughts of ambition and the grandeur of my children. I would give my soul to the Devil if it did not belong to him already, in order to exact vengeance upon those two ingrate sons. Cursed be the day when I was born, and cursed by God be the two sons I leave!'[9]

"I approached him, and leaned over the bed, already stripped of the precious fabrics that had once covered it, which the varlets had pillaged before abandoning the dying man. I spoke to him about mercy, and God deigned, by means of my feeble voice, to disarm that irritated father. He retracted the curses he had proffered and charged me with carrying to his children words of benediction; in testimony of the pardon that he accorded his sons, he gave me this seal."

"My father!" murmured Richard, hiding his face in his hands. "My father!"

"When he had pardoned them, the moribund rendered his soul to God. I remained alone—yes, alone—with the cadaver, meditating on the negligibility of human grandeurs and thanking God for only having made me a poor priest. Then, as the old woman who had me to call me had taken flight herself, taking away a silver cup, the last object that had been left to the monarch of two kingdoms. I went to the city to beg for a shroud in which to bury the man who had been Henry II.

"No one opened his door to me, in spite of my prayers, and I would have come back without the shroud if I had not encountered a dancer, who gave me, out of

---

[9] Author's note: "Numquam me Dominus mori pemittat donec dignam de te vindictum accepero. (Script, Rerum Franc, Lib. XVIII)" The quotation, which corresponds roughly to the last line gen in English, is taken from Thierry's *Conquête de l'Angleterre par les Normands*, where it is credited to Giraldus Cambresis.

charity, her mantle and a part of her veil. The mantle enveloped the royal cadaver, the embroidered fringe of the veil served to imitate a diadem on the forehead of Henry Plantagenet, King of England, Duke of Normandy, Aquitaine and Brittany, Comte d'Anjou et du Maine, Seigneur de Tours et d'Amboise.

"Since that time, Sire I have searched for you in order to bring you your father's pardon, but fortune tested you in so many fashions and took you from one end of the earth to the other. In the name of that pardon, Sire, I seek justice for the citizens of London and punishment for those who oppress your subjects, and who only make use of the sword of justice that you have confided to their hands to strike unjustly."

"I will do right by your demand, Father. Soon, I shall return to London, when I have finished with the Comte de Limoges and his Château de Chalus. But what are you doing there, archer, and whence comes the audacity that enables you to carve a piece of wood with our dagger in our presence?"

"This piece of wood," replied the archer, unemotionally, "was detached by me from the gibbet on which my sister's husband, William Longbeard, was iniquitously suspended."

"And what are you making of that wood, by carving it thus?"

"A crossbow bolt."

"Who, then, do you count on striking with it?"

"You, Sire."

A cry of indignation went up in all sides, and the men-at-arms wanted to throw themselves on Bertrand de Gourdon. Richard made a sign forbidding them to approach.

"Comrade," he said disdainfully, "you lack iron with which to arm the tip of your arrow. It's necessary for me to give you one, in order to complete that fine gibbet weapon."

He took an arrow from the quiver of one of the sentinels on watch at the entrance to his tent, from which he detached the iron tip, and threw it at the archer's feet.

"There's your weapon complete. Go away; I leave you free to enter the fort of Chalus, so that you can aim your crossbow at me at your ease. Only I warn you that if you don't attain me before the end of the siege, which will not be of long duration, I'll have you well and truly hanged, without mercy. I give you my royal word on that. Let's go! Let everything be prepared! We attack in one hour!"

Bertrand de Gourdon bowed, and then knelt before the priest and asked for his benediction. The old man extended his tremulous hands over the archer's forehead.

"Bertrand, faithful and loyal soldier," he said to him, "may God protect you and turn away from you the misfortunes you have just attracted upon your head by imprudent words and culpable and presumptuous thoughts."

The archer got up, and then, looking around proudly, he traversed the armed crowd that surrounded him and went at a tranquil and slow pace to the drawbridge of the citadel. There he sounded his horn in a certain fashion; the drawbridge was lowered to allow the archer to enter, and then immediately raised again, for the army was beginning to move; clarions and trumpets sounded on all sides, and King Richard was seen, mounted on a magnificent horse, going from one to another, exhorting the soldiers to do their best, promising them victory and showing himself the most ardent of men-at-arms.

Separated from the faithful Bertrand de Gourdon, with whom he had supported so many rude proofs since their departure for the continent, the old priest went to sit down sadly on the steps of an altar elevated, according to custom, facing the royal tent. From there his gaze overlooked both the camp and the besieged citadel. At the sight of the carnage that was in preparation, the man of peace felt the discouragement by which he was overwhelmed increase even further.

Alas, he thought, *the blood of Christians is about to run in abundance for a frivolous motive, and the King, who is rendering England so unfortunate by his absence, is not hesitating to risk in this skirmish a life on which the salvation of London might depend, My God, how mysterious your judgments are, and how insufficient and feeble the human reason is that tries to penetrate them. May your will be done, then!*

The priest hid his face in his hands and remained absorbed for some time in pious meditations, which were suddenly interrupted by fanfares and instruments of war. At the same instant, a thousand strange noises unknown to the old man mingled with the bellicose clamors of the brass instruments and the cries of the soldiers. There was the whistling of the machines that were hurling enormous stones, the thunder of the battering-rams that were striking the weakest parts of the rampart with their bronze heads, and, finally, the hiss of the arrows that were going relentlessly and reciprocally to thin the ranks of the assailants and the besieged.

King Richard was everywhere that there was peril. Sometimes he ran to regulate himself the employment of a badly directed machine; sometimes it was an attack attempted weakly, of which he stimulated the energy.

For an hour the combat, on either side, had been furious, when suddenly, on a high but slender tower that served less for the defense of the citadel than to provide a facility for observing the movements of the enemy, an archer was seen to appear. He was holding in his hand a small white flag, which he unfurled in the air, and on which the priest read the words: *In the name of William Longbeard*. Then the archer took up his crossbow, wound it, placed on the weapon a bolt that he drew from his quiver, and waited.

Irritated by that bravado, all the Norman archers directed a cloud of arrows at Bertrand de Gourdon, whom they had recognized, none of which reached him. Irritated by that lack of skill, King Richard seized a crossbow and directed a bolt at Bertrand himself, which was blunted by the man's coat of mail. Bertrand picked up the royal arrow that had fallen at his feet, changed its iron tip, placed it in his own crossbow and launched it at the group that surrounded Richard, but with the evident intention of not hitting the King. The bolt wounded a page in the throat, who fell.

Furious, Richard unleashed a second arrow against the audacious archer. This time the weapon struck Bertrand in the thigh, and blood was seen trickling over his knee-guard. He pulled the bolt out, put it in his crossbow as before and aimed at the king's horse. The arrow hit the noble animal in a gap in the armor that defended its breast, and King Richard rolled in the dust with his mount felled.

Then Richard was seen to get up, covered in blood and soiled by mud, and, in one of the violent and terrible fits of anger that was all too reminiscent of the blind rage of a lion. He signaled to his archers to recommence their attack against Bertrand. A cloud of arrows flew, whistling, around the intrepid soldier, but without hitting him.

It was in the midst of that mass attack that Gourdon was seen to take an arrow of a spatulate form from his quiver and take aim at the king. Immediately, Richard uttered a cry of pain and was received, unconscious, in the arms of those surrounding him. The arrow had pierced the monarch's shoulder all the way through.

The King was carried to his tent. The bolt was extracted from his arm, and was recognized as the one that Bertrand had carved in front of the King. A dressing was placed on his wound.

As soon as Richard recovered consciousness he asked whether the attack had been continued, and learned that it had been suspended. Without wanting to listen to anyone, and without even paying attention to the prayers and tears of Queen Bérangère, he had a horse brought and went to show himself to his soldiers, who recommenced the combat furiously, avid to avenge the insult hey had received by virtue of the king's wound. In spite of the pain he was experiencing, Richard directed the movements of his troops personally, and the battering rams soon made two large breaches in the side of the ramparts, by means of which the Normans precipitated themselves into the city.

Although the besiegers surrounded him on all sides, and those who were in Chalus were put to death pitilessly, Bertrand de Gourdon, without seeking to flee, still remained standing at the crest of the tower, and seemed to determined to await death there, when King Richard had the trumpet sound and gave the signal to suspend the carnage. Then turning toward the knights who surrounded him, he said: "I don't want any harm to be done to that archer. Let him be brought to me without maltreating him, and without saying a word to him about the fate that awaits him. Only let a herald of arms cry to him that he has to render himself a prisoner of King Richard."

A herald did, in fact, approach the foot of the tower, and after three appeals of the clarion that he had a trumpeter who accompanied him sound, he cried: "Bertrand de Gourdon, King Richard wants you to be told that you are to render yourself to his mercy."

Bertrand measured with his eye the abyss formed beneath his feet by he collapsed fortification, and thought for a moment about precipitating himself, in order to avoid the torture that he doubtless expected, but he was suddenly seen to kneel down on the platform, and he was heard, after a brief prayer, to say: "I shall not turn my head away from the chalice, Lord; I shall drain it to the lees, for you did not recoil before any torture for the salvation of humankind."

And he went down the steps of the tower placidly, opened the iron door himself to the assailants, and allowed his hands to be bound without putting up any resistance. He was taken immediately before the King, who had just reentered his tent and as surrounded by the queen and all his servants, for the fatigue of the assault had poisoned the wound dangerously, and rendered its cure difficult.

At the sight of the archer who had wounded Richard, everyone uttered a cry of horror, and the queen hid her face, but the monarch drew Bérangère against him and lifted up her hands gently.

"There is no need to be afraid of a brave soldier," he said to her. "Bertrand de Gourdon only did his duty, and I attacked him first. Bertrand, you are free. You can leave for England with this old priest, and you will see me arrive in London before long myself in order to know the justice of the plaints that you have both come to enable me to hear. Yes, if William Longbeard has been put to death unjustly, William Longbeard will be avenged, even if I have to hang the Archbishop of Canterbury himself. In the meantime, take this purse and go. God be with you, for you are a skillful archer and a courageous man-at-arms. On my soul, I would have been afraid in your place on the platform! King Richard envies you, for you have made the best of the day."

With those words he extended his hand to Bertrand, who knelt down in order to put his lips to it respectfully; then the priest and the archer left the royal tent and headed toward the principal exit from the camp.

Chapter Six
A Third Martyr

When the soldiers saw the man who had endangered the Lionheart's days leaving peacefully, evidence of discontent burst forth on all sides, and the crowd moved to block his passage with evident hostile intent. The archer contented himself with putting his hand on his danger, ready to unsheathe it for his defense, and continued walking toward the exit. He was about to reach it when a stone came to strike his head and threw him rudely to the ground. Immediately, everyone rushed upon his person, struck him with daggers and started to exercise upon him he most frightful cruelties. In vain the old priest tried to stop the wretches by invoking the name of King Richard. No one listened to him, and he nearly fell victim himself to their insensate rage.

Finally, the cries of the assassins reached the Lionheart's tent. Suspecting the truth, he tore himself from the hands of his servants, who were bandaging him, and ran to the place where the archer was being murdered, but he arrived too late. Bertrand de Gourdon was dead. At the sight of his cadaver, Richard, crazed by anger, started striking with his sword all those who had taken part in the murder, and only ceased when he fell unconscious.

More than two hours went by before, having been carried back to his tent, he came round. An ardent fever was soon manifest; delirium took possession of the monarch, and for a week he never ceased, in the transports that agitated him, to beg William and his father for mercy, believing that he saw them incessantly standing by his bedside.

Finally, he recovered his reason, and the first sensate words he spoke were to ask whether his days were in peril. This is what happened, according to Gauthier d'Herminsfort, a contemporary historian.

"Sire," the Archbishop of Rouen replied to the king's question, "put your affairs in order, for you are dying."

"Is that a threat or a joke?" replied Richard, who still doubted, or rather, would have liked to doubt, that redoubtable truth.

"Nor, Sire, your death is inevitable."

"What do you want me to do, then?"

"Think of the daughters you have to marry and do penitence."

"I've already told you that I have no daughters."

"Sire, you have three daughters and you have been nurturing them for a long time. Your eldest is ambition, the second avarice and the third lust."

"I give the eldest to the Templars, the second to the gray monks and the third to the black monks."

"Don't talk thus," said a voice, "don't talk thus, Sire for your death is approaching. Think of your salvation."

"Who addresses that threat to me?" asked Richard, astonished.

"The man who received your father's last confession, and who has come to receive yours," replied the old priest of Saint Mary-le-Bow, advancing to the royal bedside. "Elevate your soul to God, Sire, for it is time; do penitence, and confide yourself to eternal mercy."

Touched by the old man's words, the King began to weep, and said: "I am very repentant and you shall see the proof of it."

Then he ordered everyone to leave, and, left alone with the old priest, he made a confession that lasted nearly two hours. When it was concluded, he wanted his feet to be bound and that his body, naked and suspended in the air, should be flagellated until the blood flowed. That flagellation was recommenced three times on his orders; afterwards he was dragged by a rope to his confessor, who had gone in search of the last sacrament, and who criticized gently and put an end to the rigors to which the royal penitent had condemned himself during his absence.

Richard received the last sacraments with testimonies of the most ardent fervor.

The next day, the old priest conducted to the Abbey of Fontevraud, in order that it might be placed beside the remains of Henry II, the coffin that contained all that remained on earth of Richard Coeur-de-Lion: his cadaver.

Chapter Seven
The Angel

Sitting sadly on the shore of the sea, Asrael, since the fatal exile that kept him far from Heaven, had not once opened his wings, with which he veiled his face. Still a stranger to the periods of time that regulate the life of mortals, three months had passed in that fashion for the cherub, whose tears never ceased to flow. The murmur of the waves that came to break at his feet, harmonized with his profound despair with a sort of charm, and his gaze, accustomed to the intoxicating splendors of Paradise, preferred a complete obscurity to the dull clarity that was known on earth by the name of daylight. He resolved to wait thus for the accomplishment of the decree of the Eternal and not to mingle with the fragile creatures among whom his imprudent charity forced him to remain for such a long time.

At least, he said to himself, *my brothers who descend to earth will not be witnesses to my shame. There will never see on my forehead the ignominious stain with which the lips of Satan have perhaps soiled it forever; and if I must never reenter Heaven, if William's family becomes extinct before four martyrs have emerged from its bosom, well, I shall remain in this solitude until the consummation of the centuries, deploring my fate and my destiny.*

While he was delivering himself to those deadly ideas of discouragement, he suddenly heard the sound of the golden harps that the angels unite in Paradise with the songs of the cherubim; that celestial harmony caused him to shiver with an emotion that was simultaneously sweet and painful. He sensed the resolutions of despair that he had previously formed vanishing from his will; his wings were parted slightly, and his eyes turned toward the sky. He perceived, in an aureole, three angels who were guiding a soul. Asrael fixed his gaze upon the divine cortege for as long as he could; then, when everything was effaced in the distance, by virtue of a involuntary movement, he took flight and followed the celestial group at a distance, all the way to the gates of Paradise.

There, two of the blessed, with martyrs' palms in hand, received their new brother, extended their arms to him and placed a luminous crown on his head, similar to the ones that radiated n their foreheads.

"Bertrand," they sad, "beloved brother, whom God has blessed forever in having abridged the time of your exile and having opened the gates of Heaven to you gloriously. Come, you who were brave and faithful, courageous and loyal on earth, unshakable in your Christian faith and defender of the oppressed. Enter into the felicity that will never end, for your death has expiated the little weakness inherent in your human nature, and the Normans who tortured you have placed an eternal crown on your head, like God. Come, take your place in the celestial militia alongside Paul, who fought with the sword, and near Maurice, who bowed his head under the sword of the decimator rather than betray his faith. Come, for our phalanx already counts three martyrs."

And the angels repeated: "Hosanna! A new phalanx will not be long in mingling its hymns of gratitude and amour with our canticles. Hosanna! The angel our brother, who is weeping and suffering on earth, will see his time of expiation and ordeals abridged and will return among us. Hosanna! Transports of felicity will burst forth in the celestial militia, for it is written that it is necessary to rejoice when a stray lamb returns to the fold."

As the songs reached him, Asrael felt moved and consoled. The discouragement that had overwhelmed him before was gradually succeeded by a sweet hope, and for the first time, prayers came to his mind and his lips. He knelt down on a cloud, his white and delicate hands united against his breast; he raised his head and his beautiful blond hair unfurled in long ringlets over his shoulders and his face. When he had concluded the fervent orison that emerged from his heart he got up, full of resignation and strength; then, shaking the pleats of his white tunic, impregnated with vapors that were exhaled by the earth, he contemplated for some time, with mute adoration, the waves of crimson and gold that the rising sun cast upon the oriental gates of Heaven.

"Thank you, my God!" he cried. "Thank you for having rendered me hope and strength, for having taken pity on my shame and my weakness! Thank you, for having abridged the term of my ordeal already, while in my ingratitude I doubted your mercy. Thank you, for I will labor henceforth in the work of my deliverance, and direct toward your holy dwelling the family to which, in your infinite views, you have attached my destiny. And you, my celestial brothers, beautiful angels, for whom I am separate for a time that might yet be long, unite your prayers with mine, for prayer softens punishments and redeems faults. Implore for me the pious and divine mother of God, the virgin of mercy who always places herself between the repentance and the justice of Jehovah. Obtain from that mother of the afflicted, not my return to Heaven—I have lacked faith and it is just that my sin be expiated—but the disappearance of the horrible stain that soils my forehead and drives me to despair.

Let Satan's horrible kiss by effaced, let my shame no longer be visible to all, in order I can lift my head, curbed by shame…and your brother will ask no more of your intercession. And his destiny can be accomplished without Asrael uttering a murmur."

He prayed again when he suddenly felt the bitter fire that was burning his forehead ease. A divine freshness replaced the painful wound of the infernal stigma. The cherub, full of hope, deployed his wings and took flight toward a spring, in the bright and pure waters of which he saw his image reflected. O joy! The imprint of the demon's kiss had almost disappeared! Only an imperceptible white scar remained on Asrael's forehead.

The angel hovered for almost an entire day above the spring that reproduced his divine forms. He could not weary of contemplating, in that transparent mirror, the beauty that had been so cruelly deleted by despair and expiation. He yielded himself to a thousand innocent and pure joys. Sometimes he lifted on to the summit of his head the undulating locks of his blond hair and disposed them as a crown; sometimes it was the pleats of his light white tunic, previously soiled and floating at hazard, that he readjusted with a skillful hand around his slender and noble waist. Then, after that, he brushed the water of the spring with his feet and rid them of the dust that profaned their delicate forms.

Only night, with its somber veils, was able to put an end to the cherub's purifications, and when, in the midst of the splendors of the setting sun, he elevated his soul toward God, prayer came easily and sweetly to his lips, and his vice united with the choirs of the angels, his bothers, who were celebrating the marvels of nature and the infinite grandeur of the one who drew Heaven and earth from nothing.

After concluding his prayer, the angel got up, full of hope and strength.

"Shame on my weakness," he said. "Already, divine mercy has come before the culpable, and the culpable should only think of seconding that mercy. Since my salvation depends on the family of William Longbeard, since it is by that route that my fault arose and by that route that pardon must arrive, I want henceforth to unite my destiny with it; I shall become its protector; I shall protect it against the traps of the Evil Spirit."

Preoccupied with those ideas, the angel deployed his wings and was disposing himself to fly to an elevated rock in order to discover with his divine eye where the last survivor of William's family lived when he heard frightful laughter grating under the earth. He lowered his eyes and saw the demon Astaroth hidden among trees, the leaves of which were withering as if ardent coals had touched them.

"Search," howled the evil angel, "search, handsome cherub, honored already by my kisses, and who will see himself reduced again to delivering yourself to my caresses in order to discover the place where the daughter of William Longbeard, the daughter of Saint William the Martyr, resides. Oh, don't go pale, for you won't know, first of all, what I don't want you to know, even on that condition, and secondly, that the child isn't baptized, and belongs to me. You were too quick to believe in my good faith, Asrael. The war I'm making is a war of cunning more than an open warfare of confrontation. Truly, you aren't an adversary worthy of me. It's necessary that I give you some advice, in order that the struggle becomes equal.

"While you were despairing and weeping, instead of flying to the church and inspiring the priest with the idea of baptizing William's daughter, I was thinking of means of making sure of my prey and keeping the victim that I had ceded to you for a few minutes at the price of the tender kiss you received from me. When Godwin and his wife, on leaving the church, went to climb into their boat to return to their dwelling, I accompanied them; I sat down in the poop and held out my arms. Suddenly, the demons recognized their monarch, the winds blew violently, the waves swelled, the tempest raced and lightning burst forth in all directions.

"Soon, the boat broke up on a rock, and Godwin and his wife perished, arming themselves with the accursed sign of the cross and invoking the mercy of your God. They went up to heaven. But the child, the child that was not baptized, belonged to me. I had only to allow it to sink to the bottom of the sea and its soul would have gone to augment, in the darkness, the number of pale phantoms that the lack of baptism has banished from Heaven forever. But that wasn't what I wanted.

"What does one more victim of the original sin matter to me? No, it's necessary that William's child—Saint William's child!—be damned of her own free will, by her own sins! It's necessary that she gives herself to Hell and not that fatality pushes her there! I showed myself charitable, therefore! Ha ha ha ha! I'm still laughing—I did a good deed! The child, attached by Godwin to a plank, was about to break against a rock and I placed myself between the rock and her. It was against my breast that the waves pushed her! My arms received her, my breath warmed her, my kisses appeased her cries. A tender mother—ha ha ha ha!—couldn't have lavished more care and testified more tenderness. Well, what do you say to my charity, handsome cherub? Could an angel of the Lord have done better?"

Asrael smiled with disdain. "God is combating with me," he replied, "and all your ruses, all your perfidies will not prevail against his power. I shall save William's daughter in spite of you, and I shall place the aureole of the elect on her head."

"It's necessary, for that, to overcome a few obstacles, which are not without difficulty, I warn you of that frankly. First of all, it's necessary to divine where the child is living, to what hands I confided her, and then to get close to her. Now, as she hasn't received the water of baptism, the guard of her cradle doesn't belong to the angels but to demons, and I doubt that, even for one of your kisses, those who are watching over your predestined will allow even the shadow of your wings to approach her cradle. So, search, Asrael; since the Almighty is fighting for you, vanquishing me should be a facile matter, and I don't doubt that your candor will easily triumph over my cunning."

And he had recommenced laughing his accursed and insolent laughter when his pale face suddenly became even paler; a convulsive agitation twisted all his limbs. He fell to his knees on the ground; he extended his arms toward the sky, and his lips, tightened by dolor, murmured words of supplication. God had extended his hand and the reproved struggled in the chastisement due to his blasphemies.

"Mercy! Mercy! Obtain my mercy!" he murmured. "Let these frightful torments cease and I'll tell you everything. I'll take you to the place where William's daughter lives; I'll order my legions to stand aside from her cradle. Mercy!"

Asrael leaned toward Astaroth. "May God, wretch, give you mercy," he said, "and may his clemency deign, by my intercession, to suspend the tortures in which

73

you're struggling. But I don't want you to reveal your secret to me. Keep it. I'll be able to discover it I spite of you, and save William's child in spite of you."

With those words of the angel, the demon's suffering eased. He fell breathless on to the sand, and a few moments went by before he recovered the strength to get up. He finally did so, but slowly, with his head bowed to hide his shame from the cherub's gaze. Then, suddenly, he opened his vulture's wings, and launched himself into the air with a precipitate bound, where he soon disappeared, like a black dot, in the clouds.

Asrael, uncertain, looked around with an irresolute gaze, which he then raised toward the sky.

"You alone, God," he said, "are strength and verity. I can do nothing without you, so deign to inspire me! For since my exile from Heaven, my gaze is feeble and has lost the power it enjoyed in happier times!"

Chapter Eight
The Child

In the land of Wales, on the shore of the sea, there was a little cabin—or rather, four stakes dressed with animal hides, which a fisherman and his wife sometimes planted in one part of the strand, sometimes in another. An old boat was always found sunk in the sand near the cabin, far enough away from the waves for the frail skiff not to be carried away but close enough for it to be put to sea without too much fatigue and effort. When no storm rumbled in the atmosphere, when he waves bobbed with tranquility and without anger, Gurth was seen to take his nets, which he disposed at low tide and then came back to recover them, when the high tide had covered them and left a few fish in them. He took that prey, brought it back to his wife, who grilled it over a few embers, and then, after a short meal, he went to lie down on the seaweed on a rock, gazed at the sky with a discontented expression, and ended up going to sleep.

But what if the sky was covered with clouds, the wind roared, the sea was swollen and unquiet, and its waves began to collide? Then Gurth woke up, and a strange joy took possession of him. His eyes shone with a sinister gleam; ferocious laughter contracted his lips, covered with a lush russet beard; joyful cries emerged from his breast. Then he was seen to take off his tight-fitting sealskin garment and lay his broad and powerful shoulders bare. He summoned his wife to help him launch the boat; he seized the oars, and soon the frail skiff was bounding over the furious sea, carrying with it the two savage creatures previously extended so peacefully on the seaweed.

While Gurth steered the little boat, his wife Herlich interrogated the extent of the waves incessantly, searching to see whether the beacon of some ship might appear in the distance. As soon as Herlich perceived the agitated light of one of those beacons, she suddenly hoisted an immense horn lamp to the top of the mast, and Girth steered the boat with great skill through the reefs and rocks among which he navigated habitually, the slightest details of which he knew. Almost always, the captains of ships that had gone astray on the coast allowed themselves to be taken in by that infernal ruse and advanced confidently toward a shore near to which they saw a ship sailing without danger, of which he could not make out the form, but which he judged to be of considerable size, given the nature and dimension of its beacon. Soon, the keel of the ship confided to the imprudent individual came to break up on the rocks, and the sea covered the debris and the men.

Then Gurth's boat stopped, was brought back to the shore and run aground on the sand. Herlich gave her husband a long club and took for herself a hook attached to the end of a rope; then the two of them waited. If the waves brought debris, Herlich threw her hook with a marvelous skill, seized the items, brought them ashore and carried the wreckage behind a rock or to her cabin. If it was a man that the sea pushed toward the shore, Gurth threw himself upon him, and whether the unfortunate was unconscious or he extended his hands and asked for help, the brigand struck him pitilessly with his club and despoiled his cadaver.

One evening, the day had been good; a ship had come to sink very close to Gurth's cabin; not only had he later found on the eight or ten unfortunates fallen under his blows a good deal of gold and precious objects, but Herlich's hook had brought two crates full of salted meat and several leather bottles full of wine.

Rich enough to deliver themselves joyfully to an orgy, the two ferocious creatures were about to return to their tent with their booty, without worrying about the other debris they could see floating among the waves, and commence a feast, to the sound of the tempest and the lightning, their accomplices, in which drunkenness and its furies would not be long delayed in taking part, when the waves suddenly cast up at Herlich's feet a little child, who began to utter plaintive cries.

Gurth seized the club in order to strike it, but his wife's heart, hardened as it was, felt moved to compassion and she stopped her husband's arm.

"Let's not kill children," she said.

These were the first words of pity that Gurth had heard emerge from his companion's lips, so he looked at her with an air of surprise, laughing.

"This is new!" he howled, in a voice that covered the oars of the tempest. "What do you want to do with that screeching runt, Herlich? Let me crush it."

He raised his foot in order to crush the child. Herlich seized her hook and threw it at Gurth's head, and while the latter wiped his bloody forehead, she picked the child up and warmed it against her bosom. The brigand, whom anger had initially caused to go pale, soon started laughing, and held out a hairy hand to his ferocious companion.

"Well struck, Herlich, well struck. If my head weren't as hard, I think you'd have broken it. I forgive you, but don't do it again. Come on, throw that little mewling cat away; the sea can do what it likes with it.

Come and drink the shipwreck victims' wine with me and see whether their provisions are good."

"Gurth," replied the savage creature, passing one of her arms around the fisherman's muscular neck, "it's necessary to let me have this child. I'll bring him up, he'll grow tall, and when we're old, he'll steer the boat for us and bring the flotsam of the wrecks to our cabin."

"That's a singular idea, of which I wouldn't have believed you capable," Gurth put in, evidently softened. "Do as you wish. Keep the child, as long as its cries don't trouble my sleep." He added: "And let it be a boy, for otherwise, I'll wring its neck. Come on, let's go; I'm dying of hunger and thirst is tightening my throat."

Herlich let Gurth enter the cabin and deposited the child in a hollow in the rock that was full of moss. She took off the coarse mantle that was hanging over her shoulders and covered her protégé with it carefully, planted a kiss on the little white forehead and went to join Gurth, not without looking back twice to make sure that the child was asleep.

When she went into the cabin she found Gurth devouring a piece of salted pork with a bottle that was already empty lying beside him. She encouraged him to drink again, pretending to deliver herself to intemperance as well, and the brigand soon fell over, dead drunk. Immediately, she left the cabin and went to find the child, which had woken up, and was holding out its arms to her with a smile, as if she were its mother. A tear gleamed in the eye of the woman who had never wept; that tear slid over her brown cheeks and dripped on to her bosom, like a shiny pearl.

"Yes," she said, "you can smile at me and hold out your arms, for I'll love you and watch over you as your mother would have done, your poor mother, whose cadaver the waves are doubtless carrying away. I'll love you, for I've been alone in the world since the day when Gurth came to steal me from my family, a poor defenseless girl that he made his companion. For you, I won't get drunk anymore; for you, I won't kill any more, for blood brings bad luck, and then, I don't want you to commit crimes and to fear the justice of men and the justice of God, as I do. I'll hide your sex carefully from Gurth, who'd kill you if he knew you were a girl. I'll bring you up beside me like my child until the age of five or six. When bad examples might have some influence on you, the good God will inspire me as to what I ought to do for you. I'll do it, even if it costs me my life."

As she spoke she poured into the infant's mouth, drop by drop, a little of the milk that came from a goat, the only living creature that inhabited the tent with Gurth. Herlich placed the child on her knees as if in a cradle, rocked her to send her to sleep, and ended up falling asleep herself.

It was broad daylight the following morning when Gurth emerged from the profound slumber into which the previous evening's drunkenness had sent him. His eyes swollen and his head heavy, he paraded an astonished gaze around the tent, for he expected to find Herlich lying at his feet, numbed by the wine, as usual. He got up, went outside and called Herlich several times; not seeing her come, he headed for the rocks, where he did not take long to find her, asleep, with the child in her arms. Gurth frowned.

"Whence comes this singular tenderness for a child she's never seen?" he muttered. "Is she going to abandon my cabin every night for that little creature? Herlich was abrupt, pitiless, with no weakness; I've seen her a hundred times stripping cadavers that were still palpitating, without showing the slightest sign of pity, and here she is making herself a cradle and sleeping in the open in order to care for a runt. Oh, women! It's necessary never to believe in them; an instant suffices for them to change. Hey, Herlich!"

Herlich woke up, and hastened to place the child in the nest of moss, for she read anger in her husband's face.

"The next time you leave my cabin to me and spend the night with that child," he told her, "first I'll break the head of the kid against a rock, and then I'll tie you to a stake and you'll make the close acquaintance of the cord of your hook or the wood of my oar."

Herlich looked up at Gurth ferociously.

"You've often beaten me, and I've borne your blows without avenging myself," she said, "but if you touch the child, I advise you to kill me with him, because otherwise, passers-by will soon see a cadaver in your cabin, even if I have no other weapons than my hands."

"Ha ha!" said Gurth, pleased to see anger and menace animating his woman's features. "That's how I like you, Herlich; you're truly beautiful now, hair in disorder and fire in your eyes, face pale and hands convulsively agitated. You no longer look like an old London nurse crouching on the doorstep of a shop to change the nappy of a merchant's son. Come let me kiss you, my fury!"

And he pressed her in his muscular arms with a force that would have stifled any other woman, but the robust Herlich's waist barely buckled.

"That's enough quarreling, let's go; come and help me replant the pickets of the cabin, which the violence of the storm has shaken. Then we'll throw back in the sea the cadavers that the tide hasn't carried away yet, and bury our superfluous provisions and our gold. It's necessary that no one divines the wealth of the poor fisherman Gurth until we can go and lad the opulent life of a rich ban in Normandy, for with gold, King Richard will make me a baron, Herlich. Gold makes everything possible at King Richard's court!"

Before following her husband, Herlich deposited the child on the bed of moss, and after having made sure that she was asleep and kissed her forehead, she headed for the cabin. She suddenly felt a delightful fresh breath of wind pass over her head and caress her face. That breath caused Gurth's savage companion to experience sensations that were unknown to her. It was the wing of the cherub, who was traversing the air and coming to watch over the child.

Chapter Nine
At Sea

Six years went by, during which the child cast into Herlich's arms grew up, and ended up even winning the grim affection of Gurth, thank to her prettiness and her naïve cheerfulness. The mildness and the lack of strength of the little creature, whom he believed to be a boy, were not of a nature to please the robust and brutal brigand, but the caresses of Edward—that was what they had named "him"—her unalterable gaiety and grace, spread throughout her person, caused the words of disdain or anger provoked by the weakness of the little girl, clad in the costume of Welsh peasants, to die on his lips.

Edward buckled under the burdens that Gurth wanted "him" to carry, and was unable to handle the oars that were too heavy for her arms, but by sway of compensation she held and directed the tiller with as much skill as the brigand himself, and was able to climb to the top of a mast with the briskness and agility of a squirrel. No danger astonished her and no obstacle stopped her; not a day passed when she did not bring Herlich a few seabird chicks taken from the highest and steepest rocks.

With her blonde hair scattered over her shoulders, clad in a doublet that outlined the form of her slender waist, and britches that left her legs and feet bare, when she was not leaping from rock to rock she practiced with the bow or the crossbow, and hardly ever missed the target at which she aimed. Gurth took her with him every time he went fishing, but when a tempest arrived and the brigand lit the searchlight of his mast in order to cause a shipwreck, Herlich, under the pretext that it was necessary not to expose a frail creature like Edward to the perils of the sea and the outrage of the wind, always obtained that the child should be left in the cabin. The true motive that made her act in that fashion was that she did not want to associate the young girl with scenes of crime and murder, because she did not want to soil the purity of heart of the child she had adopted.

Yes, Herlich, Gurth's wife, who had once struck shipwreck victims who implored her for mercy, without flinching and without any emotion, no longer felt the same now. She would have given half her life to find herself in the depths of some placid village, and only to be a poor woman sitting by her fireside with a distaff in her hand. A thousand maternal anxieties filled her heart regarding the future of the child that she saw growing up beside her, and who would not take long to be corrupted by Gurth's example; for Gurth's joy was extreme when he saw Edward putting a cup full of wine to his lips and repeating the blasphemies that were mingled with the brigand's slightest speeches.

Those anxieties regard the future of her adopted child rendered Herlich sad and thoughtful. She was often seen spending entire hours sitting on a rocky point, her head hidden in her hands, letting her thoughts wander. Then the cherub Asrael came to sit beside her or hover above her head, in order to stimulate with his divine breath the generous flame that pity had lit in the woman's heart.

One evening when Gurth was absent, she suddenly quit the rock, set the boat afloat and called to Edward.

"My child," she said, "it's necessary for us to row hard, for we're going on a journey that might be long."

The child wept with joy, for she only felt at ease when she was in the boat and on the waves.

Inspired by Asrael, Herlich had decided to take advantage of Gurth's absence to flee, to attempt to reach the coast of France and seek on some deserted shore of that country an existence devoid of crime and remorse.

There, she said to herself, *I shall live on the labor of my hands. I shall go fishing; I shall mend the sails of fishermen; I shall even beg if necessary, but at least I shall save this little girl from the remorse that is gnawing at my heart; I shall not have to repent of having caused her doom. God, who is inspiring me, will protect me.*

And for the first time, that woman, who had not prayed since the day when Gurth had brought her, bleeding, to his cabin, that woman habituated to pillage and murder knelt down piously, extended her hands toward the heavens and tried to murmur a prayer. Edward, who saw her do it, placed herself beside her, imitated her and recited the words that she heard emerging from her adoptive mother's mouth.

"Lord, Lord protect us!"

Soon, the boat, detached from the ring that retained it to the shore, was set afloat and launched on to the water; the sail opened and inflated, and the ebb ride carried the skiff out into the open sea with the rapidity of an arrow. But Astaroth, who saw his prey escaping him, and was subject to all the more rage at Asrael's triumph because that triumph would put an end to the angel's exile and bring him back to Heaven, went to Gurth, who was coming back, inspired thoughts of anger and crime in him, and hastened his march by pushing him with his invisible hands.

Gurth arrived on the shore at the moment when Herlich and Edward were beginning to ply the oars in order to reach the open sea and give more speed to their boat. Without understanding the motives for their flight, he nevertheless understood that they were both fleeing. Immediately, he took an arrow from his quiver and fitted it to his bow; the arrow whistled, and would have reached its target if Asrael's hand had not deflected it; but the furious Astaroth launched himself on to the boat with one bund and pushed Herlich into the sea.

Herlich uttered a scream: "My God! My God!" and then she disappeared beneath the waves, which closed over her.

While Edward yielded to despair and wondered anxiously whether she ought to continue her route or obey Gurth, who was calling to her from the shore, the furious Gurth started swimming, heading for the boat. At that moment the sky was covered with flashes, lightning burst forth, and it was not long before two cadavers came to break against the rocks: hideous and bloody cadavers in which no one would have been able to recognize the disfigured bodies of Gurth and Herlich.

Meanwhile, Edward, lost in the midst of the waves, who had just en his benefactress perish, raised his hands to the heavens and repeated his adoptive mother's last words, as he had repeated her prayer that morning, for the angel Asrael was still sitting in the poop of the boat; but Astaroth, standing at the prow, troubled the mind of the little girl in order to drive away any religious thought, and hurled thoughts of terror and desolation upon her. Without the cherub, he would have tried to tip the child into the waves, for he was beginning to fear that she might escape Hell, but he dared not attempt that bold project; he recalled the cruel tortures to which he had already been subjected before the eyes of the exiled angel, and a convulsive tremor seized him merely at the thought of that horrible suffering.

Both of them, in presence, therefore awaited the outcome of that struggle between Heaven and Hell. For Astaroth, defeat would shame him and expose him to the pitiless mockery of the other demons for eternity. If Asrael were defeated, it would be necessary for him to wait for the consummation of the centuries before reentering Paradise, for Edward—or, rather, Edwige—was the last survivor of William's family...

Astaroth folded his arms over his hideous breast; Asrael knelt down and raised his eyes hopefully toward Haven. But God did not want everything to be concluded that night; the sea gradually died down, the waves lot their agitation, the thunder ceased to rumble and he lightning was extinguished. Edwige, exhausted by fatigue and dolor, went to sleep; and when she woke up, the boat was stationary among rocks.

When the young girl awoke she looked around in surprise; the vents of the previous night seemed to her to have been a troubled and dolorous dream. But when she saw that she was not asleep, when the memory of Herlich's death was presented distinctly to her mind, she began to weep bitterly.

Asrael, moved to pity, detached the boat with the tip of his wing and directed it toward a nearby bay, which served the frail skiff as a port. Edwige jumped on to the shore, and saw a young boy going past at a run; she tried to call to him, but the cry she uttered was so hoarse and so terrible that it frightened the child, and put him to flight. The latter's parents, alarmed to see him come back pale and trebling, inquired as to the causes of his terror, and he replied that a monster with long hair was on the sea shore, ready to devour anyone who approached it.

Everyone immediately armed themselves and ran to the shore; they stopped with astonishment at the sight of Edwige, whose strange and marvelous beauty took on a wilder character under the last rays of the setting sun, which were casting glorious crimson reflections over her. Her long blonde hair scattered, standing up and leaning on an oar, she gazed for some time, smiling, at the crowd of assembled fishermen, and walked toward them confidently.

By virtue of a mechanical movement of terror, the fishermen recoiled before the unknown creature; Edwige continued walking nevertheless, surprised by the fear that she had inspired, and tried to take in her arms a child whose precipitation had caused it to fall at her feet. As she bent down to pick up the frightened child, the father hurled the harpoon that he was holding in his hand at Edwige and struck the child in the middle of the breast.

She fell under the blow and struggled for a few moments on the sand, which she covered with her blood; but it was a rapid crisis, over which she soon triumphed. Habituated to suffering, the young girl overcame the pain that she was experiencing, got up, and pulled her harpoon out of her wound. Seeking with her gaze the man who had struck her, she recognized him, pursued him into the middle of the crowd and soon threw him down at her feet. Then there was a frightful tumult around her; everyone attacked her; alone against all of them, she did not take long to yield to the weight of numbers. She was knocked down, tied up, tightly bound to a stake, and the fishermen, still under the influence of anger, started debating between themselves as to the fate of their captive.

While some proposed putting her to death immediately, others wanted to preserve her for long and cruel tortures. Edwige, exhausted by anger and the loss of her blood, fell into unconsciousness. An old woman took pity on her, leaned over her in order to bandage her, and opened the coat that she was wearing.

"It's a woman! It's a woman!" she cried then.

And she interrogated Edwige; but Edwige did not understand the language that the old woman employed to speak to her, and responded in a faint voice with a few words in Saxon. Those words were not understood by those who surrounded her.

Fortunately, an old English priest, whom the death of King Richard and the catastrophes that had ensued since that time had prevented from returning to England, attracted by the tumult, quit the little hermitage that he had established among the rocks and hastened to extract their victim, if there was still time, from the fishermen. The angel and the demon, who were hovering above the shore, recognized the old priest of Saint Mary-le-Bow.

Asrael uttered a cry of joy, but Astaroth laughed bitterly.

"Don't think you're victorious yet," he said. "In spite of the presence of that auxiliary, Edwige has not been baptized, and she has just shed blood; my influence can therefore be exercised upon that individual predestined for hell, while you'll be forced to remain inactive in her regard."

As he spoke, he descended close to the young girl, and, without ceasing to be invisible, he surrounded her with his filthy arms and troubled her with the current of is infernal breath. Edwige, who had just succumbed to a second faint, opened her eyes and felt herself animated by a strange force. Her heart was beating rapidly, her blood burning in her veins; her gaze as illuminated by a sinister gleam. The women who were surrounding her recoiled in fear, and the old priest remained alone with her.

"Come, young woman," he said to her. "You have no more anger to fear. Come, a shelter awaits you. I'll take you to a nearby cloister, where you'll find cares for your wounds and your soul. Come with me."

Edwige made a movement to follow the old man. The demon stopped her and tightened more narrowly the embrace with which he surrounded her.

The old man took the child by the hand, but Astaroth murmured fatal words in Edwige's ear, and she pushed the old man away so rudely that he fell, and his head went to strike the angle of a rock and broke.

Furious at the sight of that murder, the fishermen threw themselves on the murderess, whose bloody body soon fell beside the old man, who was dying.

Triumphant, Astaroth was already leaning toward Edwige to take possession of her soul; Asrael knelt down beside the old man and murmured in his ear: "She isn't baptized; save her."

The priest, at that celestial inspiration, lifted himself up, dragged himself toward the expiring Edwige, and allowed a few drops of the blood that was flowing from his own wounds to fall on to the unfortunate child's forehead.

"I baptize thee in the name of the Father, the Son and the Holy Spirit," he said, and died.

"A tear once saved you," cried the angel, "and it's a drop of blood that has redeemed you. God be praised forever, for the secrets of is Providence are divine and impenetrable."

Then the roar of the vanquished Astaroth was heard, who returned to Hell to hide the shame of his defeat, and the cherub Asrael rose into the heavens again in order to take to the feet of Jehovah two radiant souls, while the angels, his brothers, sang their most harmonious canticles and mingled with their divine voices the sublime chords of their golden harps.

HEADS OR TAILS
A Flemish Tale

> At the first glance, the players read a horrible
> mystery on the face of the novice.
> Honoré de Balzac, *La Peau de Chagrin*

> One of my ancestors borrowed twenty thousand
> ducats and only gave his moustache as a pledge.
> His creditor never had the slightest anxiety, and
> he was paid on the due date.
> Thomas de Carcassol.[10]

I. The Game Won

"Isn't it true, Antonio, that seeing those men standing around is already a spectacle full of emotion , those men whose features are contracted in a convulsive impassivity? And then, the gold that clinks and stones! The great silence of a decisive coup! The dull murmur that follows a game won! The voices clamoring! The players throwing their gold on the baize. The felons drawing away with their paltry prey, braving scorn for a hundred ducats. Apprehensions, transports, torments and sarcasms; and all that carefully retained in the breast, hidden from all eyes, kept to oneself, to oneself alone! All that during a fête, among women with bare shoulders, in a warm and soft atmosphere, all that and the vague

---

[10] Like many of the author's citations, this one is entirely fictitious.

chords of guitars, flutes and viols, and the buzz of a thousand voices.

"But to mingle with that group oneself; to throw a large sum oneself among the heaps of gold; to hold in one's own trembling hands the cards that will adjudge those riches' to pant with expectation oneself and shiver at each of the rapid chances that succeed one another; to be the object of ardent prayers; to become for a few minutes as powerful as destiny, to be cursed like Satan or blessed like the savior—oh, that is another emotion altogether! That is living, that is feeling—isn't it true, Antonio?

"Well, a quarter of an hour ago I played a better game than Lansquenet, for better than gold. I wagered my life, my life of a young man of twenty-five, my life of a Spanish captain, with its extravagances, its orgies and its nosy escapades; my life, with its nocturnal serenades, its duels and its rendezvous; and all that in a moment, in a second. A second sufficed; a chance decided. I lived more in that second than you have done in your entire life.

"And I won. Let's go! Let's go! Wine, beautiful women! Call all our comrades! Let's have guitars, dances, kisses, cries, drunkenness! A blow-out until tomorrow, until the day after, as long as you want! I've won! I've won!

"I've won, I tell you, I've won that game, and against a young man like me, my handsome cousin Pezarre del Montes, the man who was to share with me the heritage of my old uncle Don Gordon, the man who was to marry the beautiful Marguerite Raparlier! And now, the inheritance, Marguerite and my life of a young man of twenty-five is all mine, and mine alone.

"He came to find me a little while ago, the insensate. 'I'm jealous of you, for you love Marguerite. I hate you, because you're going to share my uncle's inheritance. As long as you're alive I'll never savor Marguerite's kisses; I'll always remember the gaze that she darted at you just now.

"'You'll never be happy either while Marguerite sleeps in my arms, as long as you prowl around my swelling pale with jealousy and despair. You'll never be able either to dissipate cheerfully a fortune shared with me.

"'Let's see, do you want to bet? Complete happiness for one of us: for one of us the heritage, Marguerite and the death of a rival; for the other, the dagger, or even worse, the cloister. Let this coin decide. Do you want to?'

"'Done!'

"He tossed the gold coin into the air. Heart palpitating, chest taut, I shouted a word mechanically; I followed with my dazed eyes the ducat riding and spinning. It fell back, bounced and stopped. Antonio, I didn't know which of the two words I'd said: heads or tails?

"And he was there, fixing his convulsive gaze on the coin, a gaze so strange that I couldn't divine whether it was joy or despair. Suddenly, he cried: 'Malediction! Ah…!'

"That frightful cry made me bound with joy, intoxicated me with a happiness that resembled rage.

"I had won, won…yes, won! As he had said, it was all mine: the heritage, Marguerite and the death of a rival.

"Wine! Wine! Kisses! Mad joys! Orgy! Orgy! Until tomorrow, until the day after. Call our comrades, let them all come. I've won! I've won!"

At those cries of joy, several Spanish officers came running and surrounded Don Carlos urgently. For Don Carlos of the ardent imagination, the profligate and witty, Don Carlos the agile, impetuous and perfect cavalier, was an object of envy and affection for the whole regiment. Everyone quoted his quips, everyone listed his mistresses, and no one wanted to cross swords with him, given that more than one had attempted it and always ended up on his back.

Don Carlos, by means of a gesture, recommended discretion to Antonio, and then started to tell I know not what mad story to his comrades to explain his noisy delight. Soon, bottles of wine covered the long table in the tavern; games of Lansquenet were organized, and a murmur of voices informed the neighbors of the Lion d'Or that, in spite of the night and the curfew, the Spanish dragoons were having a party.

Such a racket was happening very close to the house inhabited by the lovely damoiselle Marguerite Raparlier; nevertheless, it did not trouble in any fashion that young woman's reverie. That was, you see, because amour and vanity were cradling her with their sweetest charms. Plunged into one of the large and voluptuous armchairs of the epoch, she had not even noticed that the daylight had gone and that it somber night had fallen. Happier than can be expressed, she was letting her imagination go to the most eccentric projects, and all those projects were associated with the idea of Don Pezarre, her fiancé Don Pezarre. Proud of the amour of such an accomplished cavalier, proud of his high rank and noble lineage, she delivered herself with abandon to the caressant promises of the future. Rich, beautiful and beloved, nothing was lacking but the crown of a marquise, and Pezarre, her Pezarre, would place it on her head.

And the day of the wedding was finally fixed, irrevocably fixed. A week from now, she would receive the felicitations of all Cambrai, who would hasten to compliment the daughter of the alderman and the wife of the marquis. But there he was! And, getting up with a joyful agility, she ran to meet him

"Pezarre! My Pezarre! Why that pallor? Why this silence? Your hand is shivering in mine! Holy Virgin Mary, why? Speak, speak."

Pezarre turned his head away and put a trembling hand to his forehead. After that, he took a few aimless steps, and then he said: "Adieu!"

"Pezarre! Just Heaven. why this fear? Why this embarrassment? Why that adieu...? He's going away! He isn't listening to me! Pezarre! My fiancé!"

"I am that no longer."

"Oh!" she said, putting her hands together. "Oh, what are you saying? What! Have I heard correctly? Listen, Pezarre woe betide you! I've confessed, in front of everyone, that I loved you; I've prayed, I've begged to be yours; they all said: she's marrying him, her, the alderman's proud daughter, is marrying a captain who doesn't possess anything but his cape and his sword; they've even said it in front of me; I've suffered all that without a murmur. And now, like a coward and a felon, you're abandoning me! Oh, yes, woe betide you!"

Bewildered, trembling with rage and dolor, Marguerite could not contain her tears any longer, which escaped and spread over her burning cheeks.

"Woe betide me!" repeated Pezarre, after a long silence, absorbed by the most poignant despair. "Woe betide me! Woe betide me. You smiled a little while ago at that frivolous fop Carlos; you received his insolent homage with vanity. He's of royal blood, he's the most brilliant cavalier in the whole army, he goes everywhere repeating that he loves you...I couldn't contain myself and I said: let one of us die today, immediately!

"The wound I have in my arm, didn't allow me the possibility of combat for at least a month; it was necessary for me to get out of that execrable anxiety. So I said: 'Let fate decide!' Malediction! Carlos won!"

Then he told Marguerite at length what had happened between himself and his rival. Marguerite let him speak, and when he had finished, she said:

"And you doubtless believe, noble Seigneur del Montes, that I will ratify that fine treaty; you believe that I will humbly become the prize of a gambler, like a gold piece. Come on, you're joking, and you're forgetting who I am. Gamble your heritage as much as you please, but you've dared to mingle my name with such follies?"

"Adieu, Marguerite!"

Those words, stifled by despair, were Don Pezarre's response.

The alderman's daughter let him take a few steps, but when she heard the door close on Pezarre, all her fine courage gave way to dread and she ran to her lover and brought him back.

"Listen," she said. "You can't die. I don't want that. You're mine, you belong to me, you're my fiancée, my husband. Everything you've done is a folly of young men. Don Carlos can't seriously demand the accomplishment of such a treaty. Let's go find him. Let him take your fortune and mine, all that I possess. But you, you..."

A glance that she darted at Pezarre told the poor young woman that no hope remained in that direction.

"Well," she added, throwing herself at Don Pezarre's knees, "let's flee. The night is dark; take this gold, these diamonds, let's leave without telling anyone, not even my father, and may he not die of it. You'll change your name; we'll go to find a shelter in some unknown country; wherever you wish, it doesn't matter...you're hesitating? Oh, you don't love me; for do you believe that it costs me nothing, to flee like a fallen woman, to permit everyone to say of me tomorrow: 'Marguerite Raparlier, who was so proud, has allowed herself to be abducted by a Spanish cadet'?

"Come on, come on, don't go: stay, stay! A little while longer! The hour of death isn't fixed for today, for now. Wait until tomorrow; take pity on poor Marguerite. See, she's on her knees. My God! My God! How pitiless these men are" Oh, stay, stay! Listen, here's a means: Let's flee, and throw my veil and your mantle into the Escaut. People will say: 'They've drowned.' Oh, that's a good means, isn't it? You can't refuse now, your honor will be saved. But no, no...he still refuses!

"Come back, come back, I haven't said everything. My God, inspire me, make him listen to me! Oh, I won't quit you, I won't let you go; drag me after you, cover me with your blood, strike, kill yourself in my arms if you dare. Why don't you dare? You're really pushing me away? Courage, come on, I'm embracing your knees, kick me away, courage! You've already done too much to hesitate to kick a woman!

"O my God my God, touch his heart...! Pezarre, you told me that he let you choose between death and a convent. Well, become a monk. They won't say you lack heart; you're brave, everyone knows that, and then, God will bless you...oh, he's escaping me, he's fleeing, God! My God!"

She fell unconscious, and Pezarre, who had wrenched himself from her arms, disappeared.

II. The Bullfight

Three years later, there was a great bullfight in Madrid and the vast amphitheater where that combat was to take place was filled with an immense crowd; the aristocracy in the first rank, then the bourgeois, and after that the populace.

In the midst of that noisy crowd, monks were circulating with purses in hand, going from one to another begging for the dead, for the ransom of captives, or even, for there were a large number, their convents. Although the spectators were horribly tightly packed, they never failed to get up respectfully before the monks as they moved around the seated public, or to open a passage for them when they cleaved through the crowd standing at the extremity of the circle.

All the collectors had good receipts, but one of them seemed privileged, for he had had to empty three times into the satchel of the lay brothers who were following him the sums that were deposited from all directions into the purse that he held out to everyone. He was a tall, stiff man, entirely bald, whose wan complexion and hollow cheeks revealed great austerities or a mortal illness.

He had made his way gradually around half the circle when cries uttered in all parts announced the entry of a bull into the arena. In order not to trouble the pleasure of the spectators, and harming his receipts in consequence, the monk took his place between two cavaliers, who moved aside to make room for him, and he pulled his hood down over his eyes, in order to meditate and not to participate in the worldly joys in the mist of which he found himself. That was difficult, for a single rank of spectators separated him from the balcony of the arena, and a veiled young woman who was in front of him never ceased to address passionate words to the cavalier who accompanied her.

"Oh, my dear beloved, O my friend," she said, with the exaggerated expressions of the Spanish language, expressions that become quite simple in amour. "Why, my lord, my life, how beautiful your Spain is! How easily one loves beneath its burning sky! Oh, my beloved, how sad my homeland is compared with yours. No, I don't want it anymore; adieu Flanders, adieu forever!"

The monk straightened, shivering; then, he put his elbows on his knees, in order to hear more clearly what the señora who was speaking was saying.

"And nothing is lacking my happiness, nothing," the young woman continued, placing her blonde head voluptuously on the cavalier's shoulder; "nothing, my love, for you're handsome, you're rich, you're noble, and you risked your life in order that I might be yours! And you supported for six months—as long as that, my Carlos—my disdain and my regrets for the love of another."

The monk uttered a roar that caused the gazes of all the spectators to turn toward him. Only two paid no heed to it, although they were his two nearest neighbors: the cavalier and the young woman who were saying words of amour to one another.

"But now, I only love you. The past seems cold to me; before you, I had never loved. Oh, no! You alone, you!. I do not love, and never loved, anyone but you, Blessed by the death of Pezarre, which delivered me from the misfortune of belonging to another.

The monk stood up, trembling in his every limb, his face still masked by his hood.

At that moment, there was a great noise in the arena, and all the spectators on the balcony leaned over in order to see the bull, which had been driven back against the barrier, and had just torn apart a toreador. Drawn from their sweet ecstasy by what was happening at their feet, the two lovers did as everyone else was doing and leaned over the wooden balustrade as far as they could.

The monk also leaned over, but it was to strike the cavalier with a terrible blow, who fell on to the horns of the bull, and to murmur in the señora's ear: "Remember Pezarre!"

THE DAMOISELLES DE BÉTHENCOURT[11]

In the lineage of Béthencourt
Eight virgins will be engendered;
Amours will not be seen
Like theirs.

The Wedding Night

Legend
957

Monseigneur Satan, I've come to request from Your Highness, in exchange for my soul, my body and my entire self, a benefit that will not cost you much: it is merely to give me to torment in Hell, as I wish and as I please. Jacomo Benevenutto.

Paoli Frienzi, *The Damned.*[12]

The rising sun was still tinting the clouds red when many squires, pages, varlets and hunters were already in the courtyard of the Château de Béthencourt, leading horses by the bridle, holding back the hounds and bearing hawks and tercels on their wrists. Never had a more

---

[11] This story series was originally published in three issues of Émile Girardin's pioneering fashion magazine *La Mode* in 1830.

[12] Entirely fictitious.

joyful confusion been heard than the wing-beats and piercing cries of the falcons, the snorting of the horses, the various clamors of the dogs and the hunting horns trying the fanfare that would soon be repeated deep in the woods.

So, when the lords and ladies descended the perron in order to go hear mass before setting forth on the hunt, each of them darted a long and brilliant sideways glance, which demonstrated other thoughts than pious ones, and which seemed to be saying: "Weary! Not so soon!"

Meanwhile, the Bishop of Cambrai, Monseigneur Bérangaire, a good companion if ever there was one, whose hunting doublet was visible through the surplice that he was wearing on top, trembling with joviality, repeated to them: "Have no fear, my lords and ladies, I shan't speak for long, but very dry, as you can see; to that end, I haven't put on any priestly garment except the surplice, omitting the stole and the chasuble."

Monseigneur Bérangaire was true to his promise, for, following the usage of "dry" masses said *venatoria*—masses subsequently reproved by the Holy Council, he omitted the oblation, the consecration and the communion, and everyone was very joyful and amazed when he was seen, after the duration of a *pater* and an *ave*, to turn round and say *ite, missa est*, take off his surplice and then take from the hands of the chaplain the hood and sword of a hunter.

Go, go! The horns sounded, the chargers were launched at a gallop, and immediately, the baying of the hounds let it be known that they were on the trail of a wild boar.

Among the best of the hunters was, first and foremost, Damoiselle Mélissende, the only daughter of the Sire de Béthencourt and fiancée of the noble Sire d'Havrincourt, "the genteel Renaud," as everyone called him. No one knew better than the two of them how to guide a charger white with foam, no one repeated the hunting cries more gaily and with more ardor. Mélissende counted for nothing hedges to jump and ditches to cross. Renaud was less concerned with running the beast than sparing his fiancée a peril or fatigue; keeping alongside her galloping horse, he moved aside with the aid of his pike the branches that might have entangled the lovely maiden's long black hair or struck the face that blushed with pleasure at so much concern.

Now, it happened that they encountered an old woman picking up dead wood while her son, a young man of twenty, fashioned faggots with it. Neither the damoiselle nor the knight paid any heed to them, and the poor creature, whose deaf ear and seventy-year-old eyesight did not alert her to the advent of the horses, was thrown bloodily at her son's feet.

The young villein thought that she was dead; he uttered a cry of despair and struck Messire Renaud a blow on the head with his staff, which tipped him from his charger. He would have redoubled his efforts if the screams of Mélissende had not attracted varlets who mastered the furious man, not without difficulty, and managed to bind his feet and wrists.

In the meantime, Monseigneur Bérangaire and many others strove to revive Messire Renaud, who finally opened his eyes. Mélissende, a well-educated chatelaine, was savant in medical science, and, not wanting to leave anyone else to examine the stricken man's injury, she took the head of her beloved sire on her knees, and made a long and anxious search, during which tears forced her to recommence more than once. Finally, she gave thanks to the blessed Saint Hubert, and promised him a novena and a dozen wax candles, saying: "There's no danger to his life! May God, Our Lady and all the saints of paradise be praised forever!"

"Now," she resumed, after a brief prayer, "it's necessary to return to the manor, in order that Messire Renaud can take such repose and remedies as might be appropriate. No other hands than mine will soothe his wound with balm; no other hand than mine will bring the beverage that makes dolors sleep, which I learned to make for a savant physician of Cambrensis...now forward! Messire Renaud, let two arms sustain you, that of Monseigneur my father and that of your fiancée, and let's set forth slowly and at a measured step, to go back to the manor."

"Sagely spoken!" said the bishop. "The most knowledgeable cleric could not have preached better. Marvelous maiden, depart as you have said; I'll have the villein hanged high with his neck in a noose from that tree, for the wicked action for which your eyes are now red and swollen Here comes the administrator of justice! It is, by God, his good angel that has brought him here. Work quickly and soon, worthy vassal, and fulfill the duty of your charge as necessary. The first oak will serve you as a gallows."

On hearing the bishop's words, the old woman, to whom no one had paid any heed and who had recovered consciousness, cane to put herself at Bérangaire's knees, asking for mercy for her son in the name of Jesus Christ and Our Lady.

The bishop pushed her away with his foot without response, and watched the executioner at work, who had already knotted the rope with expert hands.

The poor mother saw that there was no hope in that direction. She ran after Mélissende, and in a state to make the most implacable weep, she begged the chatelaine for mercy for her only son, the hope of her old age.

"No, on the salvation of my soul," replied Mélissende. "He tried to kill my beloved."

"Mercy! Grant him mercy!" implored the old woman, again.

For all response, Mélissende ordered her varlets to drive away the old woman, who was importuning her with her laments. On that harsh command, they began laboring her with great blows of leather straps. She fell unconscious, and when she came round, she found herself alone in the forest, at the foot of the tree from which the cadaver of her son was hanging.

I shall not tell you what she suffered, for in order to understand it, it would be necessary to be a mother and to find oneself confronted with the cadaver of one's only son...one's only son, killed for having defended his mother.

"If I could avenge myself," she said, finally, in a terrible voice...

She darted futile glances around her, still alone, feeble and impotent.

Her head fell into her hands

Suddenly, she got up and started to cry: "Satan, come to my aid! May she be unfortunate! May no maiden of that wicked lineage be fortunate! Let them all know despair—all of them, and her above all—and I will give myself to you instantly, body and soul!"

The earth trembled, thunder uttered a long howl, and flames emerged from the flanks of the earth.

After that time, no one ever saw the old woman of Béthencourt again.

The events that I have just related occurred in the epoch of the feast of the Nativity; when the feast of the blessed Magloire arrived,[13] there was scarcely any trace of Messire Renaud's wound, and it was the day of his marriage with Damoiselle Mélissende.

It would be necessary to write from the holy day of Sunday to the following Saturday, and perhaps a good clerk would not be sufficient, to recount in a suitable fashion, without omitting anything, the countless ceremonies, feasts and passes of arms that were held to celebrate such a noble wedding.

At the very end, to the great jubilation of Messire Renaud, a truce was called to such long rejoicing. Messire Bérengaire blessed the nuptial couch in the appropriate manner, after which everyone went away and the husband was admitted to the company of his wife.

Lord God! Never was one more beautiful seen!

At the sound of Renaud's urgent steps, which trampled in great haste the strewn reeds and flowers, the virgin covered her crimson face modestly with her two hands. Little by little, nevertheless, she opened her fingers, let her hands fall, and dared to open her yes.

Our Lady aid us! There was then something like a flash of lightning the color of blood. And two pale phantoms, one of an old woman clad in fire, the other of a young man, his face all black, whose tongue was protruding in the fashion of a hanged man, sprang forth between the two spouses.

The old woman wrapped her burning arms around Messire Renaud, all of whose efforts were insufficient to free himself from such an embrace.

---

[13] The Nativity of Mary is celebrated on 8 September; the feast of Saint Magloire is celebrated on 24 October.

Mélissende saw the horrible hanged man lean over her; she felt the violet lips of the revenant on her lips, and his icy arms hugged her as one hugs a wife.

Then demons, lamias, witches and other frightful phantoms arrived in a crowd and hung like clusters of fire from the curtains of the bed. Some extending hooked hands, spun around in mid-air; others sang in a low, deep voice, as one murmurs near a dying person:

In the lineage of Béthencourt
Eight virgins will be engendered;
Amours will not be seen
Like theirs.

That lasted until the first rays of dawn.

Toward Matins, when the noble Dame de Béthencourt came to see her dear child Mélissende, in order to receive her first accolade as a wife, as is a mother's due, she uttered a piteous clamor and put her hands together, weeping.

They were both there, as white as a dead man's shroud, showing gazes that are only seen in mad people.

No caress or benevolent word could extract any reasonable speech from them; to all words and all prayers they started to sing, like the revenants of their sad wedding night:

In the lineage of Béthencourt
Eight virgins will be engendered;
Amours will not be seen
Like theirs.

The Chaplain

Chronicle
1226

"And vengeance," said the witch, "vengeance!

Is it not the best morsel that has ever been prepared in the cuisine of Hell?"

"Well, let the Devil beware for his dinner, for I'll be hanged if I like the sauce you've out into it."

"Vengeance! It's the sweetest recompense that the Devil can ever accord us. I've done many things to savor that pleasure; but I'll savor it, or there's no justice, either on earth or in Hell."

Walter Scott *La Prison d'Edimbourg.*[14]

Since the commencement of the Autumn season, there had been great claps of thunder, flashes of lightning and deluges of rain such as had never been heard before. No wind or tempest had ever produced such a terrible evening, or showed so clearly how good shelter is.

That is why the varlets, falconers, huntsmen and men-at-arms were gathered in the great hall of the manor of Béthencourt. Mademoiselle Alix, the chatelaine's only daughter, sitting among her ladies in waiting, was reciting loud prayers. From time to time the handsome young woman threw holy water with a box-tree branch,

---

[14] *La Prison d'Edimbourg* (1832) is an opéra-comique with a libretto by Eugène Scribe adapted from Scott's *Heart of Midlothian*; the quotation is fictitious.

as is recommended by the Holy Church, and at every great burst of thunder, she made the sign of the cross devoutly.

Monseigneur de Béthencourt went from person to person in the hall; sometimes he stopped in order to see how the men-at-arms were making the mesh of their steel camisoles shine; sometimes he reprimanded one who had not sharpened his sword sufficiently or given a good enough point to a pike.

The chaplain, Père Benoît, who was more than thirty years old, followed Monseigneur step for step, and scolded the servants more than his master. For that reason, no one in the manor had the slightest affection for him. Far from it, for everyone repeated that the tall monk with the shaven head, on which only a thin crown of bright red hair was visible, with hollow eyes and a burnt complexion, was a maleficent felon, employing the practices of the holy mass for the vile usages of sorcery.

To tell the truth, Père Benoît had marvelous secrets of balms for soothing the fires of fever, for curing Saint Guislain's disease[15] and for closing broad and dangerous wounds. You might ask how and from whom Père Benoît had learned those secrets. God preserve me from so doing! But a science so astonishing, cannot, in my feeble judgment, have come purely and simply from the studies and research of a mortal.

Père Benoît stopped in front of an old soldier who was repairing a crossbow and boasting loudly that he had never released the string of his fine weapon without having hit his target.

---

[15] The name Guislain or Ghislain was often given to aristocratic children in Flanders because the saint of that name was reputed to protect those under his patronage from rabies.

"So," he said, "Saint Sebastian is my witness that since the age of seven, not a day has passed when I have not fitted a bolt to my crossbow in order to bring down an enemy or strike the wooden head of a quintain."

"I once knew," said the chaplain, "in my homeland beyond the sea, a Neapolitan archer who was as good as you, upon my soul! But he never practiced on the wooden head of a quintain; he simply recited words that he had learned from a celebrated sorcerer."

The old man winked in the fashion of Saint Thomas when he was told about the resurrection of Our Savior.

"By the Holy Mass!" said the monk. "You put in doubt the word of clergyman! Now look, I've retained those words, and although my hands have never stretched the string of a crossbow since I came into the world, we'll see whether the secret is good."

So saying, he took the weapon, and retreated to the end of the great hall, muttering: "God has the departure and the Devil the exit. *Non tradas dominum nostrum malthon, Amen.*"[16] Then, designating for a target the old man's hair-clasp, he lifted it off his head before the latter had thought of guarding against such a dangerous ordeal.

Everyone started looking at the chaplain in terror, and the chaplain seemed to rejoice in it. As for the Sire de Béthencourt, he made the observation that employing magic spells did not befit courageous men-at-arms and good Christians; to which Père Benoît replied that all means were good for the greater glory of God.

---

[16] The meaning of this prayer is unclear, but "malthon" is not Latin, being a Flanders dialect term for a serf, so the priest might be asking the Devil's protection for the man at whom he is taking aim.

Monseigneur de Béthencourt replied as a sage man and a faithful Christian, to the great edification of everyone, but not of Père Benoît, who had gone to discuss the marvelous shot with Mademoiselle Alix; although, to tell the truth, she did not listen to him with pleasure—quite the contrary.

The sound of a hunting horn suddenly extracted Alix from such annoying company; the horn made itself heard at the castle's postern.

It was a knight caught in the storm who had come to ask for shelter, Monseigneur de Béthencourt ordered that the knight be admitted without delay.

"Welcome, thrice welcome!" said the castellan, saluting his guest. "Quickly! Let the provost hasten the cooks had have supper served promptly. Alix, my daughter, prepare the hypocras, and you, good sire, quit that cloak soaked by the storm and that robe heavy with rain; let my varlets unfasten the rings of your warrior camisole; put yourself at ease, and for the better."

The knight requested from Monseigneur, in beneficent terms, permission to retain his hood of mail and his warrior camisole. "I have made a view," he said, "that no Christian will ever see my face without having expropriated me."

Monseigneur de Béthencourt made the sage response: "May Saint Michel cast into the depths of Hell anyone who does not respect an expropriation. In that case, sire knight, sit down, and let a cup of hypocras refresh you…God help me, Alix, you haven't yet prepared the hypocras! What will the sire think of our poor hospitality?"

In great emotion, Damoiselle Alix felt herself trembling, as if she had lost her reason. Finally, she pulled herself together as best she could, and in her great haste and that of her ladies in waiting, the hypocras was soon finished. After that, Damoiselle Alix poured some into a silver cup, and offered it graciously to her father's guest.

Without anyone seeing it, the knight pressed the white hand that presented the hypocras to him gently, and Damoiselle Alix murmured so quietly that no one heard her except the man to whom she was speaking: "Henryot, Henryot, this isn't prudent!"

The master-cook had already had set down on the large table, at the bench of honor, a vast silver tray carried by four scullions; on that tray, known as a *couvert* for the reason that it was closed by nothing more or less than a box, were confected with great artistry, twenty-nine different dishes and stews.

The chaplain recited the benediction; and he had no sooner made his final sign of the cross that the master-cook uncovered the *couvert*, leaned across the table, plied his cutlass and poured into bread-plates good slices of wild boar, hare and other renowned game. Only Monseigneur de Béthencourt, Damoiselle Alix, the knight and the chaplain had their share, of course, while the ladies in waiting, the chambermaids, the varlets, the pages, the huntsmen and the men-at-arms seated along the table in the place that their more-or-less elevated status warranted, were served, under the inspection of the provost, with portions of pork, beef and other strong meats, less expertly prepared.

Throughout the supper, the unknown sire was less intent in eating than fixing upon Alix two eyes that shone like true carbuncles through the mesh of his warrior hood. As for Alix, simultaneously joyful and apprehensive, she scarcely ate any more. giving all the slices put into her bread-plate and the bread-plate itself to a pretty greyhound bitch that leaned its white muzzle on its mistress's knees.

After supper, the evening prayers were recited by the chaplain, standing in the midst of all the others, on their knees. Then the pages conducted the knight with honor to a fine chamber strewn with fresh verdure and oak-leaves.

Left alone with her father, Alix requested the old man's blessing. The noble sire imposed his hands on Alix's forehead, and begged God the Father, God the Son, God the Holy Spirit, Our Lady , the mother of the Savior and Saint Bertin, patron of Béthencourt to bless his daughter. The young woman curtseyed respectfully and then went up the spiral staircase that led to her bedroom, at the top of which her ladies in waiting and chambermaids were waiting.

Damoiselle Alix's bedroom was a true abode of pleasure. The Sire de Béthencourt had been obliging enough to have to furnished and disposed at the whim of his dear child, and as befitted a damoiselle of great lineage.

Situated at the top of a small tower, the bedroom received daylight through a single window, the red and blue panes of which, blazoned with the escutcheon of Béthencourt, allowed nothing of what was happening in that virginal abode to be seen from without.

An expert workman had fashioned in brown and shiny oak the columns of the bed, which was enveloped by heavy curtains, the chairs and the dressers. The prie-dieu, each arm of which as sculpted in an admirable manner, served simultaneously to support a massive silver crucifix and a finely polished steel mirror. On the countless shelves of the prie-dieu there were agni, rosaries and reliquaries, not to mention rings, belts and cushions of long silver pins, all intermingled with blaundrell apples that exhaled delicate and sweet scents.

The ladies in waiting first removed their mistress's scarlet outer dress, the false sleeves of which hung down behind; after which they divested her of her under-chemise, of which only the bright sleeves had previously been visible.

While two chambermaids provided that service briskly, two others lifted up the mistress's beautiful black hair and enclosed it in a large night-bonnet. In truth, that was conscientious work, for that hair extended in such a smooth fashion over each temple to form two tresses falling as far as the birth of an ivory neck. There they were lifted up in their double length and rounded in a crown on the top of the head, where their knots mingled with the pleats of a long veil.

That beautiful work was undone by the chamber-maids. Then Alix dismissed her women, detaching herself the body-clasps that secured her elegant waist. When that was done, she remained pensive and preoccupied for a long moment. Henryot, whom she had not seen since her return from the house of her aunt, Dame d'Heninlieutard: Henryot de Carbins at the castle of the Sire de Béthencourt! Henryot, whose father had killed the Sire de Béthencourt's brother!

Sweet Jesus, what if anyone found out what knight was hiding under that helmet of mail! What a risk that faithful lover was taking in order to see her again! Holy Virgin, protect Henryot!

With those thoughts in mind, she knelt down on her prie-dieu and said a prayer:

"Immaculate mother of our Savior, patron and merciful saint of true lovers, Our Lady, grant me your aid! Henryot has risked himself for me in my father's castle;

Holy Virgin, let him return without misfortune, and I promise, for as long as my life lasts, to decorate your divine image every day with a head-dress of flowers; not to mention that I will never allow the candle that I have put in your chapel to cease burning."

She recited a few more prayers, after which she started looking through the windows, trying to see some glimmer of the lamp that was burning in Henryot's room, Leaning her forehead on the window, she was there, pensive and forgetting to go to sleep, when she suddenly shuddered.

Footsteps had sounded behind her.

"Holy Virgin! A Man!"

Père Benoît! What has he come to do? How did he get in?

She covered her semi-naked breasts with her arms and hands, for the monk had placed himself between her and the garments that she had taken of a short while before.

"Alix," he asked, "can you estimate accurately the perils to which I'm exposing myself in order to see you alone?"

The damoiselle lowered her eyes, for she could not sustain the diabolical gaze of the monk, and almost fainted. Gathering all her strength, however, and leaning against the profound window that extended, in a fashion, the little cabinet, she cried: "Help! Help! Lydorie! Perette! Marie! Berthe! All of you, help!"

The monk folded his arms, smiling, and allowed her to clamor as loudly as she wished.

"They're asleep," he said, finally. "They won't wake up until I want them to, for my power has put them to sleep."

He went out and returned, dragging a chambermaid by the arm over the strewn plants, who was not woken by the rude jolts to which she was subjected; then the monk threw her into a corner, where she remained, still asleep and without even uttering a sigh.

"Alix," the monk went on then, "you are alone with me, so listen; I have loved you, as you know, since the first moment I saw you. You wanted to tell your father that I loved you, but the fear of my magic power prevented you, and, by Beelzebub, you did well, for infernal spirits would have tormented you night and day.

"By saying a single magic word I could have had you for my own; far from that, I have supported your disdain and your harsh fashions, as a timid vassal enamored of a highly-placed lady might have done. Finally, for the first time, you allowed it to be seen that you have some pity for my pains and languor; your foot sought mine during supper. And see: nothing more was necessary for me: perils, the gallows, the pyre, I have braved everything! Here I am!"

"Lord God! What a fatal error! What, it was the chaplain's foot!" cried poor Alix.

"You were seeking the foot of another! You're enamored of someone else! Who? Who? Oh yes: that knight. No matter, you shall be mine."

As he spoke, the chaplain held out his arms in order to embrace her; in that movement a short dagger hidden in the folds of his sleeve fell on to the strewn plants. Alix seized it and turned it so promptly toward her breast that she pricked it, and a large drop of blood emerged.

"Take another step," she cried, "and I'll kill myself."

"Do so; better that you die for me than live for your knight."

And he advanced.

Alix recommended her soul to God and got ready to die, when the monk suddenly stopped, as if by virtue of a sudden reflection, went out, making a gesture of vengeance, and closed the door in such a manner that the young woman could not open it. She cried out in vain; none of her women woke up, put to sleep as they had been by the chaplain's spells.

He went to the knight's chamber; without waking him from his profound sleep, he was able to study his face at his ease and recognize him as Sire Henryot de Carvins.

The following morning, at the hour of Matins, the chaplain went into Monseigneur de Béthencourt's chamber.

"May Our Lord Jesus Christ come to your aid and grant you courage! You have great need of it! Yesterday's knight is Henryot de Carvins, the son of the murderer of your brother, Paul d'Esnes."

Monseigneur de Béthencourt got up, beside himself; then he suddenly got back into bed, saying: "He has received hospitality in my house; Saint Julien protects him. Let him be safe and sound. I'll avenge my brother another time. God will give me the opportunity."

The monk folded his arms and began to smile, as he had smiled in Mademoiselle Alix's room. Then he spoke.

"Henryot de Carvins has dishonesty outraged such a generous hospitality; last night he was received in Damoiselle Alix's bedroom."

"Monk! Monk! Proofs, or I'll kill you!" cried Monseigneur de Béthencourt, drawing his dagger.

"I've seen him! I swear by the saints of paradise," replied the monk, calmly and without moving a step.

"I've seen him! And then, as he left, he took out and dropped this veil, which was suspended yesterday from Damoiselle Alix's hair."

"True! Only too true! My armor! Give me my armor!"

"Felony ought to be slain by felony. He's asleep; let's go."

"Monk, that would be to avenge oneself in the fashion of a monk, and it's the vengeance of a knight that I need. My armor! In the meantime, go fetch the traitor and bring him to the entrance of the wood."

With a joy horrible to behold the monk made haste to run to the chamber of Sire Henryot de Carvins."

"Oh, handsome sire, there's no longer any need for mystery; it's known that you're Sire Henryot de Carbins, You would have done well to keep your hood of mail on in bed. Now get up! Put that warrior camisole on your shoulders and that dagger in your fist; you're awaited at the wood, to receive the recompense that is owed to you."

Henryot made a sign of despair. "I shall not make use of this sword against the father of my lady Alix," he said.

"Upon my soul," replied the monk, "you will have to face better than the feeble wrist and tremulous legs of Monseigneur de Béthencourt; you're awaited down there by a young and valiant sire, Mademoiselle Alix's fiancé, a young knight, the nephew of Monseigneur Oldebrand de Cagnoncles."

"Ah!" said the knight "Mademoiselle Alix's fiancé!"

He armed himself rapidly, and it was necessary for the monk to fasten the straps of his buckles, for Henryot was trembling with rage.

Guide to the entrance to the wood by the chaplain; Henryot rushed at his adversary, but he could not see his face because the knight was wearing a hood of mail. The combat did not last long; wounded first, although only slightly, in the side, the Sire de Carvins felled his enemy, pierced through. His hood fell from his head and left his face uncovered. Henryot recognized the Sire de Béthencourt.

But when, in the most frightful despair that had ever broken a man's heart, he turned round to kill the felonious monk, the monk was no longer there; but Henryot saw him, through the foliage, clasping the damoiselle Alix in his arms, and uttering cries.

Henryot set forth in pursuit of the monk, but the weight of his armor, a cruel pain and the weakness caused by his wound rendered his efforts futile; his knees buckled beneath him and he fell.

The monk came toward him then and cried to the dying Alix, whom he was still holding:

"He has killed your father... He has been wounded by a poisoned dagger... You will be mine and we shall perish together, you in my arms... Am I avenged?"

The Bloody Forehead

1314

The dead go quickly.
Burger, *Ballade*.[17]

Messire Gauthier dug his spurs into the bloodied flanks of his horse and cried: "Faster! Faster still, my good courser, faster!"

And yet his horse was going faster than the wind, and the sweat was streaming over its breast, and white foam enveloped its bit.

Oh, that was because for Messire Gauthier it was a matter of life and death, because he was carrying on the rump of his horse the beautiful Blanche de Béthencourt: Blanche, whose weakening hands barely conserved enough strength to cling on to her lover's armor.

And then, in the distance, menacing voices and hoofbeats could be heard, the clank of armor and, above all that, the clamors of the Comte de Béthencourt: "Stop them! Dead or alive, it doesn't matter! Better that she has a shroud than opprobrium!"

By the aid of God and all the saints! There'd the Fortress of Quiévy! Oh, the brave men-at-arms are lowering the drawbridge, ready to rush out against Messire de Béthencourt and his men! Thank you, Comrades! She's mine now!

Everyone back inside! Raise the bridge! Lower the portcullis! To the ramparts! Load the crossbows! Charge

---

[17] The line is from Gottfried Bürger's poem "Lenore" (1773)

the machicolations with stones! Give a good reception to that braggart sire who thinks that the blood of Béthencourt would be misallied in mingling with the blood of Quiévy!

"Blanche, my dear Blanche, come round now. Look, look, it's your friend, it's your Albéric who is clasping you in his arms! Nothing can separate us now. My chaplain will marry us in the eyes of God, as befits good and loyal lovers, true Christians in the bosom of the Holy Catholic, Apostolic and Roman Church."

And Blanche, pale, faint and without saying a word, let herself go, as if in a bad dream, not daring to believe that it was really her. Bounty of God! To flee with her lover, before everyone's eyes, in the presence of her father! And not to come back when the irritated old man shouted: "I curse you, unnatural daughter, you are accursed! Accursed, you hear? Accursed...!" Oh, yes, it's a dream, is it not?

This somber church, the pale candlelight, this priest who is asking: "Woman, do you take Albéric de Quiévy for your husband?" that ring that is being put on your finger...say it, say it, say it...all this is a dream...a dream that will finish...

For she can no longer support the horrible anguish.

What tumult is making itself heard...? Arrows whistling through the air; someone crying: "They're beaten, they're fleeing...! His head has been broken by a slingshot! He's fallen...he's dying..." Who?

The drawbridge is lowered; men return and come back...they're carrying a cadaver...

Oh! Her father! Her father...!

"Father! Father! Leave me alone, leave me alone! He hasn't rendered his soul; his hands are still warm...he's going to open his eyes...that gaping wound isn't mortal... He'll look at his daughter; he'll say to her: 'I forgive you; I no longer curse you...'

No! Dead, dead!

Holy Virgin, won't you take pity on a poor woman? Why do you want her to be cursed by her father? By her father, dead because she disobeyed him...Holy Virgin, help me...Come on, don't be so inflexible! You know how I'm suffering; grant my prayer!

"Oh, don't drag me away like this! Leave me with him, let me be! I'm your chatelaine; I want you to obey me! Leave me with my father...! Ah...!

She fell, unconscious.

And when she came round, it was in the nuptial chamber that she found herself; and her husband, the young and handsome Sire de Quiévy, wanted to enlace her in his arms and kiss her pale lips. Exhausted, and as if numbed by dolor, she yielded mechanically to his caresses.

It was only at daybreak that she emerged from her slack stupor.

Then she was able to weep.

Nine months later, there was a there was a great disturbance in the Château de Quiévy. It would have required less than that to disturb it.

Messire Albéric had just died suddenly, and that frightful news had caused Madame Blanche to bring into the world—justice of Heaven!—a child whose forehead was bloodied.

The surprised matrons tries to wash away that blood, but it was ineffaceable, and depicted, in a fashion horrible to behold, the wound of which the Comte de Béthencourt had died

Pray to God for the Sire de Quiévy and for Madame his widow; for it is said that she has lost her reason, and spends all day trying to wash the ineffaceable wound from the forehead of her son.

Hector de Saveuse

Chronicle
1427

Immaculate Holy Virgin, who has granted the good fortune of my life, the salvation of my soul and not true love.

Christine de Fusseleu, *Les Merveilles*.[18]

Oh, my friend, you will never know how much I love you! For you, I would give my fortune, my happiness, the repose of my entire life, my reputation, and even your love. You, you, alone, you, friend!

Love letters.

There are in Flanders no celebrations more joyful and festivities more marvelous than the Ducasse of Cambrai.[19] That Ducasse takes place on Trinity Monday. Everyone comes from thirty leagues around. Such a great influx of strangers is seen that the bourgeois, too cramped in their houses, erect canvas tents and wooden huts in their courtyards, and even in their doorways.

From Trinity Sunday onwards, the houses of the bourgeois, from the richest to the poorest, are encumbered by guests that are accommodated as best they can. Villeins and peasants who do not have the advantage of

---

[18] Fictitious.

[19] The Ducasse—the annual fair of Cambrai—is still celebrated, but in August rather than late spring, and now extends for ten days in the town's main square.

knowing anyone in the town to welcome them arrive in numerous bands.

Before passing the portcullis and the drawbridge or entering into some winding street, they quit their every-day clothes and put on the best adornments they have. The men put on breeches and doublet instead of their knee-length smocks, the women and girls wipe the dust from their faces, smooth their hair, put on lighter foot-wear and change their hat, their dress and even their chemise. For that, the men go to one side of the road and the women to the other, each back to back, and ought not to turn their heads; but, to tell the truth, people hardly take account of the prohibition, and more than one curi-ous individual delights in seeing white shoulders, round-ed arms, and better still, if possible.

Mademoiselle Berthe de Lens, the niece of Monsei-gneur the Bishop of Cambrai, Jean de Lens, had sent Mademoiselle de Béthencourt, her faithful friend, a cour-teous and urgent message in which she let her know that the festival of Trinity had arrived, and requesting her to come and spend it with her. She reminded her that for a year it had not been given to them to see one another or embrace one another.

Marie de Béthencourt had acceded joyfully to such a request, and, under the escort of forty men at arms had set forth for the Episcopal castle. As soon as Berthe saw her tender friend's white hackney and the men-at-arms coming on to the pavement of Béthencourt, she started to run, mad thing that she was, and had no contentment until she had hugged Mademoiselle Marie in her arms.

The next day, early in the morning, Marie de Béthencourt, who was sleeping in Berthe's bed, opened her eyes and began to sigh; it happened that during the night, she had dreamed about Messire Hector de

Saveuse, her knight: Hector who had requested and obtained from his lady the gift of amorous mercy, swearing by the holy evangelists, by Saint Michel and by the spurs that he wore, to marry her before the Church and men as soon as he had made a truce or peace with the Bishop of Cambrai.

That was not, to tell the truth, a short or easy thing, for Hector de Saveuse had, the previous year, taken the side of the bourgeois against the bishop. Entering the episcopal castle at the head of three hundred men, he had nearly killed the bishop himself, and that would have happened if Monseigneur Jean de Lens had not put on the doublet of his fool, Benoît Sot-Souris, and had not been taken by that fool out of the city to a safe place.

Now that he had returned to his castle with a good number of men-at-arms, and the bourgeois, out of fear or some other cause, were being peaceful and obedient, Hector had been put under the ban of the Empire, declared stripped of his titles, goods and seigneuries, and had a price put on his head of three hundred gold écus.

Curious to obtain such a large sum, a good number of bourgeois, including those at whose request Sire Hector de Saveuse had departed against the bishop, had tracked him like a ferocious beast. But the worthy knight, with a few determined soldiers, had kept them at bay and sent them packing when the opportunity presented itself, accompanied by good thrust of the lance, ax and two-handed sword. Such thoughts and such memories filled Mademoiselle de Béthencourt's eyes with tears.

With that, Mademoiselle Berthe emerged from sleep, stretching her pretty arms and yawning with a dainty mouth that allowed the sight of a double row of ivory teeth embedded in the freshest coral. She turned partly-opened eyes this way and that, as if searching for someone who was not there.

Then, putting an arm round Marie's neck and leaning on her shoulder, she remained thus for a long time. Nothing more attractive had ever been seen than those two young women, half-naked, their black hair confounded, and in their tender embrace, as if only forming one.

"Marie," said Berthe, finally, in a low and not daring voice, "dear and beloved Marie, it's necessary that I depose in your bosom a mystery by virtue of which I am content and afflicted. I am loved, Marie, loved by a brave sire of great beauty. Never has one been cited who equals him, for tender words, for thrusts of the lance and in noble renown. There is no one who knows how to love as he loves, for, Marie, in order to come to me for an hour, he risks his liberty, not to say his life.

"To diminish the perils that are against him, Berthe has counted, dear Marie, on your courage and your faithful amity.

"Soon, while everyone is out of the castle rejoicing at the festivities of the Trinity, my dear sire, disguised as he has to be, will come all the way to the castle by means of the abandoned postern, to which he has a key. I shall feign a grave illness and request your good offices, giving my chambermaids leave to go to the festivities. That way, my tender friend will not see anyone but you, and when night falls, it will be easy for him to escape."

"I will do as you request," replied Marie. After that, she asked the young woman, curiously: "What is the name of your knight?"

The demoiselle de Lens placed her lips very close to the ear of the damoiselle de Béthencourt and murmured a name.

The demoiselle de Béthencourt fainted.

She came round after long care. Then she started weeping bitterly. "Hector de Saveuse!" she said, wringing her hands. "Hector de Saveuse!"

Bethe thought that such laments came from the dangers of her amour. "Oh yes," she replied, weeping herself, "Such an amour exposes me to great dangers, but is it not better to die than not to be his?"

Mademoiselle de Béthencourt stared at her friend, and embraced her for a long time, tenderly. "I will be a faithful friend until death!" she said. And her tears recommenced.

At the hour of vespers, a man wearing a large hood entered Cambrai by the door of the Château de Selle, paid the duty of gaves without saying a word, and headed for the episcopal palace, but without seeming to do so, and pretending to be occupied with the festivities as much as was necessary in order not to give rise to suspicions.

Those festivities were, however, beautiful, and none like them had ever been seen in a city renowned for its celebrations. People first admired several *Exemples* and spectacles given at the expense and by the care of *Sermens*, or Fraternities.

At the Guitier, which others called the Saint-Fiacre quarter, wild men were dancing, wilders of two-handed words clad in white, in white chemises and white huvetes, and then a wild woman, who had no garments except for her long hair.

Further away, the millers were roasting an entire ox, and stuffing its belly with piglets, goslings, chickens and pigeons. The taverners were piling casks of wine on to a large scaffold and letting them flow as much as they could. In other places people were indulging in other frolics, such as playing the horn and dancing.

Having arrived behind the episcopal palace, and very close to slipping into the forlorn street of the postern, the hooded man—who, needless to say, was Hector de Saveuse—was obliged to stop. The procession suddenly arrived outside that street and a considerable time passed before solitude returned and he was able to bring his project to a conclusion, for the procession was long.

First came, at the front, the arbalestiers, all on horseback, the archers clad in red with yellow bonnets on their heads. Several other Sermens followed, corseted by breastplates, with yellow hoods.

After that came Monseigneur the Bishop's carriage, the papal carriage, and in the last place, the carriage of the Holy Virgin, a young woman of great beauty sitting on a throne carried by angels, representing the immaculate mother of the Savior of humankind. At times, hidden springs raised that throne to a great height, and brought it down again with grace and rapidity.

At the foot of the holy carriage, Saint Michel the Archangel was wrestling with the Devil, whose quips amused the bourgeois and the peasants. When the blessed spirit was unable to reply to the evil one, he gave him a great thrust of his copper sword, fashioned as a flamboyant rod, in the belly, and a great red flag emerged from the demon's entrails, a simulacrum of blood.

When the prayers of the clergy could be heard more clearly, and golden crucifixes, candles and chasubles gleamed behind the Virgin's carriage, Messire Hector kissed his hood again and bent his knees in the midst of the crowd, in such a way that he could not be seen by Bishop Jean de Lens or his men.

The street only became solitary enough for the knight's liking and expectation at nightfall. Then he ran to the postern and was received there by a veiled woman, to whom he paid no attention, mistaking her for a chambermaid. But a bourgeois had recognized him and had seen him enter the castle; he went to inform the bishop of that as soon as the procession ended.

The bishop, quite perplexed, had the sentinels doubled and gave the order to close all the doors and lower the portcullis. After that, not knowing where to find Messire Saveuse, he set out to search for him, dagger in hand, with a large number of men-at-arms. At the noise of such a rumor within the castle, the terror of Berthe and Hector de Saveuse can be imagined. The latter kissed the hilt of his dagger, recited a brief prayer, and prepared to sell his life dearly.

With that, the veiled woman came in suddenly. "To the secret stairway! To the postern! Take this woman's cape, knight, and give me your mantle and hood. Quickly! Quickly! I'll receive the bourgeois here.

They separated.

She put on the hood and wrapped herself in Sire Hector de Saveuse's cloak, barricaded the door with all the furniture and the waited, recommending her soul to merciful God.

The bourgeois who had recognized Messire Hector put his eye to the little window of the chamber, known in those days as a Judas.

"By Saint Sebastian!" he said in a low voice to those who were following him. Three hundred gold écus are mine. His barricades won't do him any good.

So saying, he armed his crossbow, took aim through the judas, and released the bolt. A great cry was heard; the cadaver twitched momentarily, and that was all.

Joyful cries went up from all parts.

"He's dead! He's dead!

"Dead! Killed for me! Malediction! The faithful chambermaid has paid for my life with hers"

"Killed! Marie de Béthencourt!" cried Berthe, with a horrible anguish."

"Her! Marie?" said Messire Hector de Saveuse.

And from the middle of the postern, in the ditch, the sound was heard of a man hurling himself into it.

Michel d'Esnes
Chronicle
1584

They also that render evil for good are my adversaries; because I follow the thing that good is.
Psalm 38: 20.

Nothing is as odious or the wicked as the happiness
that the virtuous man enjoys. Be careful that he does not
see it, for he will strive to destroy it
Chronique d'Albert[20]

One summer evening in the year 1584, after having
made sure that the drawbridge of the château was lifted
and made sure that the sentinels were at their posts—
precautions that the troubles in Spain rendered necessary—Michel de Landast, Sire d'Esnes went back into
the hall where his wife, Blanche de Béthencourt, was
cradling a child a few months old on her knees. The almoner, Laurent Davos, an old priest who has escaped the
persecutions of the Baron d'Inchy, was reading aloud
hymns that he had just composed, and did not perceive
that the young mother was too entranced by the caresses
of her son to lend a very attentive ear, while the Seigneur

---

[20] There are several documents to which this title might refer,
including the chronicles of Albert d'Aix and Albert de Stras-
bourg, but it is doubtful that the quotation comes from any of
them.

d'Ewars, Nicolas de Hertaing,[21] scarcely sensible to the charms of that poetry, was profoundly asleep in a large armchair which he filled with his vast corpulence.

Sire Michel took off his mantle, soaked by the rain that was falling then with extreme violence; he kissed Blanche on the forehead and slapped Sire Nicolas on the shoulder.

"Wake up," he said, raising his voice, for the good seigneur was a little deaf, "Wake up, you'll sleep tranquilly tonight. The time is over when the dread of the Duc d'Alençon will keep you in such emotion that you'll lose sleep.

The old comte opened his large eyes slowly. "It's easy for you to talk," he replied, eventually. "thanks to the protection that the kings of Spain and France have accorded you, by I know not what good fortune, you've never seen enraged warriors destroying your game, ravaging your cellar, beating your varlets and ending up expelling you from your own château…!"

---

[21] Author's note: "Nicolas de Hertaing was the son of Jacques, peer of Cambresis; he was the son of the valiant Guillaume de Hertaing, Seigneur de Marquette, who, after have fought for the cause of the reformed for a long time, because governor of Berg-op-Zoon." This story is probably based directly on material collected and published by Berthoud's friend and fellow antiquarian Andre-Joseph-Ghislain Le Glay in the *Archives du Nord*, but the activities in Cambrai of the Baron d'Inchy and Jean de Montluc de Balagny had been featured in numerous historical accounts familiar to the author, including Jacques Auguste de Thou's *Histoire Universelle* (1734). The historical Michel d'Esnes founded the present Château d'Esnes when he was Bishop of Tournay in 1614, but the events featured in the story are fictitious.

At that point Nicolas interrupted himself with a sigh, and his joyful face, on which the habitude of bonhomie and insouciance were painted, took on a temporary expression of sorrow.

"Oh well," he went on with a slightly forced gaiety, "have I not been more fortunate than others? I've found an agreeable refuge with you; I can hope to end my days here in peace...and by the intervention of Our Lady of Grace," he added, taking off the black velvet hood that covered his partly bald head. "I'll spend a few more moments chatting with you and bouncing that dear child on my knees, who will take lessons from me in hunting and drinking when he's grown up."

Outside, the rain was falling in torrents and the wind was engulfed with a long murmur in the woods that surrounded the Château d'Esnes. Laurent Devos, finally finding in Sire Michel a more attentive listener, continued reading his hymns. The Norman lord took a malign pleasure in interrupting from time to time to address critical observations to him, which Laurent, while secretly recognizing their justice, combated nevertheless with the warmth that poets and musicians ordinarily put into defending their work.

In the meantime, a man-at-arms came to announce that a large number of horsemen surrounding a litter had stopped in the avenue of the château and asking for a refuge. Laurent Devos cried that leaving unfortunates exposed to the fury of the tempest would not be a Christian action.

"There are a mother and a child who await them with much anxiety," added Blanche. And Sire Nicolas immediately said that his conscience to would be troubled by not receiving them—"Provided," he murmured between his teeth, "that there is not some scoundrel among them who will take my own bed, as was done in my poor Château d'Ewars."

Sire Michel ordered that the drawbridge be lowered, and the littler and its escort, composed of about thirty men, entered the courtyard of the petty fortress. While the castellan advanced to receive his guests, he saw by the light of the torches that his varlets were carrying a lady whose features were not unknown to him. She was leaning on the arm of the Chevalier de Villers-Houdan, a young seigneur resident in Cambresis

"Since when," cried the lady, whose naturally beautiful face was then disfigured by the most violent anger, "is the wife of a Maréchal de France reduced to waiting outside a miserable castle?" Her tone became softer as she added: "What do I see? This shelter isn't so wretched, since I find Sire Michel here. By what fortunate hazard do I have this unexpected pleasure?"

"This domain is mine, Madame, and..."

"Your domain...! What! The mysterious castellan who, in the three months that I've been living in this region, has not once appeared at my court, whom I believed to be a old man—your grandfather, at least— hiding in his manor in order not to die of right at the sight of a man-at-arms, is you, the young Sire Landast et d'Esnes!"

"Yes, Madame," replied Michel, "and if I had been able to foresee that the beautiful Renée d'Amboise..."[22]

---

[22] Renée de Clermont d'Amboise (c.1546-1595), also known as René de Bussy d'Amboise, the sister of Louis de Clermont, seigneur de Bussy d'Amboise (1549-1579)—the hero of Alexandre Dumas' novel *La Dame de Monsoreau* (1846)—married Maréchal Balagny in 1579.

"Say the Princesse de Cambrai. But let's hasten to come inside, so that I can dry my clothes, for what means is there of finding others here?"

"Dame d'Esnes will hasten to provide some, noble lady."

"Dame d'Esnes, Sire Michel! You're married? What, the gallant minstrel of Marie de Médicis, the joyous page of Philippe II has submitted to the yoke of marriage, and, jealous in his turn, he imprisons his languorous dove in his towers? Although I'm far from the court, how can I be unaware of such an event? And what beauty has fixed your choice? Is it Diane d'Estrées, Isabelle de Fuentes, Louise de Tavanes? For the ladies of the courts of Spain and France disputed the honor of captivating the most amiable of chevaliers."

Without waiting for the response, he hastened into the Gothic hall where Blanche was giving the orders necessary for the reception of her unexpected guests.

Madame de Balagny remained motionless with astonishment. The Seigneur d'Esnes, by virtue of his noble lineage, his talents and his credit, could aspire to the most brilliant parties, and yet he had not chosen his wife from among the women who were then the ornament of the courts. Blanche was beautiful above all in candor and in youth, although she wore a long veil inside her château, which descended all the way to the floor; the high collaret of Flemish ladies rose above her shoulders and a bunch of keys suspended from her belt next to a gold chaplet proved that she did not disdain supervising domestic concerns personally.

Michel understood Renée d'Amboise's astonishment, and, presenting Blanche's hand, which advanced timidly, he said, with dignity "This is my noble spouse, the Dame de Landast et d'Esnes, the only daughter of the noble and powerful Seigneur de Béthencourt.

A mocking smile contracted Renée's lips, but was immediately suppressed. She bowed, and without saying a single word, went to the apartments that had been prepared for her.

Left alone with Michel, Balagny looked around, and suddenly interrupted the silence that he had maintained since his entry to the château.

"My God, Michel, you must be mad! It seems to me that I'm dreaming. I scarcely expected to find here, living like a hermit, the page of Philippe II, the Michel d'Esnes who, by a marvelous art, was simultaneously the favorite of Charles IX and the Queen Mother—I remember that she sang your laborious motets from matins to vespers—and who was welcomed by Henri III of Mayenne, and also the King Of Navarre. Who had the favor of that prince more than you? 'I know that Michel seems slightly Spanish,' he said to Crillon in my presence, 'but he's as brave as you and me, and I can't do without him.' And what usage are you making of that favor? You're locking yourself away in an old château with a young woman of whom you're probably already weary, or soon will be. By Saint André! All that I see makes me believe that you've lost your reason!"

"God granted that no such misfortune overtook me!" replied Michel, smiling. To have quit the court in these stormy times, when I could do so with honor, was sage rather than insensate. Honored by the favor of the King of Spain, a subject of Henri IV, judge how painful my position was! I embraced the knees of the King of France and I asked for permission to retire to my lands. 'Go, Michel,' he said to me, generously. 'You will not be the last to draw your sword by my side if ever I a unfortunate,'

"So, I lived in Cambresis. Thanks to the protection of two monarchs, my château was respected by the French troops and the Spanish troops who ravaged this country by turns. Several seigneurs, my neighbors, expelled from their dwellings, sought refuge with me; one of them was Blanche's father. He died in my arms, recommending his poor orphan to me; she is as tender as she is beautiful, and my chaplain blessed our union a year ago. My dear Montluc, however monotonous my existence may appear to you, I prefer it to the intrigues and noisy pleasures of the court.

"For a long time I dreamed of a loving and good wife; Blanche's naïve caresses, the speech, which respires an ingenuous grace, my child, who already smiles at his father and holds out his arms to him, all of that, Seigneur Balagny, offers pleasures that ne scarcely suspects at the court; in the midst of luxury and grandeurs, one is far from knowing how happy one is as a husband and father. I still cultivate poetry, but not, as before, in order to acquire glory; I'm disgusted by a renown that it is necessary to purchase at the expense of one's repose. You've sought happiness by a very different route; you're in possession of al the honors you desire; I have, therefore, no more prayers to formulate, since the friend of my childhood, my dear Montluc, is happy."

Michel stopped speaking, and Balagny, without responding, continued pacing back and forth. What painful reflections were agitating him! Michel was happy; and he, heaped with favors and fortune, experienced a frightful void that, in the bosom of pleasures and grandeurs, attaches to a man when he seeks his enjoyments outside nature and duty. And then, how different Renée was from Blanche! He had loved the daughter of Bussy d'Amboise, when he married her, swearing to punish Montsoreau, her father's murderer. Soon subjugated by that ambitious woman, whose counsels enabled him to succeed in several difficult missions, and who pushed him rapidly to honors by means of her adroit intrigues and bold projects, he only any longer saw her with the chagrined and jealous sentiment that feeble souls nourish against imperious force against which they cannot sustain themselves. One does not love for long a companion who takes possession of a superiority that denies him nature. So Balagny gave himself to the most ignoble libertinage, conduct that only served to put him further under the dependence of his wife. Oh, how the Prince de Cambrai envied Michel's fate!

While he delivered himself to such thoughts a page came to announced that their seigneuries were served.

Laurent Devos blessed the table, and a long silence fell, only interrupted sometimes by the Sire d'Ewars, who praised the most delicate morsels of the venison, and was not sorry to show a great lady how, in his Château d'Ewars, he cut up a haunch of roe deer or a wild boar's head. Villers-Houdan fixed a melancholy gaze on Renée d'Amboise. In order no longer to quit that lady, whom he loved madly, the young seigneur had sold the immense properties he possessed in Picardy and had come to live in Cambrai. Since then he was no longer distant from the object of his fatal passion; he was incessantly attached to her footsteps. A thousand rumors ran around, which were repeated in whispers, for everyone dreaded offending the Dame de Balagny, who was vindictive and powerful.

By the discourse full of bitterness that sometimes escaped Renée, the chagrin with which she saw the grace, mildness and youth of Michel's wife was easily divinable. As for Balagny, fearing the unfortunate scenes and contradictions that he had to endure from his wife every time he offered an opinion, he consoled himself by drinking and darting inflamed glances at Blanche, while Laurent Devos, a stranger to everything that was happening, was doubtless meditating some new motet.

The constraint that reigned among those various individuals hastened the end of the meal, and a little while thereafter they went to the chapel, where the almoner, kneeling in the midst of the family of Michel d'Esnes and his guests, recited the evening prayer piously. He concluded his orisons by asking God to spread his benefits over our Holy Father the Pope, the king, the noble families of Esnes and Béthencourt, and over Messire Louis de Berlaymont, by the grace of God the Archbishop of Cambrai...

"Wretch!" cried Renée, suddenly, without any regard for the sanctity of the place. "I'll do justice to your insolence! What! I hear prayers, before me, for a traitor sold to the Spaniards, for the hypocrite prelate that I expelled from Cambrai! Why not pray also for the King of Spain and the Ligue? This, Michel, is how you show yourself worthy of the king's favor? Someone seize this audacious chaplain!"

And, directing her men-at-arms—who, as was customary, were present at the prayer—to advance, she ordered them to take possession of the old man, which they immediately did, in spite of the supplications of Blanche, those of Seigneur d'Ewars and the energetic protests of Michel, who drew his sword, swearing to avenge the rights of hospitality, so outrageously violated. In vain, a few faithful servants, armed with the first objects they found, ran to arrange themselves beside him; their efforts could not deliver the old priest.

Balagny, animated by drunkenness and irritated by the reproaches that Michel addressed to him, hurled himself upon him, wounded him, and with the aid of Villers-Houdan and part of his escort, disarmed him, not without difficulty.

Laurent Devos, his hands together, considered that frightful scene with the silence of despair, but when he saw his benefactor covered in blood, Blanche unconscious and poor Sire d'Ewars trampled underfoot, he tried to launch himself toward Renée, who, profiting from the confusion, had surprised the château's guards, put men of her escort in their pace and returned, insulting him verbally.

The unfortunate fellow was retained by his guards. Then, fixing glittering eyes upon her, he cried: "Tremble, woman unworthy of that name! You have profaned the house of God, brought trouble and despair among those who welcomed you, violated a refuge that two powerful monarchs protect, and charged with irons an old man, a priest of Jesus Christ! And why? Because he prayed for his legitimate pastor, persecuted and banished far from his unfortunate flock. You want my death! Well, satisfy your rage; but hasten to enjoy your crimes. In a few more years you will no longer have any treasures or grandeurs, and it is you who will have destroyed everything yourself!"

He was dragged away. The next day, before dawn, Balagny had the drawbridge and the château's other means of defense destroyed; then he departed, taking his prisoner with him.

That evening, the family of Michel d'Esnes, assembled in the chapel, recited the prayers for the dead. They were for the almoner, Laurent Devos.

Further men-at-arms of Balagny's were combined with those that had been left in the Château d'Esnes, and happiness fled forever from that dwelling, formerly so peaceful. Michel implored the protection of the king more than once, but his complaints never reached the king. Gabrielle d'Estrées was the friend of Renée d'Amboise. In any case, Henri IV had a considerable interest in protecting Balagny, and Michel was oppressed more than ever. Only one hope remained to him, which was to take his supplication to the foot of the throne personally, but his wound prevented him from putting that project into execution for a long time, and when he wanted to depart he was, alas, a prisoner in his own château.

A few years went by. One day, Spanish troops surprised the Château d'Esnes; Balagny's soldiers were massacred. It was the Comte de Fuentes, united with Michel by the narrowest amity; he came at the head of an army to lay siege to Cambrai.

Execrated by the inhabitants and only having a garrison of six hundred men, Balagny did not put up a long resistance. The gates of the city were soon opened to the besiegers. He took refuge in the citadel, believing that he would find abundant food supplies there, with which he could await the help of the French, but the avid Renée had sold them to the Spaniards, and she died of rage when she saw her husband reduced to capitulation. She was thus the cause of her own ruination, as Laurent Devos had predicted.

However, Balagny, abandoned by his men, detested everywhere and dreading to fall into the hands of the

Spaniards, escaped on horseback, followed by a single page. Fearful of being recognized in spite of his disguise, he was trying to reach the frontier when he believed that he saw that the road to the Château d'Esnes was less covered with soldiers than the rest of the country. That was easily explicable by the known amity of Fuentes for Michel. Knowing how generous the latter was, he resolved without hesitation to ask him for shelter until he could cross over into France.

When he arrived at Esnes, what a sad spectacle was offered to his eyes! The woods had been felled, the fields were uncultivated, and the fortifications half-destroyed. The ruins of Esnes were not the work of time and their aspect was far from inspiring the sadness that is not without charm; the destructive hand of man was recognizable everywhere; the heart was constricted by dread and fear in considering them.

An old man, preceded by a ecclesiastic, was marching in all haste toward the château. Balagny approached the man and recognized, not without difficulty, Sire Nicolas de Hertaing. He was no longer the good seigneur once so jovial and so pleasing. His cheeks were hollow and withered, and his almost-extinct eyes could not distinguish the stranger who addressed him.

"Leave me alone," he said, in a surly tone, "by Our Lady of Grace, I don't have time or the desire to listen to you. What have you come to seek here? Hospitality? Balagny's soldiers have destroyed and devastated everything. Without Fuentes, God bless him, the poor Dame d'Esnes wouldn't have a bed to die in..."

"I'm unfortunate, Sire Nicolas..."

"That's what they all say!" cried the old man. "As if we didn't have enough misfortunes of our own! I tell you that poor Blanche is dying; she couldn't resist all the woes she has had to support: her château filled with soldiers blaspheming night and day; her husband wounded, captive in the dwelling of his ancestors; and her dear son who died suddenly..."

Leaning toward Balagny. He added in a low voice and a confidential tone: "They doubtless poisoned him, like Villers-Houdan; may God grant peace to the latter but he, at least, merited such a fate for having united himself with those accursed by Heaven..."

Balagny stopped his horse and ceased to follow Sire Nicolas, who was still walking and talking, He turned to his page,

"Such a refuge doesn't suit us, Marguerite"—for his page was a woman in men's clothing—"It's Renée, again, who has done all this evil…"

Then, after a moment of silence, he said: "Let's keep going forward, come what may."

And they soon disappeared.

It is known that Balagny returned to Henri IV's court, where he married Diane d'Estrées. Soon weary of his new union, he did not take long to retire to the comté de Marle, where he delivered himself to the most shameful debauchery.

After the death of his dear Blanche, Seigneur d'Esnes, inconsolable and disgusted by the world, went to live in Douai; he entered into Holy Orders and consecrated his time to belles-lettres and good works. In spite of his resistance he was appointed Bishop of Tournai; it was there that he died, pronouncing the names of Blanche and his son.

Sire Nicolas de Hertaing followed Michel to Douai, then to Tournai, and lived for several more years, but he was no longer heard repeating the joyful discourse that

he had once loved so much, and a bitter tear ran down
his cheek every time he mentioned Blanche.

But he talked about her often.

A Soirée chez la Comtesse du Barry

Anecdote
1770

"Hang, hang," said the judge, "he's stolen six écus; hang, hang, he's earned it." And he left the tribunal in order to try to seduce the president's wife, whom he had been coveting for a month.

Le Robin.[23]

Buried in the cushions of a large armchair, on the evening in question, Louis XV was sad and thoughtful. The lewd teasing of the Comtesse du Barry,[24] and the prettily comical mannerisms that suited the favorite so well, all went completely to waste.

The position was untenable.

Also, the worthy governor of the children of France, the Duc de La Vauguyon,[25] was raising his eyes of

---

[23] "Robin" is a familiar term in France for a lawyer.

[24] Jeanne Bécu, Comtesse du Barry (1743-1793) was the last and most notorious of Louis XV's "*maîtresses-en-titre*" (official mistresses). Abundantly slandered by illicit publications, she was eventually guillotined during the Terror on trumped-up charges. The present story was probably inspired by an episode in chapter IX of the fake memoirs attributed to her by Étienne Lamothe-Langon, published in 1829, which became a best-seller, in which the comtesse and the king read letters intercepted by the postmaster general, Baron d'Oigny.

[25] Paul-Francois de Quélen de La Vauguyon (1746-1828) was one of the gentlemen attached to the household of dauphin, and served as the tutor the future Louis XVI.

Heaven so forcefully that he no longer showed anything but the whites, exactly as he would have done at Notre-Dame, his hands joined and kneeling on velvet cushions. Even more disappointed than him was the stout Duc de Richelieu,[26] a sexagenarian Céladon, less old than his sixty years in the young fashions he adopted, for there is nothing in the world as insupportable as an superannuated libertine who cannot adapt to his age; perhaps I would find more supportable a respectable dowager, too respectable, making eyes and with a low neckline like a young and comely woman.

I do not know embarrassment parallel to that of seeing a person suffering ennui whom one is trying to amuse, and whom it is one's duty to amuse.

Nevertheless, nothing worked, and the comtesse, despairing of conquering the royal ennui, made the decision to beat a retreat. It was necessary to have recourse to cunning; she had recourse to it. She leaned over the hearth, as if to examine the progress of the coffee that was boiling in a little silver pot. In that position she uttered a cry; the blood, she said, had rushed to her head, and was making her suffer horribly. No migraine had ever been so sudden; she had never made such a fuss.

But the king only suffered a little less ennui with her than when he had been suffering alone, and it mattered little to him that his favorites were dissimulating frightful yawns and that his mistress was suffering from a headache. He did not even stir in his armchair, and he remained half-asleep and half-awake, without paying

---

[26] Armand de Vignerot du Plessis, Duc de Richelieu (1696-178) was a close friend and influential advisor of Louis XV; often at odds with the king's previous official mistresses he developed a close relationship with Madame du Barry.

any heed to those who were trying to cheer him up and without giving them the slightest excuse to leave.

Finally, there was a modest little knock on the door and the half-honey and half-vinegar voice of the lieuten-ant-general of police coughed dryly and humbly.

The comtesse launched herself at the door with a bound, opened it herself to Monsieur de Sartines,[27] and could not refuse herself the pleasure of tangling her fan, as if by chance, in the lieutenant-general's enormous wig. That was easy, because he advanced profoundly bowed down, with his head a little lower than the comtesse's hand. The playful creature burst out laughing on seeing the fan, in the midst of a cloud of powder, swinging from a large hank of artificial hair. It was very funny, for a royal smile parted the lips of Louis XV. As for La Vauguyon and Richelieu, they laughed so much they had to hold their sides: the king had smiled.

Far from being disconcerted by such a merry wel-come, Monsieur de Sartines seemed very proud of it, and after having saluted the king he deposited the wad of papers that he was holding on a table. Only then did he rid himself of his strange aigrette, imprinted a respectful kiss ion it and returned it to the comtesse; that was ac-companied by a very insipid and very affected compli-ment.

---

[27] I have retained Berthoud's spelling of the name of Antoine de Sartine (1729-1801), whose position as the Lieutenant-General of Police from 1759-1774 made him belatedly leg-endary as a character in feuilleton novels, Boulevard du Tem-ple melodramas and early crime fiction. His reforms of polic-ing in Paris had little apparent effect on the crime rate, but he did introduce a regime of assiduous street-cleaning that was a significant measure of public hygiene.

"Baron d'Oigny is ill," said Monsieur de Sartines thereafter, readjusting his wig. "Two bleedings and four fainting fits have retained him in bed. He charged me with bringing you a few dispatches drawn from his post."

The king extended a nonchalant hand toward the table, and they hastened to roll it nearer to him. The comtesse went to put her elbows on the back of Louis XV's armchair and, leaning over her royal lover's shoulder, she ran her eyes over the papers he was holding; when he had not read as rapidly as her, she forced him cheerfully to turn the page without having finished.

To begin with that reading did not amuse either the king or his mistress very much. The letters fell from the royal hand with disgust almost as soon as it had picked them up and went to cover the parquet. Monsieur de Sartines, the Duc de La Vauguyon and especially the stout Richelieu competed to pick them up. Nothing was as funny as seeing their triple inclination every time a piece of paper slid from the hand of Louis XV. The malicious comtesse took a liking to that grotesque behavior, and more than once she pretended to throw a letter in order to laugh at the sight of the three courtiers bending over fruitlessly.

Meanwhile the king read one letter more attentively, although it was rather short.

Monsieur de Sartines hazarded a glance at the piece of paper sufficiently interesting to fix the king's attention. After that furtive examination he smiled like a man who knows what is what. Then turning to La Vauguyon and Richelieu, he said to them in a low voice, with a self-important grimace: "A love letter! A priceless adventure of that bad lot Vaudencour." In a louder voice, addressing the king, he said: "It's only a copy; your majesty's indisposition has not permitted me, for more than a fortnight, to bring the postal packets. It was necessary to have them sent to their addressees, but I've extracted, as you can see, those that are worth the trouble. In any case, you can know the whole story, for it has reached its end."

Madame du Barry fixed her large eyes on Monsieur de Sartines, and the king lifted himself up slightly in his armchair.

Proud of having attracted such marks of attention, Monsieur de Sartines thought that he ought to precede his story with a preamble. "It is," he said, "a poignant story. It has a heroine of great sentiments, almost a heroine like those of Monsieur Voltaire's tragedies."

At that name, disagreeable to him, the king frowned automatically.

"For," added Monsieur de Sartines, hastening ahead of the king's thought, "he and people of his sort have a mania of blackening paper with all the mad ideas that run through their heads, and believe themselves to be very important."

Louis XV smiled, and his smile made Monsieur de La Vauguyon feel queasy, so he hastened to overbid Monsieur de Sartines' idea. "Let us hope," he interrupted, "that one day he will be brought to justice, France only needs eight men of letters at the most, and they ought only to write under the supervision of the police."

But the king was no longer smiling, because he had not listened, and the comtesse scowled, because Monsieur de Voltaire had sent her an adulatory quatrain the day before. Poor La Vauguyon nearly fainted, and in order to conclude, Madame Dubarry said dryly: "Monsieur de Sartines, I would prefer to hear your story."

"You know that the Comte de Vaudencour married a Flemish heiress last year…"

The Duc de Richelieu interrupted Monsieur de Sartines. "I was the one who made his marriage with Mademoiselle de Béthencourt. My God, he was paid well by the dowry's income of two hundred thousand livres; the poor fellow had debts up to his ears and had no idea how to get out of it. I chanced to think of one of my distant relatives, very aged, very infatuated with her nobility—one of the most ancient, if she can be believed, but one of the most obscure. I wrote to the relative, without saying anything to my young friend Vaudencour; the latter's name and my intervention smoothed out all the obstacles. One morning, I had him climb into a carriage with me. En route for Flanders! And when I saw him admire the old castle and ecstasize over the immense properties that depend on it, I said to him: 'My friend, all this is yours: a signature, a mass and a week with a provinciale; that's the price.'

"May Heaven preserve you, Madame la Comtesse, from ever spending a week in the provinces, especially in Flanders. That fresh and pure complexion would turn as crimson as the cheeks of a peasant, and that little mouth would lose its ravishing form by dint of yawning. Imagine the mores that there were a hundred and fifty years ago, dresses tailored as in the days of the regency, a prudery as under the old court of Madame de Maintenon.

"Mademoiselle Adélaïde de Béthencourt was a tall, pale brunette with promising dark eyes, but all of that was stilted, stiff and starched. When we went in and the venerable mother introduced Mademoiselle de Béthencourt to us, with reverences to make one die laughing, she got up gauchely, bowed even more gauchely, blushed like a milkmaid and kept her eyes lowered constantly, only responding in monosyllables. An unimaginable corset tightened her waist. Following the custom of the region, in order to prevent her from bearing her head too far forward, she had been equipped with an iron collar covered in black velvet; the appendage of that strange carcan was supported by the corset and forced the head backwards. As for the coiffure and garments, they were unusual, upon my soul,

"A stroll in the environs of the château, and visiting a few invalids to bring them help, were her pleasures. Knitting, reading for hours, preparing unguents, the tradition of which was conserved in the family, and jam-making, were her occupations. The local curé, even stiffer and more awkward than her, was her entire society.

"The marriage was made, and she allowed herself to be married without manifesting any joy or pain. I believe that the only thing that she enjoyed was quitting her inconvenient iron collar.

A week after the wedding we departed for Paris again, pretexting Your Majesty's orders. On the way, Vaudencour recounted incredible things about the innocence of the girl."

Monsieur de Sartines hastened to recover the floor that Monsieur de Richelieu had stolen from him.

"Well," he said, "six months ago, the Vicomte de Germignies and a few other fools of his species were having a little supper together. Monsieur de Vaudencoeur, about whose marriage they were joking a great deal, started talking about his wife as an invincible virtue, and furthermore, so well-guarded by her mother that even the most adroit would be unable to do anything.

"The Vicomte de Germignies was sitting beside the Marquis de Chabannons. 'I'll wager,' he said to him in a whisper, 'that within three months that doll so extolled is mine.' Monsieur de Chabannons accepted the wager for five hundred louis, and the next day, Monsieur de Germignies announces that he's departing for a terrain that has just been given to him by his uncle, Prince de Rohan, Archbishop of Cambrai. But it's the road to Flanders that he takes. His carriage breaks down, as if by chance, outside Béthencourt; he claims to be wounded, dying. He's transported to the château, and the most touching and devoted cares are lavished on him when it's discovered that he's a friend of Monsieur de Vaudencour.

"Three months later, the Vicomte de Germignies demanded five hundred louis from the Marquis de Chabannons. The latter wanted proofs, Monsieur de Germignies showed him the letters. His partner claims that they've been faked. 'Well,' cried Vicomte de Germignies, "I'll doubt the wager and she'll come at find me at my petty house.'

"In order to succeed in that he wrote to Madame de Vaudencour that he was ill, and that his malady was commencing to be mortal; then, graduating the tone of his letters with the supposed progress of his illness, he ends up saying that he's dying, and only has one regret, that of not seeing again someone he loved so much. It was then that she replied with the letter that Your Majesty is holding."

The Comtesse du Barry took the letter and read:

"Philippe, I've committed a great sin, a sin of which the remorse renders me very unhappy. I have lost all repose, but I would count all that for nothing, my sweet friend, if you were happy; and you are ill and dying. To

see me would console you, you say? Philippe, you shall not die without being consoled; I will see you one last time. I have sacrificed to you my conscience and my repose; well, I will give you the sole possession that remains to me, my reputation—and may I die thereafter. I am taking advantage of my mother's absence and I have gained, at a price of gold, one of my domestics. Oh, Philippe, Philippe, what am I going to do?"

"That letter remained in my hands for a few days and as only forwarded to the vicomte on the very day when Madame de Vaudencour was due to arrive, Monsieur de Germignies was at table with the Marquis be Chabannons. Their heads were heated, and by virtue of an imprudence that only the state they were in renders comprehensible, Monsieur de Chabannons went to fetch Monsieur de Vaudencour. They started drinking even harder, and when a domestic came to whisper in the vicomte's ear to tell him that a carriage had just arrived at the door of his house, Monsieur de Vaudencour cried that he wanted to see the good fortune of his friend Germignies. Monsieur de Chabannons encouraged that insensate desire, and in spite of Germignies' efforts, they ran out to the carriage."

"Well?" demanded the Comtesse du Barry, made very indignant by the story.

"Well," said Monsieur de Sartines, "a duel ensued in which the Vicomte de Germignies was slightly wounded.

"And Madame de Vaudencour?"

"She has what she merits," the lieutenant of police replied, coldly. "She's imprisoned in a convent."

"The Vicomte de Germignies and the Marquis de Chabannons are scoundrels! It's necessary to punish them. It's necessary no longer to receive them at court,

Sire. You'll send them back to the provinces, won't you?"

"My word, no," said Louis XV. "It's a folly of young men. The affair has been put to sleep; let it remain there. Let's not give Messieurs the writers, Voltaire and others, an opportunity to laugh at the expense of the court; they're already too disposed to do so."

"They'll be exiled from the court of France," said the Comtesse du Barry, leaning toward Louis' ear, and, in a tone that was simultaneously serious and joking she said: "or I'll exile you from my bed."

"Monsieur de Richelieu," said Louis XV, getting to his feet "You're a friend of the Vicomte de Germignies and the Marquis de Chabannons; advise them on my part to go and make a tour of their terrains and not to come back without my orders." And then, leaning on the arm of the Comtesse du Barry, he said: "Bonsoir, Messieurs!"

The Boatwoman

Adventure
1816

Alas, of so much amour here's the recompense!
Phaon is at the altar; he invokes the hymen;
Of another at that moment his hand meets the hand;
Over their inclined heads the veil deploys,
In their eyes an odious joy glitters...
How they tremble, as only a furious lover can;
The people, fleeing, utter cries of horror.
The Virgin will curse this fatal wedding,
And the faith of oaths casually profaned
By all their blood...blood, you, daughter of Apollo?
And what altar received the oaths of Phaon?
What rights can the culpable couple invoke
Who by night, O modesty, fled her mother's roof.
S. Henry Berthoud, *La Fiancée de Leucade*.[28]

You do not know what happiness there is in seeing one's homeland after six years of absence, especially when it is the land of Flanders.

For Flanders is a beautiful land. You would say the same if you had seen its melancholy sky, its fields of

---

[28] This poem appeared in full in the *Mémoires* of the *Societé d'Émulation de la ville de Cambrai*, then kept by the author and printed by his father. The same 1831 issue contained one of the stories from *Contes misanthropiques* and a poem by Delphine de Girardin.

wheat, which the wind stirs like waves, its plains gilded by rape or whitened by fecund poppies.

Flanders has hills in the flanks of which hang boscage and hamlets, which steep paths climb that extend like gigantic serpents; it has valleys bathed by rivers and rich canals; it has plains with beautiful pasturage, marshes with clouds of fog.

Over the foreheads of the young women of Flanders floats a red veil, which the wind inflates and causes to play around their black hair. And then, it is necessary to see them assembling around there waist the endless pleats of the brown cape or the multicolored drapes of the mantle.

The costume of the inhabitants is still the ancient *braie* of the Gauls, a short tunic by which the breasts are gripped, which falls freely around the shoulders and terminates above the knee. A white garter with no button designs the muscular leg beneath the contours of its fine cloth, and the hand, hardened by the plow, leans on a large oak staff.

No, you do not know what pleasure there is in seeing Flanders again after six years of absence, seeing it again in autumn, the autumn more beautiful in Flanders than spring in other lands.

Let me tell you how the foliage reddens then, and turns yellow, how the wheat is accumulated in ricks, how, in the partly scythed fields, a shepherd in perceived next to his mobile cabin, looking at the sky and meditating, his arms folded and his brow inclined toward the earth.

Let me tell you how one shudders with joy at some naïve gleaners' virelay, at the distant sound of a mill, and carriages rolling far away, without one perceiving them.

As for me, exiled from beautiful Flanders six years before, I was going there to rediscover a wife, an angel...Clara de Béthencourt. Never, since my departure, had her name been spoken in my hearing. And yet, six years before, she had sought very often to discover whether she would not see me close to her. On seeing me, a blush covered her forehead, her gaze became tender and a smile parted her lips...

I had never told her that I loved her; she had never pronounced the word amour, and yet we were like old friends that misfortune had tested, like two orphan siblings who transferred all their tenderness to one another. I for her, and she for me, was happiness the universe...

It was necessary not to think of our union; I was poor...

I would not have be able to surround her with well-being and amour, she so happy and so playful, ignorant of poverty and the bleak cares of need. The plays that moved her, which refresh and exalt the imagination; the balls at which young women ornament their semi-naked shoulders with diamonds; the apartments on the floors of which soft carpets extend; the windows whose long curtains enlace and fall...to be mine it would have been necessary for her to renounce all that. I had not wanted that.

So I had quit Flanders.

An insouciant artist, I had climbed the mountains of Switzerland, I had traveled in Italy, I had shivered under the skies of Scotland; and everywhere I dreamed about the beautiful and of Flanders. Once, amid the ruins of the Coliseum, I sketched a Flemish cottage, with its clay walls, its thatched roof and its brick chimneys, from which the peat exhaled its yellow smoke.

A mortal languor gradually took possession of me; my forehead became pale and my limbs paltry. My breast was painful; my convulsive hand could no longer hold the brush, which had become too heavy for my debilitated fingers. The physicians declared that their science could do nothing to cure me. I had homesickness; I could only obtain my cure from my homeland.

I have seen it again! Oh, you cannot know what happiness there is in seeing one's homeland after six years of absence.

I asked for information about her, Clara de Béthencourt. Betrothed to another, to a rich young man, a military man; the marriage is tomorrow.

I shall only see her once more, I said to myself, at the church, on the day of her marriage, tomorrow. I shall hide behind some stout pillar; she will not perceive me. The sight of me might remind her of memories of six years ago; it might perhaps trouble her happiness; it might sadden her, and I do not want to sadden Clara for a day, even for a moment, even if that sadness is caused by a memory of me, by a tender memory, by a memory of the time of our love.

Oh, it was then that I felt my isolation bitterly—me, a poor orphan. No mother to hug me in her arms; no sister to embrace me; no friend to hold out a hand to me; not one voice to bid me welcome. No one remembered my features; no one had retained a memory of my name.

My heart constricted, I left the town and stated to wander along the bank of the Escaut. Gradually, my agitation became less embittered, and I allowed myself to yield to the charm of the spectacle that was offered to my eyes. It was a spectacle full of poetry, one of the sublime scenes that cannot be seen with indifference even by the man most poorly organized to savor the beauties of nature. The air was pure, calm and warm; the mist circling the horizon like an immense curtain confounded its white and transparent vapors with the luminous fluid of the moon, and rendered the light that it spread even vaguer. It was not precisely shadow, nor light, but a mixture of all they have that is most delightful. The image of the moon was reflected on the water as a long oval, the golden fissures of which swayed at the slightest ripple; finally, a religious silence reigned throughout that vast extent, except that at long intervals, the melancholy cry of a bird nested amid the verdure rose up like a lament.

Twenty times I had visited those places. I had never suspected the magical charm that the night and the silence must spread over that beautiful canal, which extends through a picturesque valley between two rows of trees, and over the boats, the floating habitations of a nomadic people.

The bronzed features of that nation, its mores, its costume and even its language have been conserved, strange and without alteration, in spite of time and contacts with the inhabitants of towns. Alternately heaped with superfluities and subject to great privations, the boatmen spend their time in the midst of rude labor or slack idleness. Ardent, choleric and voluptuous, they nourish in the cold climate of the north the burning passions of the Midi; and it is not only their sun-tanned complexion their pale blonde hair and their large black eyes; nor their short broad garments laden with brandenburg fastenings and the enormous rings in their ears that render plausible the supposition that their ancestors were the Bohemians by which Europe was inundated in the fourteenth century.

I was delivering myself entirely to the power of the exaltation, a privilege of adolescence, which returns too rarely to make our heart beat faster at the positive age when experience and its sad realities have disenchanted the soul of so many happy illusions, when all of a sudden, I saw a young woman lifting the trapdoor of a boat. She held it above her for a few moments; her gracious profile was outlined in silhouette amid the gentle and value light that illuminated the scene and seemed disposed like the luminous colors that a painter graduates cleverly around a miniature.

No sound could be heard.

She emerged with precaution, and her gaze interrogated, slowly and by degrees, the expanse that surrounded her. Suddenly, she maintained the immobility of attention; her arms were folded over her breast; her short garments left her legs and bare feet uncovered; her long, semi-scattered hair fell over her shoulders; and on seeing the moon gild a part of her garments with its rays, while the rest remained in somber obscurity, one might have mistaken the young woman, upright and motionless, for an ancient bronze statue.

A joyful gesture suddenly escaped her. Throwing down a plank that formed a narrow and unsteady bridge between the boat and the bank, she flew into the arms of a young man.

In order to consider the young woman more at my ease, without any danger of being seen, I had hidden behind a hedge; it was at the foot of the hedge that the two lovers came to sit down.

At first I only heard a confused noise of kisses, tears and words punctuated so as to stammer with a profound emotion. After that there was a moment of silence.

"I see you again, Paul; I finally see you again after three months. For it was three months ago, you know, that our boat quit this shore, three months that we've been separated. But finally, here I am beside you, my head reposing on your shoulder, my hand in yours! Oh, how happy I am!"

The man named Paul received those caresses with embarrassment and coldness; at least, it seemed so to me. But she was too happy and too emotional to perceive it; entirely given to the ecstasy of being with him, she continued the tender and diffuse speech, that does not dry up, so pleasant is it to let it flow, when one finds a lover again after a long absence.

"I've suffered a great deal during these long three months. When evening came, when everyone gathered on the largest boat to tell and listen to surprising stories, I kept apart and I thought about you. I remembered the night when, pale and covered with blood, pursued by the English, who wanted to kill you, you threw yourself on to the boat where I was alone. I remember, too, the fashion in which you told me that you had to get away from the town because the enemy had just taken it...and then, Paul, I remembered that night of fear and amour..."

The young woman continued talking for a long time, and in her expansive joy she listed all the circumstances of her amour. For me there was the greatest charm in that story, told with all the naïve abandon of a young woman in love, and to which the boatwoman's accent added a further grace that I cannot describe; for the boat people have something of the pronunciation of the Midi. It is a sort of slow melody, a veritable rhythm at which a stranger hearing it for the first time marvels.

"But you're remaining pensive in listening to me," she said then. "You're not as joyful as me? Well, listen, Paul, you'll become cheerful, you'll be very surprised, very happy. Now, Paul, I'm rich beyond my hopes, rich as I never dreamed of being when we were forming impossible projects of happiness. An old aunt has just died; she had two daughters and both had died a month before her. I'm her only heiress! She left eight boats! Tell me, do you know what eight boats are worth? Good, you don't know. Listen, Paul, they're worth eighty thousand francs. Combine with that the value of my two, and then you'll see how rich we are.

"Now, I can be your wife, for we can sell all that. An officer can't marry a boatwoman, I know that, Paul. Your wife! Oh, how happy I'll be to be able to say to everyone that I love you, that I belong to you, and that you're mine! To lean on your arm, to see the sentinels salute you while bearing their weapons! Paul, my Paul, how happy I'll be!"

And he, who had suffered as much as a man can suffer, pushed her away gently, for she had thrown herself into his arms, and he said: "It'll soon be daylight; it's necessary to quit one another."

At those icy words, the poor young woman shivered; her brown cheeks paled, and her hand dropped her lover's hand, which it had been holding.

"Paul, you're not replying to me...?" she murmured.

She could not finish, her voice failed.

"Lucile, it's necessary for you to depart tomorrow at daybreak. I'll come to rejoin you, but it's necessary for you to go. It's necessary."

She did not reply, and began to weep bitterly.

"You'll know why," he continued. "I can't tell you this evening. You'll know, Lucile, and you'll tell me that I did well to demand that you go."

She looked at him anxiously.

"Today, now, tell me, tell me and I'll go, I swear."

"If my happiness is dear to you, Lucile, it's necessary for you to go; I'm asking you, for mercy's sake." He said the last words with a sort of tenderness.

"I'll go," she said.

After that, she drew away at a slow pace, pulled back the plank that served as a bridge between the bank and the boat, and the trap-door closed again.

He remained there, motionless and thoughtful. Then he made a gesture of resolution and despair, and disappeared at a rapid pace.

The next day was the wedding day of Clara de Béthencourt, whom I had loved so much.

When I entered the church, the marriage had already taken place. An immense crowd filled the church, countless curious people were gathered around the grille of the choir. I advanced without fear of being seen.

Heaven! Clara's husband was the boatwoman's lover!

She, so worthy of being loved, for whom I had sacrificed everything, the wife of a wretched suborner!

I would have liked to be able to cry, but I could not; despair and indignation were suffocating me too much for that.

Everything that was happening around me seemed to be a maleficent dream. A heavy fire weighed upon my forehead; my eyes could barely see; a cold sweat was steaming over my trembling limbs.

Suddenly, a woman hurtled into the church; she uttered screams, she cleaved through the crowd, she arrived as far as the spouses and fell motionless at their feet.

I had recognized the boatwoman; he too had recognized her—for he remained there, motionless, as if thunderstruck. No pallor similar to his has ever contracted a human face.

The ceremony was only interrupted momentarily; the priest continued his offices.

After that, Paul took the hand of the woman he had just married. As he traversed the nave to rejoin the carriage he darted anxious glances around him, as if to discover what had become of the boatman.

A young man whom I recognized by his white gloves as a member of the wedding party approached the husband and murmured in his ear: "Don't say anything to your wife; it might affect her. The madwoman is dead."

A convulsive movement shook all Paul's limbs, and he fell unconscious.

Clara's eyes filled with tears, and it was necessary for her mother to support her.

"Have no fear," said Madame de Béthencourt to her daughter, while Clara knelt down to make her husband inhale smelling salts. "The young man has not been able to resist the tender emotions he is experiencing. Make way, Messieurs, stand aside. A little air and he'll recover consciousness. The emotions that joy causes are sometimes dangerous."

The Widow

Story
1829

Beautiful pastorella
That amour made to charm you,
Besieged by such cruelty
In the season of amour
A chorus will complete it
And my regrets.
        Morel, Canon of Montpellier[29]

Past felicity
That cannot return
Torment of my thought.
What have I done to lose the memory of you?
        Boileau[30]

Alas, my Charles, the wealth that I desire so
much, which I would give all the world to
possess, I have disdained, I have misunderstood.
Oh, tell me, tell me will you not return them to
me? You would make me the happiest of women.
Love letters.

---

[29] This translation from Occitan is approximate, at best.

[30] This stanza can, in fact, be found in the *Oeuvres poétiques* de Nicolas Boileau-Despreaux, but only in a footnote, where it is credited to Philippe Desportes (1546-1606). It is also quoted in Stéphanie de Genlis' *Annales de la vertu* (1781), but she credits it to Jean Bertaut (1552-1611).

In the midst of the joyous insouciance of an independent life, in the midst of the pleasures that if offers, of the piquant incidents that daze, of its indolent whimsy, to which one delivers oneself with so much abandon, what young man has not felt the imperious need for a placid, mild and legitimate happiness? What young man has not dreamed, even in the embrace of the most intoxicating of mistresses, of a woman beautiful in tenderness, modesty and candor.

Yes, of long, tranquil days, entirely devoted to study; in the evening, the caresses of one's child, a leisurely meal, a mean alone with one's wife; after that, a walk in some solitary place, endless chatter full of confidence and amour. And them a fresh slumber, and when one opens one's eyes again, to contemplate, smiling, the white and semi-naked shoulders of one's wife, to hear delightedly the vermilion mouth of one's child respiring!

Fortunate Ernest! Soon that happiness would be his. In a few days, he would be Caroline's husband.

And everyone tells him so! Is there a young woman anywhere whose eyes have more tenderness? Whose gait is more naïve and more elegant? When she sings, her voice stirs the soul. As she dreams, her forehead supported in her hand, one senses sentimental tears welling up, one experiences I know not what emotion, which tightens the breast delightfully.

Caroline, dear Caroline! Oh, how he wants to surround you with happiness and amour,

Many a time, he has thought that he loved; but never, no, never, has he loved as he loves her. He understands now. Yes, amour is a grave and sublime thing. Outside of duty there is no amour, ineffable amour, like the amour that he experiences.

So he will annihilate everything that reminds him of his liaisons and his pleasures of old. Locks of hair, rings, letters, he will deliver everything to the flames. Only he will look at them, and read them, one last time. After that, all will be said.

There is an indescribable charm for him in these dried flowers, these knotted ribbons, once received with transport, in these unevenly written lines, once opened so precipitately, which the eyes devoured, which made his heart beat faster—and which he now unfolds nonchalantly and scans with a vague smile on his lips.

The flames had destroyed everything.

All that remained, at the bottom of a drawer, were the letters of Maria de Béthencourt, of Maria, his first love.

That one, he had loved; perhaps he loved her as he loves Caroline—for she also was to have been his wife, she too was to have realized the dreams of happiness that his poetic imagination formed.

Their families rejoiced in seeing them together, in projecting in low voices the day when those dear children would be married; and when he heard those words, he was the happiest of men.

It happened that an officer, young, sprightly, rich and of noble birth became smitten with Maria de Béthencourt, and from then on Ernest had much to lament. For the young woman dreamed while he was talking to her about amour, and her distracted gazes seemed to be listening to see whether they could not hear the gallop of an impetuous horse. She preferred to the most delightful walk the sound of warrior fanfares and the tumultuous movement of squadrons with golden breastplates and scarlet plumes. Yes, now nothing any longer charmed her like soldiers who drew together, drew apart and extended their ranks amid the clamors of command, horses pounding the pavement, sabers clashing. Then her eyes sparkled and a blush covered her cheeks.

Maria de Béthencourt married the captain.

Ernest had a great deal of difficulty consoling himself for that. For a long time he remained in a profound sorrow, full of suspicion and discouragement. Poor young man! He no longer believed in amour.

But finally, he was loved by Caroline, the angelic Caroline, and from then on he became happy again, as before. Happier, perhaps—for the memory of what he had suffered rendered even more precious to him the possession of a wealth that he had despaired of ever encountering, a wealth that he had, alas, revoked in doubt even the possible existence.

But finally, only one more day to pass, and he would be happy, he would be Caroline's husband—tomorrow! Tomorrow!

Caroline would realize the dreams of happiness to which Maria's letters had once delivered him...the letters that he could not help rereading again.

There was a tone of conviction therein, an enthusiasm that could not be feigned. Yes, the woman who spoke of love like that knew how to love.

She had preferred splendor to happiness, might she be happy! She had been seduced by intoxicating charms, might her illusions never dissipate!

And he reread them once more, and could not resolve to deliver Maria de Béthencourt's letters to the flames.

While they plunged him again into memories full of melancholy and tenderness, someone came to hand him a note.

No! It was not an illusion...her handwriting! The same seal that she used, and even the signature of the sweet name of Maria.

One evening he had said that he found the charm of English orthography in his fiancée's name, and since the evening he had aid that Marie de Béthencourt no longer had any other signature than *Maria*.

If you want to receive a friend of your youth, a friend distanced from you for five years, she arrived this morning at the home of Madame Saint-Yves. Maria.

That was what Ernest read in the note.

He went immediately to the address it indicated. Maria was there, alone. She was dressed in black.

There was a moment of embarrassment and silence between them, and then a few cold and constrained questions.

Afterwards, they began to converse more fluently, like two proven friends who had rediscovered one another after a long absence.

Maria had been widowed eight months before. Her husband had left her a considerable fortune. She had no child.

"You've been happy, then, for five years?" asked Ernest.

"Happy?" repeated the young woman, in a melancholy voice. "And you, Ernest?"

He shivered, for she had named him, as she had named him in the time of their amours.

He hastened to talk about Caroline; it seemed to him that if he deferred it any longer he would be behaving badly, that he would be at fault with regard to his fiancée. He recounted the happiness that he expected with Caroline; he told her how gentle, tender and naïve she was, but his words had none of the fervor and enthusiasm that had previously exalted his imagination.

Then he began to depict the pure, calm, delectable life that was reserved for him with Caroline. This time, he could not remain cold before the depiction, and gradually, his expressions became warm and impassioned.

Tears rolled from Maria's eyes. She also began talking about happiness, but a happiness that she had never encountered, a happiness that only two beings who understood one another obtained, a happiness that she had once believed possible, which was not made for her—she understood that now, alas.

"At least," she added, with difficulty, "you'll always be my friend, won't you, Ernest? In whatever position you find yourself, whatever distance or duration separates us, you will always have a memory of Maria."

Ernest felt too much emotion to respond. He held out his hand to Maria. That movement allowed the widow to see a ring the Ernest was wearing on his finger. It was Maria, Maria de Béthencourt, who had given him that ring, in other times.

It was necessary for her to stand up and pace back and forth for a few minutes; otherwise, she would have choked.

Then she came back and sat down in front of Ernest; and, preoccupied by sweet and bitter thoughts, she was pensive for a long time.

Then, tearing herself from her reverie, effortfully, she rang for her domestics, gave them orders, and, smiling sadly at her friend she said. "Adieu. Adieu, Ernest, forever!"

At those words he was struck by stupor and dazed by a thousand confused thoughts.

"Adieu, Ernest," she said again, "For I'm in haste, and the carriage is ready. Adieu forever."

She had difficulty holding back her sobs.

Their hands clasped one more time; then the carriage departed. She had disappeared for a long time when Ernest was still there. motionless, his gaze fixed on the extremity of the horizon, where he had ceased to perceive her.

Dejected, experiencing an insupportable void, he went to join Caroline. She thought he was ill, for she saw him sad and pensive all evening.

More than once, the following day, he felt the same sadness, and abandoned himself to the same reverie; and when left alone with Caroline in the nuptial chamber, he surrounded her with his embrace, he murmured: "Maria! Maria!"

The next day, when he awoke, with the smile of happiness on his lips, he delivered himself with his young wife to the sweetest expansions, and while she leaned a semi-naked arm on her Ernest's shoulder, she reminded him of the mistaken name of the previous evening.

"Oh," she said, pretending to sulk and without believing in the least in the reality of the reproach she was making, "there's apparently someone you love more than your Caroline, isn't that true, wretch?"

He fell back into his reverie.

Then, suddenly, enlacing Caroline in his arms, he cried: "To you, to you alone, for life!"

The Red Nose

A Flemish Adventure

I. The Château de Boussu

It would be difficult, if not completely impossible, to find a town, a convent, a village or an old château in Flanders to which no legend is attached in which the Devil and monks play the principal roles. The story of the foundation of the manor of Boussu is not the least curious of those legends.[31]

The Château de Boussu elevates its towers and dismantled fortifications on the banks of the Hayne, between Valenciennes, the coal town, and its rival Mons—Mons, whose bituminous coal gives a bright, energetic flame of brief duration, while the sulfur of the Valenciennes mineral burns with less brightness and vivacity, but with a slowness very favorable to economy.

Once, the Château de Boussu was regarded as an important military position. When Louis XI besieged

---

[31] Boussu is nowadays in Belgium; the Château de Boussu allegedly dates from the tenth century, but its history is hazy prior to it falling by inheritance into the Hénin family, eventually becoming the property of Pierre I de Hénin, Comte de Boussu, a Knight of the Golden Fleece. Following its destruction in 1478 it was rebuilt by the architect Jacques de Broeucq but was burned in 1554, although its ruins still exist, despite being dynamited in 1944 when it was a Luftwaffe munitions dump. The legend cited by Berthoud is entirely his own invention.

Condé in 1478 he began by taking passion of the Château de Boussu and rendering himself master of it,
thanks to his favorite maxim: "There is no impregnable
citadel that a mule laden with gold can enter." In 1657,
Don Juan of Austria established his headquarters at
Boussu. In 1709, during the war of the Spanish succes-
sion, the elector Maximilian came to occupy Boussu.
And finally, in 1792, it was in the same vicinity that the
battle of the Moulin de Boussu was fought, in which the
Duc de Chartres, today King Louis-Philippe, saw fire for
the first time.

At the present time, save for a drawbridge that can
no longer be lifted, towers, ramparts and useless machicolations, nothing remains of the ancient military
strength of the antique Château de Boussu. An old suze-
rain fallen into decadence, its armor, once so redoubtable, inspires nether dread not respect; people no longer
bare their heads in passing before the feudal escutcheon;
people no longer point to the manor from a distance with
a gesture of admiration, exclaiming: "There's the powerful Château de Boussu." If anyone still stops before its
walls, it is a peasant who comes to nail the worm-eaten
pontoon with a crossbow bolt, an artist traveling at random in Flanders, or frivolous young women who sing
the words *manor* and *castle* in stupid ballads, and whom,
since chance has presented them with the opportunity,
are not sorry to know what an ugly mass of stones the
banal expressions designate that they have pronounced
so many times at a piano without having understood
them.

Listen to the tradition, however; listen to the tales of
the old folk of the village, and you will know that the
Château de Boussu was not built by mortal hands; you
will know that the Devil himself, taking the trowel and

pounding the mortar, placed those enormous sandstone blocks one atop another, the weight of which alone sustains them today, for the years have eroded the cement that united them and reduced it to dust.

One day, a brilliant tourney had assembled in Cambrai the elite of the seigneurs of Flanders, and after having jousted and combated until the hour of vespers, those seigneurs were delivering themselves to the joys of a magnificent banquet when a monk suddenly appeared in their midst, his head shaven, his feet bare, and a crucifix in his hand. His robe, almost in tatters, allowed the sight of the profound scars with which his limbs were furrowed: scars whose bizarre forms revealed an ingenious cruelty. The monk had arrived from the Holy Land; he had succeeded, after extraordinary perils, in saving himself from the slavery in which the infidels had retained him, and his first concern, on finding himself back in his homeland, in Flanders, had been to come to cry "Vengeance!" in the midst of Christian knights, and to preach a crusade to them. The libations of the feast had disposed the numerous seigneurs of the tourney to enthusiasm marvelously. They all stood up in a unanimous movement crying: "*Diex edt volt!*" All of them placed the red cross on their shoulder, the emblem of the vow they were contracting; all of them swore to embark for Palestine within a month.

As the preacher observed to them, God seemed to have assembled around those who consecrated themselves to his service all the facilities possible to hasten and smooth out the dispositions to be made before the departure; thus, the Jews attracted to the tourney, which was a good business opportunity for them, were there to make loans under caution and in exchange for a pledge; the ladies gave their knights sashes and amorous gifts

175

personally; monks inscribed testaments, received pious legacies and gave absolution for sins.

It was customary, when one entered Holy Orders, to put oneself under the special protection of one of the saints in Paradise. By a natural extension, and since the vow of the crusade was a vow, if not monastic, at least religious, the crusaders imitated that example and each of them chose the blessed in the intercession of whom he had the most faith; the Flemish saints were the first ones chosen: Notre-Dame de Grace, Notre-Dame de Bon-Secours, Saint Waast, Saint Druon, Saint Hilaire and many others.

After that, one comes to the rest of legend. Everyone was already furnished with a patron, except the young Sire de Boussu, who still had not quit his cup, or thought of imitating the laudable example of the other seigneurs.

What about you, Sire de Boussu, to which saint in Paradise will you cry: 'Help!'"

The Baron de Boussu wiped his lips, moist with wine, and cried: "To Sainte Maxellaude!"

"She has been chosen by the Comte de Niergnies," responded several voices.

"Then the Comte de Niergnies is going to reckon with me."

It was necessary for the monk, the preacher of the crusade, to throw himself between the two knights and adjure them in the name of God, to whom their swords belonged, not to drawn those swords against brothers and Christians.

"Well," said Baron de Boussu, "since no more saints in Paradise remain, I'll take the Devil for a patron."

Words impious to that degree made everyone sign themselves devoutly, but that did not stop Baron de Boussu, and he added: "I take the Devil for a patron! Yes, Satan himself...for you'll understand that for a Sire de Boussu, a vulgar patron is insufficient; I put under his safeguard my body, my wealth, my domains, my wife, my daughter and my honor; everything except my soul. Satan is my unique patron. May Satan be my aid!"

"I will be there, Boussu," said a terrible voice that emerged from the bosom of the earth, and chilled everyone with fear.

A few months later, they departed for the Holy Land, and what became that crusade was what had become of other crusades; to wit, in Palestine: wounds, misery, discord, prison and the plague; and after six years of absence, on the return, pillaged domains, seduced daughters, seduced and unfaithful wives. Each of the crusaders struck his breast with dolor and wondered bitterly why God should have compensated in that way those who had quit everything for his service.

If those protected by Heaven have received such ugly gifts, thought Baron de Boussu as he headed toward his domain, *what will become of me, who only have Satan for a protector? Insensate that I was, doubtless not a stone of my castle remains and I probably won't find my wife or my daughter.*

He was so convinced of that that he let his horse idle as it would and dared not prick it with his spur in order to arrive more rapidly in the presence of his domain.

Suddenly, cries of joy were heard; a brilliant troop of vassals opened in two military lines, and in the middle of them appeared the chatelaine of Boussu and her daughter, as beautiful as an angel, who came to throw herself into the arms of their husband and father. Baron de Boussu dared not believe his eyes, and thought that he was the victim of a dream.

It was better still after he had visited his domain, and had found it in a state of strength and prosperity much better than when he had departed. He had not enough surprise and admiration to suffice for what he experienced.

Then the door opened of an edifice constructed since the baron's departure, and a venerable old man appeared on the threshold and invited the baron to come in.

The baron found himself in a hall with arched windows, scarcely illuminated by paned of darkly colored glass, and on each side of the hall, on marble beds, were statues representing cadavers half-eaten away by worms, hideous faces and iron forks arranged with care.[32] While he examined these things with an anxious curiosity, Baron de Boussu saw his guide change aspect and become a spirit, his head circled by an iron crown.

"I am Satan. Have I given you good protection? Did I lie in saying: 'I will be there, Boussu'?"

"No, upon my soul," cried the baron. "I have received loyal and generous protection from you; better protection than the protection of the saints invoked by the other knights, saints who have allowed domains to be pillaged, wives seduced and daughters..."

"Don't blaspheme," said Satan, with an unequaled courtesy and delicacy. "Don't blaspheme, for people will say that I only rendered you service in order to doom your soul."

---

[32] Author's note: "This hall still exists at Boussu; it is adjacent to the chapel."

"You have been loyal and I shall be grateful, for in future I will take for emblems in my shield the cups that inspired in me the good counsel to choose you for a patron; I will deck that shield with two golden horns, and I will take for a motto: *I will be there, Boussu.*"

In 1790 the Boistrancourt family,[33] whom heritages had rendered proprietors of the Château de Boussu, emigrated and only returned to France in 1814 with the Bourbons. All that remained of the family then were three individuals, an old spinster fifty years old, the dowager Mademoiselle Aldegonde; Baron Paul de Boistrancourt, her nephew; and Madame de Boistrancourt, Paul's mother and the widow of the dowager's brother.

Madame de Boistrancourt was German and belonged to a rich Viennese family. She had married Monsieur de Boistrancourt in 1795. A short time after that union Monsieur de Boistrancourt's blind devotion to the Bourbons had taken him to the Vendée. There, taking weapons in hand and at the head of a band of insurgents, he had been gunned down on the battlefield. On the day when the news of such a great misfortune reached his wife, the unfortunate woman gave birth to a child who was baptized with his father's names: Paul Amédée.

In spite of the brilliant parties that were offered to her, Baronne Julie de Boistrancourt never wanted to remarry. She had been far from finding happiness in her first union. Young, light, frivolous and habituated to the dissolute mores of the French court, the Baron could

---

[33] In the early nineteenth century the present-day Château de Boistrancourt did not exist and Boistrancourt was merely a hamlet in the Nord. The characters in the story are fictitious.

neither understand nor even suspect Julie's tender and delicate soul. He honestly believed that he was fulfilling the duties of a gallant man with regard to his wife in showing himself mild and facile toward her, not lacking in attentions in her regard, and above all in surmounting with his baronial crown the two millions that she brought him in dowry.

For that marriage was a marriage of convenience, almost a misalliance, which would certainly not have be contracted at any other time by the Baron de Boistrancourt et de Boussu. But his domains had been sold and little more remained to him than his cape and épée; he therefore married Mademoiselle de Berkem in spite of the slightly Judaic origin for which she was reproached. In order to purify himself from the impure contact of that plebeian gold, he resolved to consecrate a part of it, if not the whole, to the good cause. More than a million had already been dissipated when the baron was killed.

Baronne Julie devoted herself entirely to the education of her son, a frail and cherished creature on which the affections of the young woman were concentrated. She never quit him for an hour since the moment of his birth; she nourished him on her own milk; she gave him the first elements of instruction, carried out studies in order for that instruction to be sufficient, and it was only with tears that she saw herself forced later to summon masters of different sorts to her aid and in lessons for which she was unable to substitute.

The result of that was that Paul's character was impregnated with a tenderness and a chastity that the ordinary education of people is far from communicating to them, and that he was imbued with his mother's ideas, ideas a little romantic for a woman and much too romantic for a man. In making her son the best possible, in accordance with the ideal of perfection of which she had dreamed, she did not think about the disappointments and despair that might lacerate that naïve soul borne to a dangerous exaltation.

The baronne was not completely blind to such dangers, but she was blind with regard to the means of preventing them, means that she judged infallible.

Paul is rich, she said to herself, *he can do without men and spend his life quietly in the obscure and placid retreat in which I have raised him, far from the impure contact of society, far from vices, far from the contagion of examples that would wither his exquisite sensitivity and give him a false and deadly direction; it is up to me to direct that sensitivity; it is up to me to present him with the object to which it ought to report; it is up to me not to leave to chance the choice of the woman he will love. When Paul is nineteen years old I will establish a relationship between him and some tender and beautiful young woman, a young woman raised by a sage mother devoid of ambition. Paul will love her, for he will find no one around her more worthy of being loved. Paul will marry her, and if God does not call me to him before the epoch when Paul reaches the age at which the passions lose their powerful effervescence, my son's happiness will be assured and I will have been able to preserve him from the heart-rending dolors that are ordinarily only spared to cold and egotistical hearts.*

The baronne's plan of education succeeded until 1814, to the great admiration and the great joy of the dowager Mademoiselle Aldegonde, who possessed for Paul all of the exaggeration of tenderness of old aunts for their nephews, and who saw in that education the beautiful ideal of aristocracy.

Nothing equaled the candor and the exquisite sensitivity of Paul when he arrived at the age of nineteen; nothing, either, would have equaled his beauty without a certain timidity that gave an embarrassment to his bearing and caused it to lack elegance, but not a certain charm. His regular features could only be reproached for a slightly unhealthy pallor, and the tender expression of his large blue eyes and his smile were reminiscent of his mother's gaze and melancholy smile. Fits of impetuosity sometimes carried him too far, and took their source from the hot-heated character he had inherited from his father and the excessive condescension of his mother, his aunt and everyone surrounding him. His gaze was then seen to ignite and his fists to clench; his cheeks became pale and his convulsively contracted lips could no longer form words; but a tear from the baronne was sufficient to calm that great anger, and Paul, ashamed and repentant, came to take refuge in his mother's bosom and weep there, as if he were only twelve years old.

It was necessary, moreover, to see him attentive to fulfill the slightest desires of his aunt, and especially his mother; no young mother ever had such refined cares, such delicate urgency. The flowers that she liked best she was always sure of finding in her embalmed cabinet. In the morning, she saw reproduced in his album the sites she had remarked the previous day in her evening stroll; and her son spent two or three hours every day singing or improvising on the piano; then the baronne came to lean over Paul's chair, intoxicated by harmony, and to gaze with an ineffable bliss at her son's features, animated by inspiration, reflected in the mirror placed behind the piano.

Paul made his ordinary reading German, Italian and French poets. German was his natural language, and he spoke the other two, especially French, with a great perfection, which she owed to daily conversations with the dowager Mademoiselle Aldegonde. Walks in company with his mother and a few excursions on horseback, always with his mother, completed the employment of the young man's time, and did not only offer him distractions, for they almost always had the goal of visiting and consoling indigent or invalid families. An aged physician, poor although very learned, who had not quit his clientele but had quit his profession in order to become Paul's tutor, usually accompanied them, and created a sort of clinic for Paul, thus giving him quite extensive medical knowledge.

It was in that fashion that the nineteen years went by that preceded the French Restoration of 1814. Mademoiselle Aldegonde saluted that unexpected restoration with the most joyful acclamations, and came to join the host of French people that an absence of twenty-five years had made strangers for their homeland. By dint of credit, initiative and importunity, she succeeded in recovering possession of the Château de Boussu and its former domains, which had remained national property, and only a small portion of which, by a hazard of good fortune had been alienated and sold. She wrote that great news to her sister, and insisted that she came immediately to take possession of the Château de Boussu and enable her son to inhabit the fief of his ancestors.

Madame la Baronne de Boistrancourt did not quit Germany without anxiety, and above all without regret. It required more than one further letter from her sister-in-law to persuade her to make that grave decision. Finally, she resigned herself to it, and set forth with her young son, whom the voyage filled with joy.

One can imagine the dilapidation that the Château de Boussu presented, uninhabited for twenty-five years. The dowager Aldegonde shed tears on seeing the blazoned tapestry corroded by damp, which left the walls bare; her regrets were far greater when the ruins of the principal keep appeared to her eyes, already covered with grass and brambles. Eighteen months were scarcely sufficient to repair the damage of time and the devastations of the peasants, who had scaled the walls of the château by night and taken possession of everything offered to their convenience in order to build and furnish their houses.

After eighteen months, however,[34] when the dowager, who could no longer resolve to quit Paris for more than a few days, came to spend three weeks with her nephew and sister-in-law, she was agreeably surprised by the state of repair in which she fund the château. Externally, all of its feudal aspect had been conserved: the towers, the crenellations and the drawbridges; the escutcheon flanked with horns and the golden cup had been replaced above the door, and Gothic letters of enormous dimension enabled anyone who raised their eyes to read the celebrated inscription: *I will be there, Boussu*.

On the other hand, the interior had been declared with all present luxury and refinement: elegant wallpaper, furniture no less elegant, a library and a billiard room displayed their modern comfort behind the old

---

[34] This eighteen moths skips over the Hundred Days of Napoléon's return, when the château was presumably untouched by the conflict, although it was not so very far from Waterloo, which might well have been visible through the telescope cited later in the passage..

feudal mantle. Finally, instead of a dense thicket whose somber and uncultivated aspect saddened the eye, an English park had been designed on an immense scale, in which the fecund meadows that extended as far as the banks of the Hayne extended their fresh grass and cheerful verdure.

After a few laments regarding the fiscal physiognomy given to the Château de Boussu, Mademoiselle Aldegonde ended up reconciling herself entirely to that not-very-feudal wellbeing, especially when she saw the delightful apartment that had been prepared for her and the balcony from which, with the aid of a telescope that her nephew had not failed to place there, she could almost count the innumerable villages of Belgium. She found it so comfortable that she even delayed her departure for Paris for a week, and promised to return before winter.

She did indeed return, and by virtue of her arrival and the news that she brought, a complete change was operated in Paul's destiny, and all the projects that Madame la Baronne de Boistrancourt had formed for her son were destroyed.

That is what we are going to relate.

One evening, the baronne was sitting by the fireside, because the first chill was beginning to make itself felt, and the first chill is keen in Flanders. The baronne, supported softly by the cushions of a vast armchair, was listening to Paul, whose fresh and sonorous voice was reading with a great deal of expression an elegy by Millevoye, a transitional poet whose verses obtained a success in that epoch of transition that they would doubt-less no longer obtain today.[35]

Paul's mother contemplated with a proud maternal smile the exaltation expressed by the young enthusiast's physiognomy. She experienced a secret joy in seeing that nineteen-year-old breast swell, and that nineteen-year-old heart beating more rapidly under the spell of the mysterious words repeat in each of the poet's verses: amour, woman, happiness transports of the soul. Yes, she experienced joy, and a great joy, for the young woman of whom she had dreamed for her son, that tender and beautiful young woman, well, she had found her! A few more days and without warning him, without him being able to suspect it, she would take Paul to her. A few more days, and the projects that she had formed for her son before he was even born, while he was quivering in her maternal womb, would be realized.

Her son! Oh, how she loves him! How happy and proud of him she is! Where can a soul be found purer and more naïve than his? Where can ideas more elevated and a nobler soul be found? With what grace his pensive head rests on the white and delicate hand that sustains it! How well his black hair goes with that white forehead! His voice has tones that make one shiver, his gaze electrifies...oh yes, she loves him, her son! Oh yes, she is happy and proud of him.

Suddenly, a door opens noisily, and Mademoiselle the dowager appears in a theatrical manner; for Mademoiselle the dowager loves noise and *coups de théâtre*. She embraces her sister-in-law, she embraces her nephew, and then, suddenly drawing away from their em-

---

[35] Charles-Hubert Millevoye (1782-1816), greatly admired by the French Romantics who survived him.

braces, she says: "Ah, ah, my nephew, I thought of you during my sojourn in Paris, Let's see, what do you desire the most?"

Paul searched.

"You're searching, my lad? Well, I've divined it. Look."

She opened the door, and an old brigadier of hussars came in, and with him entered two valets de chambre carrying a complete uniform: the saber, the dolman, the colback.[36]

"Kiss me, my lieutenant!" she cried.

Paul threw himself into his aunt's arms with a joyful effusion, and hastened to put on the hussar's coat and to fasten the great saber at his waist.

In the meantime, Madame de Boistrancourt wept bitterly and repeated: "My sister, my sister! What have you done?"

"I've made a young man of that girl. Why are you so desolate? See how that uniform suits Paul! How many heads he will turn! Come here, so that I can kiss you again."

The harm that the dowager had done was irreparable; Madame de Boistrancourt understood that. Could anything in the world engage a young man to renounce the saber that his hands were brandishing, the elegant and rich uniform that he had just put on? So she only tried with the suspicion of failure to turn her son away from the career opened to him by his aunt. To her gravest remonstrations and most tender supplications, Paul

---

[36] The French colback (the word is derived from the Turkish *qalpaq*) was a military head-dress similar to, and just as ludicrous as, the English busby.

responded with supplication no less tender and no less persistent.

It was necessary to yield.

Poor mother! How much she suffered during the three days that preceded Paul's departure! How much she suffered at the moment of the separation! How much she suffered on the evening when it was necessary to go home without having kissed her son, and with the horrible thought: *I won't see him tomorrow! I won't see him the day after! Henceforth, we're separated, for I'll only see him at long intervals and for a few days. Henceforth, he'll have other guides than his mother, other amities than his mother's amity.*

Poor mother!

II. The Garrison

For anyone who has never seen a dinner of sub-lieutenants, especially sub-lieutenants of hussars, it is impossible to imagine the confusion of conversations, the tumult of voices, the bursts of laughter, the animated discussions of forty persons all talking at once, all laughing at once, all arguing at once. Combine with that the glasses clinking with a dry sound, the chairs scraping on the pavement, the domestics being abused, and you will still only have a very incomplete idea of the amusing tumult in which good cheer, wine and a communicative joy warm scatterbrained young heads and bring into contact crazy thoughts, the sharp and continual collision of which renders them crazier still.

In 1815, an epoch in which corps of young officers were composed in part of young noblemen infatuated by their names, without the habit of discipline, who took pleasure in displaying the aristocratic impertinence of men who had finally resumed their places and who spat in the faces of the plebeians who had taken them, the behavior of sub-lieutenants of hussars caused scandals that surpassed all measure. Woe betide the towns where they were garrisoned! The spectacles were devoid of tranquility, and impudent indiscretions doomed young women, rightly or wrongly. If husbands became annoyed, they were offered a saber-thrust or a pistol shot, and given that those who made a profession of fighting were able to make better use of their weapons than peaceful merchants, the husbands always came off worse.

The regiment of the Royal Hussars prevailed over all the other regiments in its reputation for turbulence. Commanded by a young colonel who gave them an example in escapades, mostly rich and competing in extravagance, the officers of that corps had put in emotion the little town of Hazebrouck, and not a day passed when the honest Flemings did not have new scandals to deplore. Each of those triumphs was celebrated with noisy banquets, during which the wine of Champagne and a competition worthy of the days of the Regency caused new exploits to be plotted and encouraged the young hotheads in such a beautiful path.

On the day of his arrival, it was in the midst of such a repast that the chaste and naïve Paul found himself. Stupefied by what was offered to his eyes and what struck his ears, he felt sadness and disgust to begin with, but soon, the fear of ridicule, awakened by a few smiles and a few gazes, took possession of him and made him affect to understand and approve of the debauchery of words and conduct that was displayed before him with so much complaisance. His modesty embarrassed him. A bitter sentiment, a mixture of regret of the life he was commencing and repentance of the education he had received, an intimate struggle between good and evil, squeezed his heart and his breast.

The evil prevailed, and carried him away by virtue of self-esteem, for, it is necessary to say with dolor, virtue has its shame even more than vice. A man often has to blush more at his good principles than his bad ones, and the fear of ridicule, with the power of example, perverts even more than the passions.

Sitting at table between two of the noisiest of his comrades—Baron de Niergnies and Come de Hautcourt, for whom his aunt had given him letters of recommendation—Paul allowed his glass to be filled, and emptied it as if he had been habituated to the active effects of Champagne wine. How could he make the confession of a bourgeois temperance in the midst of persons who extolled drunkenness and drew vanity therefrom? He drank, therefore, and an unfamiliar warmth came to course through his veins and warm his brain. Then his ideas changed and took a strange direction; he doubted his firmest beliefs; he accepted all the ideas that were awakened before him, and the memory of his mother quit him.

His mother! Oh, how she would have suffered at the sight of her son, the object of so much love and so much care, his cheeks crimson, his eyes red, his tongue heavy; her son, listening with avidity to obscene words, infamous songs, striving to master that new language, and making his comrades, past masters in that genre, laugh at his awkwardness. How she would have suffered when it was necessary for him to lean on an arm in order to arrive at the spectacle, where soon, quitting the hall, he went up on stage with Messieurs de Niergnies and Hautcourt.

It was during an entr'acte, and various groups of women were occupying the stage while the scene-shifters were making a great racket changing the sets, vast frames hung with canvas and covered with crude pictures to which an artist had devoted a dozen pots of paint and three months of his time. Those backcloths were four in number: a blue drawing room, a black prison, a green forest and a red public square. By virtue of a talent for combination that sometimes produced the most comical ensembles, decorations were formed from all that composed of gardens, palaces, farms, landscapes, deserts, mountains and all the locations that the play in perforce required.

For the garden, they set up boldly between two windows of the drawing room the delicate and rounded crown of a tree from the forest; for the mountain they built on trestles an inclined and tilted wing of the public square of Toulouse. When a fortified château was required, the prison was employed, and so on. Narrow strips of canvas, now gray but once splashed the Prussian blue clouds, served in turn for the ceiling of the drawing room, the vault of the prison, the summit of the trees in the forest and the sky of the public square. Four chairs, two padded armchairs, two stools, one wood and the other painted and supposedly pictorial; a grassy bank, an old carpet serving to cover the throne, two ex-tablecloths dyed red and extended over two tables, completed the comical equipment, with two ladders, a hundred ropes, a hammer, nails and iron pincers.

For it was not an easy thing, truly, to maneuver all that canvas, to keep upright the badly-squared wings, which could not be given any other support but narrow and tottering poles. Certainly, it required a retribution of thirty sous a day for the poor journeyman committed to that task to have industry and invention, especially when the spectacle required visible changes. In that great circumstance he replaced the machines with arms; a man as stationed in each wing, and at the sacramental blast of the whistle, the wing was withdrawn and a second thus uncovered. It was fortunate when such an abrupt movement did not cause one or other to fall, at the risk of breaking the actors' heads.

That would truly have been a pity, for the actors were better than the theater, and the women especially distinguished themselves, if not by their art, at least by their verve. As for their costumes, they caused the despair of the ladies of Hazebrouck by a very Parisian refinement and luxury, and in which the munificence of the officers of the Royal Hussars paid a considerable part in regard to their taste and expense.

Thus, the officers of the Royal Hussars exercised over the stage a power even more absolute than the omnipotence they arrogated in the hall. Anyone who dared to hiss one of their protégées immediately exposed themselves to the insults of the stalls, three-quarters of which were filled with hussars, and to the direct provocations of the officers who garnished the orchestra and the boxes. As for signs of approval, the braided sleeves and deerskin gloves gave the signal for them, the only one that found an echo. If one pleased the corps of officers, complete success, without fear of the cabal; but woe, and thrice woe, betide anyone who did not obtain their grace; it only remained to return to the wings, pack one's bags and seek fortune elsewhere.

Judge the flatteries that such an absolute and redoubted power received! Nothing was done in the stage other than by virtue of it and for it. If there was a military role in the play, one donned the uniform of the Royal Hussars, with its sky blue dolman, its fur colback, its richly embroidered trousers and its large saber, bumping against a brilliant sabretache. If it was a matter of citing a regiment the name indicated by the author was substituted by the name of the Royal Hussars. Finally, in the entr'actes, an actor came to sing, white flag in hand, the *Serment français*, a patriotic hymn in the way of seeing of the time;[37] it was the one for which the Royal Hussars were known to profess the purest and warmest royalism; singing the *Serment français* was a means of caressing that royalism.

The power of the Royal Hussars was exercised with no less absolutism behind the scenes and on the stage. To begin with, it exercised a monopoly, and no frock-coat would have been admitted alongside the elegant coats of the hussars. Let us see: apart from soldiers dressed to the knees in the costumes of bit-part players, half-Neapolitans and half-troopers, wearing high toques and tunics; apart from the servants, apart from the dressers, indispensable machines as indispensable to the theater as the scenery and the prompter's hole, who is coming and going around the actresses? Who is conversing with them? Who is teasing them? Who is making them listen? Who is making them redouble their simpers, heads titled and fans wafting in their hands? The officers of the Royal Hussars! No one but the officers of the Royal Hussars!

A fortunate privilege, in truth! For they are pretty creatures, witty and playful, letting themselves go to their existence of joy and poverty with a enviable insouciance. To the devil with tomorrow! To the devil with soon! As long as they can be at their ease, the joyous

---

[37] Probably Alphonse Butignot's *Hymne à la France* (1814).

young women, as long as their lovers do not beat them to violently and as long as gambling laves them the wherewithal to but their mistress supper, to the devil with worries and life is good! What can be worth more to them than health, amour, carelessness and joy—yes, what more could millions, status and glory be worth? A Royal Hussar takes the place of all that. Their millions are their lover's gifts, those gifts that make them beautiful and even assure them of a superfluity: a future of a week! Their rank and their glory are the applause of the Royal Hussars; they are the homages of the young and becoming officers who lead lives of folly and pleasure with them.

Be welcome, therefore, young man who does not wear a moustache yet, and for good reason. Be welcome, you whose senses ignite at the sight of those bare shoulders and bare arms, you who quiver with new sensations at the bold words, the free manners and the tender gazes that allow you to ignore your womanly education. Be welcome, for there is a better intoxication here than the intoxication of Champagne wine; and it is not in vain that a thousand ardent and new desires throw your naïve and still virgin soul into a voluptuous anxiety.

So, how he devours those attractive women with his eyes! How he takes part in their conversations! How he forgets his timidity! How he squeezes their hands in his trembling hands! No more remembrance of his mother. No more remembrance of is ideas of old. Amour, pleasures, embraces, always and incessantly, that is what he wants. Which of them will love him? Which of them will put her head on his shoulder? Which of them will give him her fan to hold, murmur words in his ear, call him "Paul" tenderly? Which of them will treat him as they all treat his comrades?

Oh, it doesn't matter which, it doesn't matter—but one of them, one! For without that, he will be unable to suffer what he is experiencing. Is there not, Madame, a need to love? Tel me, then, who you love my beauty. Tell me, and if you want, I will be the happiest of men, for I need amour, you see. It's necessary that someone loves me, and I'd like to be loved by a pretty brunette like you, with big black eyes, like you, with a slim waist and a tiny foot, like your slim waist and your tiny foot. And given that you love me—for it's necessary that you love me—let me kiss those ravishing shoulders, let me pass over your dainty finger this ring, which will help you to remember me.

She lets him kiss her shoulders without too much rigor; she lets him put on her finger the rich ring that casts beautiful reflections. She escapes from his arms, she runs away, but slowly enough for him to be able to run after her and catch up with her; to catch up with her and punish her by giving her new kisses. He is promising, on my soul, the young man. He will make a god hussar. His comrades smile at his impetuosity; the actresses ask them: who is that handsome officer? And he, expansive in such successes, becomes even bolder, and puts his arm around the waist of the pretty Zerbine. Oh, what delirious sensations he experiences! How happy he is! How happy he is!

"Bravo, my dear Boistrancourt, bravo!" Baron de Niergnies comes to say to him. "Bravo! Poor Saint-Vallier, who departed for Paris yesterday, has found a worthy successor. Bravo, in truth, for she's nice, that Zerbine, and you'll have a mistress who will do you honor there."

Incited by such eulogies, by the instinct of the senses, by the fumes of the Champagne wine, and above all by success, Paul became even more enterprising, and dared what the least modest of his companions would not have dared, to the extent that the actress thought that she was dealing with one of those bold rakes who is not duped by the best-feigned resistance. Fascinated by the impetuousness of the young hussar, she immediately treated him as a conqueror and adopted with him the familiarity of a fiancée. Paul used and abused his advantages so forcefully that Zerbine made the decision to draw him toward a hole in the curtain through which he pretended to look through; there at least, half bent over and his face applied to the thick curtain, she could partly dissimulate Paul's kisses and bold caresses.

They were next to the curtain, their hands enlaced, cheek to cheek, their breath confounded, Paul in an inexpressible excitement, Zerbine in a disturbance no less inexpressible; for Zerbine was a good and tender young woman, during her short amours as passionate as the heroine of romance, capable of the greatest sacrifices, ready to lose everything she possessed for the man she loved…if she had possessed anything. Unfortunately, she loved intensely, but she did not love for long. Great passions pass quickly, especially in the theater. Zerbine compensated for the excessive energy of hers by the brevity of their duration. In the meantime, she was joyful, scatterbrained, not caring what anyone said, or, rather, never stopping at the slightest of her thoughts, having no concern for renown or money, or anything whatsoever, except amour.

Paul said to Zerbine the words that make no sense but cause so much emotion; Zerbine listened to him without understanding him, or understood him without listening to him; responding with pressure to the pressure of his hand, and turning sparkling and troubled eyes toward him when another actress, perhaps jealous of their pleasure came to beg Zerbine to surrender the hole in the curtain momentarily.

"It seems to me that you're not looking," she said, maliciously, "And I'm curious to know whether the *red nose* is at the spectacle again."

"The red nose!" responded several voices, with a comical interest. "Has the red nose reappeared at the spectacle? It hasn't been seen for several performances."

"It's there! It's there!" replied the other. "There it is, as usual, enveloped in a great black veil and a huge cloak. Behind it is the old man who renders it such scrupulous and assiduous cares."

"What is the red nose, then?" Paul asked.

"It's a woman who constantly occupies the box you can see over there, in the darkest party of the hall. The woman never shows her face, and none of us has ever seen any of her features, except Zerbine, who, desirous of knowing a face that someone takes so much care to hide, went to station herself one evening very close to the box of the red nose, toward the end of the play."

"And in spite of a full quarter-hour of sentry duty, I didn't know anything, for the old man took extraordinary precautions to arrange the veil of the unknown woman so as to allow nothing of her face to be seen. But—Heaven protects innocence—a door to the corridor opened suddenly, producing a sudden air current, which lifted the veil abruptly, and I saw, or thought I saw, a frightful red nose in the middle of a disfigured face. The old man lowered the veil with a rapid gesture, and, noticing the cry of surprise that escaped me, said "Silence!" harshly, with an unequivocal sign to go away. There was something so imperious and so grave in the gesture that I went away, feeling stupid."

"Zerbine's story is very nice, but very improbable, it must be admitted; it's probable that she mistook what she saw, for if the woman in question is ugly to that extent, the old man who accompanies her wouldn't give her such scrupulous cares, which can only come from an extreme jealousy. If anyone, even without intent, advances his head toward the mysterious box, it excites the discontentment of the man and he seems ready to demand a reckoning. If you're not convinced, tell me how you can reconcile with such ugliness the scrupulous, tender and continual care of the old man for that woman. I stand by what I said: Zerbine was mistaken, the red nose isn't the red nose; she's as beautiful as an angel and the old man is jealous."

"If I were an officer in the hussars...," objected another actress.

"Well, what would you do, my beauty?" asked Paul, familiarly.

"I'd penetrate the mystery and I'd know the truth about the red nose."

"Damn! I'm a officer in the hussars, and I'll know what it is," said the young officer, adjusting the centurion of his saber, his head even more intoxicated by the success he had obtained than by the fumes of Champagne wine, which were nevertheless very inebriating.

"I challenge you to do it!"

"You challenge me! Paul said, suddenly decided by those words to undertake the escapade. "You challenge me! Well, you'll see. He took two steps, but then he stopped, suddenly hesitant.

"I'll bet five hundred francs that you don't succeed in seeing her," cried Baron de Niergnies."

"I'll take the bet!"

Paul descended from the stage, went into the hall and told the woman charged with that office to open the door of the mysterious box.

"That isn't possible, Monsieur, "the box is taken."

"It doesn't matter."

"Monsieur, I can't."

"Yes you can. Take this gold piece and open it."

The opener gave in. Paul went into the box and sat down on the bench at the back.

"Monsieur," said the old man, with an extreme politeness. "You were brought here in error. The box is taken."

"Monsieur, I haven't found a place in the hall and I'm putting myself where I can."

The old man sensed a vigorous response on his lips, but he darted a glance at his companion, readjusted the veil that concealed her, closing it more hermetically, and placed himself in such a way as to hide her completely from the officer, who bore evidence traces of drunkenness on his face. But that was not to Paul's liking, who saw the gazes of all his comrades fixed upon him: gazes that would have made him commit the most incredible follies. He changed his seat abruptly, placed himself beside the unknown woman and asked her: "How do you like the play, Madame," before the old man could oppose it.

The young woman turned slowly and with surprise toward the man who had spoken to her.

"Amusing, Monsieur" she replied, in a child-like voice of great purity. "Very amusing, but the weakness of my eyesight..."

The old man, who was suffering greatly from that conversation, came to place himself once again between her and the officer.

"You know, my dear," he said, interrupting her, "that we need to get home early. Your health demands it. It's ten o'clock. Let's go.

The young woman sighed, and getting to her feet resignedly, she got ready to follow the old man. In the meantime, Paul attached his brazen gaze to her and strove to see her features through the veil; but the veil was not sufficiently transparent, and Paul obtained no reward for his curiosity.

The old man and the young woman had almost gone out when Baron de Niergnies, placed in the next box, advanced his head and said to Paul: "Lost! You haven't seen her."

"Lost? No!" Paul replied, and with a precipitate gesture, he lifted the young woman's veil.

He saw a face entirely furrowed by recent scars.

The old man threw the veil over the woman's face precipitately, leaned toward Paul and said to him: "Tomorrow, at daybreak, Monsieur, outside the Paris gate."

III. The Duel

"Already!" said Zerbine, at daybreak, to Paul, who wanted to quit her. "Already!"

"Very regretfully, my friend, very regretfully; but that damned old man will be waiting for me! And it's necessary not to make someone wait, you see, at one's first affair."

"Go, then, miscreant, and come back quickly, for you don't know how much I love you, and what my fears will be until you return."

"*Au revoir*, beloved."

He gave her one long, tender, final kiss, and then he left.

"In the meantime, the old man had written a few letters, had himself dressed by a domestic almost as old as him, and rendered with precaution to a room separated from his by five or six apartments. There, he opened the curtains of a bed, carefully, considered the features of the young woman who was sleeping profoundly, with tears in his eyes, and then directed his gaze toward a frame in which there was a painted portrait of a rare beauty. Then he went out with the same precaution and went out of the town, to the place that he had indicated to Paul.

Paul was waiting for him with two of his comrades. They saluted one another silently and the old man said, in a grave tone: "Messieurs, all explanation is I believe, unnecessary. Monsieur has insulted me without motive; he must give me satisfaction. I have the choice of weapons; here are two pistols. At fifteen paces. We will fire together, at a signal."

"So be it. But you have no witnesses?"

"I'm a stranger here and I don't know anyone; would one of you, Messieurs, be kind enough to serve as my second?"

"Me, Monsieur," said one of the officers. "My name is Baron de Niergnies."

"Messieurs, I believe that it is unnecessary to state my name, for I cannot do so without danger; not that I fear confiding my secret to me of honor, but..."

"Keep your secret," Paul replied. "I insulted you without knowing you; I owe you reparation without knowing you."

The terrain was measured; the adversaries took their places; the signal was given. Two detonations rang out, and the old man fell, struck in the chest by a bullet.

At the sight of that man, bloody and perhaps mortally struck, a frantic despair took possession of Paul. Numbed by the previous evening's drunkenness and by a night of amour, he had not reflected until then on the consequences of his conduct. He suddenly found himself confronted by those terrible consequences, looking at the cadaver of an old man.

"Pardon me!" he cried, trying to stem the blood that was flowing from the wound. "Pardon me, Monsieur; I'm a wretch, an infamous coward. Pardon me, oh, pardon me!"

"I don't hold it against you, Monsieur, but you have done more harm than you think. My daughter! My poor daughter!"

He lost consciousness, and he was transported to his home half-dead, with the gravest fears for his life, for the surgeon announced that until three days had elapsed he could not prognosticate the results of the wound. "Or rather," he said, "in three days it will be over."

In a state difficult to describe, Paul wanted to accompany the old man to his home, and there, in spite of all objections that could be raised, he established himself next to his bed, and declared that he would not budge until he knew that his victim was out of danger. His despair was expressed with so much energy, and that resolution seemed to be dictated by a dolor that was so tinged with dementia, that no one dared oppose it and snatch him away from the invalid.

He therefore found himself alone in a vast, somber chamber, in which no sound troubled the silence of death except for the cries that the injury sometimes wrenched from the wounded man.

Alone!

Alone after a day of debauchery! Alone after a night of debauchery! Alone after a duel, a duel with an old man! Alone next to that old man, who was dying!

Alas, what would his mother say, his poor mother, if ever these fatal events reached her? To see all the seeds of virtue that her son owed to her destroyed in a single day! To learn that in a single day he had become a drinker, a libertine and the cowardly killer of a venerable and defenseless man! Oh my God, my God, she would die when she knew that!

What infamous conduct he had shown in this affair! What scorn he merited! Should he have aimed at the old man? Should he not have turned his pistol away and aimed far from him? But no, he had taken aim and he had desired to strike. Why? Alas, why? Because of the fear of being suspected of incompetence, because he had imagined that he heard whispered on all sides: "He isn't of prime strength; how awkwardly he holds his pistol!" Yes, it was for such a wretched motive that he had not followed his first and generous impulse; it was for such a motive that he had felt his arm lowering his weapon mechanically, that his gaze had attached to the old man's pistol, for such a motive that he had killed him! Woe! Woe! Woe!

While he found himself prey to such dolorous thoughts, the door of the apartment opened precipitately, and the young woman of the previous evening came in, but without a veil, in an extreme disorder. She ran to the old man's bed, took one of the hands of the moribund, and repeated with a heart-rending anguish: "My father! My father!"

Then, without seeing Paul, she leaned over the bed, she interrogated her father, she lavished tender words on him, she listened to the inconsequential words that delirium caused him to proffer; and when she had understood that he could not hear her, she fell into a chair, wrung her hands and let her head fall on to her breast, which was uplifted by sobs.

Paul considered that spectacle painfully, his hands joined.

By virtue of his position, he could only see from behind the slender figure of the young woman, folded up in a naïve attitude full of abandon. One of her small white hands was dangling alongside her knee, and her beautiful golden blonde hair spread freely over her semi-naked shoulders, poorly covered by a night-dress donned in haste. Then, in one of the nervous twitches ordinary in pain, the young woman raised her head and her profile appeared to Paul's gaze. Placed before a window resplendent with the midday light that profile was in shadow, and only presented an obscure silhouette, of an extreme regularity, which borrowed even more elegance and grace from the elegant and graceful contours of the neck that sustained it.

Eventually, she stood up and approached her father's bed, and Paul was able to see her face in its entirety; then he recognized that the scars with which the young woman's face as furrowed were far less ugly than he had thought the evening before at the play. Those scars, the redness of which time was beginning to render less pronounced, and the traces less distinct, only spoiled slightly features of a great mildness. Her blue eyes, which were half-closed, and whose sight seemed very weak and almost blind, offered when open an angelic expression of candid bounty—to the extent that the astonishment that the sight of her initially caused her to experience soon gave way to a sentiment of interest and charm.

Such is the nature of the human heart that, while he was considering the young woman, Paul forgot his remorse, and almost forgot the invalid next to whom he was keeping his vigil. He approached her and said: "The invalid's respiration is freer now."

At those words, the young woman, who had thought that she was alone, leaned forward, blinking, in order to discover who was speaking. Paul's uniform astonished her, and when she recognized the officer who had insulted her the previous evening, the officer who had killed her father, she recoiled with a sentiment of terror.

"Stay, Madame, stay," Paul said to her, "and don't testify such horror to me. I only merit pity. If you knew what remorse I feel!"

As he spoke, he wept bitterly.

The young woman took a step to come back, but he turned toward her father's bed; at that moment, her father sighed, with a long effort. Then, opening his eyes, he recognized his daughter and held out his hand to her. She threw herself upon that hand and covered it with kisses and tears.

Then the old man looked around, and perceived Paul.

"Monsieur," he said to him, "what will become of his poor orphan?"

"Oh, don't speak thus, Monsieur, don't speak thus! She isn't an orphan, she won't become one. God will take pity on my suffering. He'll listen to my prayers."

The old man shook his head, in a manner to show that no more hope remained to him.

"You'll be cured, Monsieur, but if it were otherwise, if a misfortune that will poison my life forever has just arrived, then, Monsieur, I make you this oath here, before God and before this bed of dolor, that I will become henceforth for Madame a tender and devoted brother, a brother who will only have one goal, one idea and one duty: to make her forget her misfortune, or at least to soften its bitterness. My fortune will be hers and my mother will become her mother. Oh, you don't know, Monsieur what a mother mine is. She is an angel of generosity, virtue and tenderness, an angel who will love her as much as she loves me, and even more, if that is possible, for I shall beg her to do so on my knees."

The old man looked at him fixedly.

"You have a good heart, young man, a heart that is worth more than your head. May you persevere in the generous resolutions you express. Then death will be less bitter for me—because my daughter has no one in the world but me to love her and protect her. If God calls me to him and you do not keep your promises, nothing remains for her lot but misery. Uncertain of the outcome of our combat, I wrote yesterday to a friend of mine who lives in Germany. Take this letter. Read it. And if I die, don't abandon my poor Adèle."

"I would be a coward if I broke my word," cried Paul, "A coward into whose face everyone ought to spit. Yes, I will repair my fault. Yes, from this moment, Adèle will become my sister, my beloved sister."

And in his enthusiasm, he took the young woman's hand and pressed it to his lips.

The old man extended his arms as if to bless Paul and his daughter. Suddenly, he lost consciousness, for his efforts speak had fatigued him greatly.

They summoned the physician; he declared that a second similar crisis would kill the patient; he enjoined the young woman to quit her father's apartment in order that the sight of the person the old man loved so much would not cause him any further emotion. It was necessary for Adèle to obey, and Paul remained alone with the dying man.

Night had come in the interim. Only a faint and vacillating lamp illuminated the rather vast room, and cast dubious gleams of over the dull and somber walls. There was no mirror in the apartment, although it did not lack refinement. In the other rooms that Paul had traversed he had remarked the same absence of such an indispensable ornament.

Without pausing to dwell on that eccentricity, Paul sat down next to the lamp, opened the letter that the man had handed to him and read the following.

IV. Adèle

To Michel Daubenou, at *** in Germany.

For two years I have not received any news of you, my dear Daubenou; are you still living in Germany? Will this letter reach you? And yet, if you don't receive it, my daughter, my poor daughter, will remain without support, without shelter, without bread. I am going to fight a duel, my friend, I am going to fight a duel with a young officer in the hussars who insulted my daughter in a cowardly fashion yesterday.

I'm an old insensate, am I not? For love of my daughter, I ought to have supported that outrage done to my daughter; I should have scorned a madman whose drunkenness was evident. But what do you expect, Daubenou? Age has not yet chilled the old blood in our veins to the point that it does not boil at an insult. And then, it was to my daughter to whom the young man addressed his insult, to my beloved daughter, my joy, my pride, an angel of virtue and misfortune.

Is it necessary to admit it to you? He bore on his colback the white cockade that I cannot see without shivering, since it tells me that all our sacrifices for liberty are lost forever. Yes, Daubenou, we have given in vain for liberty more than our lives, in vain we have overcome for its sake our mild and peaceful inclinations, in vain we have said like Danton: "Let our memory perish, as long as our fatherland is saved!" We demanded the head of Louis XVI, we have shed blood over our name, and today, all of that remains futile; today, everything is as it was before a revolution so dearly paid for.

You cannot know, my friend, how insolently these aristocrats, crushed for so long, are rearing up again. You cannot know how they are hastening, in institutions and even in mores, to destroy everything that had been created of liberty and to reconstruct everything that was destroyed of slavery. Judge, then, my friend, what the aspect of that execrable sign, and the insolence of the man who wore it, caused me to experience! I said to him: Tomorrow! And that tomorrow has arrived, and in an hour, I, a poor old man, will doubtless receive death. Let him be on his guard, however, for I shall try to aim true and to steady my trembling hand.

Alas, my friend, why did I not believe your sage counsel? Why did the love of the fatherland make me quit Germany, where I had married, the land where I had spent fifteen years of happiness? Was not the place where the remains of my beloved wife reposed my true fatherland? But no, France offered herself incessantly to my imagination; I had a need to see France again, the memory of which filled my septuagenarian eyes with tears, the France that preoccupied my dreams, the France far from which I was languishing, like a son far from his mother.

I departed, Daubenou, and scarcely had I saluted the house of my fathers than the enemy rushed upon France and put to fire and blood the nation before which all Europe had trembled for such a long time. The little town where I lived, Avesnes, was besieged. The old republican, my friend, took a rifle and went to the ramparts to fight for the fatherland. His speeches and his example contributed more than a little to the vigorous defense of the inhabitants, but his strength betrayed his courage and he fell ill with fatigue and despair, for munitions were lacking and the courage of the citizens was beginning to buckle.

I had been lying on a bed of dolor for two days, unable to move and plunged into a complete delirium, when the enemy commenced bombarding the city, weary as they were of a stubborn resistance. I was listening with understanding, so much had my reason gone astray, to the terrible din of the artillery when all of a sudden, a strange shock shook the house in which I was living, causing the roof to collapse and burying under its ruins the somber cellar to which I had been transported. Alas, those ruins had trapped the fire with me, and my bed was already catching fire; the bite of the flame had already rendered me a sentiment of myself; I was already crying for help, when my daughter, who had just quit me, hurtled through the blazing debris, and, finding a supernatural strength in her filial tenderness, took me in her arms and succeeded in getting me out of that place of destruction. A few more paces and we would have reached a safe refuge...woe! A burning beam fell, struck Adèle in the face, and threw us both to the pavement.

Almost dying myself, I spent a week by my daughter's bedside, a week of execrable doubt as to her life or death. Finally, I had the certainty of conserving her, but in what a state, my God! Almost blind, and her beautiful face disfigured forever—disfigured! And yet, that was her greatest dread, and during enormous suffering she never asked "Will I live?" but only "Will I be disfigured?"

It was necessary to flee again; not this time before conflagration and death but before persecutions. A Conventional had become a pariah, an accursed individual whom it was meritorious to persecute. What could I do? It was impossible to return to Germany by traversing the enemy armies that covered Europe. I changed my name, and with a fairly considerable sum that I had been able to save, I went to Hazebrouck, where I adopted the most retired life.

There, my friend, I soon found myself under the weight of a new dolor. From morning until evening, the poor young woman never ceased to repeat heart-rending remarks about the loss of her beauty, although previously, insouciant and playful, she had scarcely seemed to be aware of the splendor and purity of her features. Doubtless the commotion of a blow received to the head, the crisis of the peril in which she had found the supernatural energy she had needed to save me, had shaken the fibers of her brain too violently.

"I'm ugly!" she repeated, from morning until evening, with a heart-rending expression. "I'm ugly!" She hid her face, she wept bitterly, she wanted to die rather than to find herself an object of disgust and horror.

Judge how I suffered, Daubenou.

The physicians of Hazebrouck did not inspire much confidence in me; in any case, I did not want to confide my sad secret to them. I summoned from Paris one of the physicians most celebrated for his treatment of maladies of that sort. He shook his head on seeing Adèle and told

210

me that the art could do nothing; that it was necessary to wait and put hope in nature and time, and he departed, leaving me with death in my heart.

Adèle's dementia was still increasing. The unfortunate young woman filled the house with her cries: "I'm ugly! I don't want to cause horror! I want to die!"

The art had abandoned my daughter, but I resolved not to abandon her. Only one means might succeed, and that was to make her believe in the return of her beauty. I formed the design of putting it to work, and this is how I went about it:

First I rendered all communication impossible between Adèle and any other person than a physician, a devoted old maidservant and myself. That was very easy for me, since my situation had commanded a solitary life. Then I caused the few mirrors that were there to disappear from the house. In order to do that I gave orders via the physician to preserve Adèle from the dangerous state that those mirrors produced on her weak sight, almost reduced to compete blindness.

"Afterwards everyone began to respond by laments to Adèle laments on the loss of her beauty; we no longer denied that she had become ugly, we admitted it; we were afflicted by it, in such a manner as not to inspire any suspicion of my projects and the ruse to which I wanted to have recourse.

"One morning, when I went, as was my habit, to embrace Adèle in her room, I attempted to insinuate to her that her scars were becoming less hideous. My daughter's eyes sparkled with joy, but she soon fell back into her habitual sadness and murmured, weeping: "It isn't possible."

"A few days later, the old maidservant hazarded the same observation, and the physician confirmed it. A faint but sweet hope slid into Adèle's heart. After that, the young invalid became less languid, and gave some hope of conserving her life and seeing an end to the consumption that was causing her to perish.

I continued to put the same ruse to work. Gradually, Adèle became convinced that she had recovered a part of her beauty, and that a complete cure would soon render it to her entirely. Then a further incident nearly destroyed my work; Adèle started demanding incessantly to look at herself in a mirror. Neither my observations not my pleas, nor the threats of the physician, who represented the accomplishment of that desire as the most dangerous for a damaged eyesight, could calm her and persuade her to renounce hat design. Surprised by our resistance, she did not take long to become distrustful and to conceive suspicions. What could I do?

"I made a desperate decision in which I was seconded by Adèle's near-blindness. I had a copy made of a portrait of my daughter, painted in Germany by a celebrated artist. I had the costume in which the portrait had represented her substituted by the one that my daughter wore at present, and the whole was stuck behind a mirror, part of whose silvering I had removed. Trembling for the success of the deception, for a failure might have plunged Adèle back permanently into dementia, I presented the mirror, prepared in that fashion, to Adèle. She uttered cries of joy, and wanted to look again at the image, the sight of which had charmed her so much. Suddenly, I cause to fall upon her gaze, so that they wounded her, the reflections of an ardent mirror. The dolor made her put her hands over her eyes, and I took advantage of that gesture to remove the glass and the portrait.

Convinced of the return of her beauty, and convinced of the danger that the aspect of a mirror presented to her, Adèle, reassured henceforth, lost her dread and her dementia, and only formed wishes henceforth for the cure of her eyes. Her health returned completely, and with it, everything of the most afflicting that the scars on her face offered began to disappear. I was sure that within a year, those scars would no longer present anything very visible, and would have disappeared almost entirely

Convalescent, Adèle became fatigued by the isolation and captivity in which I retained her. She wanted to go for walks, and to the theater; the physician made me fear the consequences of a refusal. I could not, moreover, allege the dangers to which my title of Conventional exposed me; for two years I had been left in peace in Hazebrouck; it was not credible that anyone would think of persecuting me henceforth. It was therefore necessary to yield to Adèle's desires; I took her out for walks and in the evening to the theater, but in a box reserved for me alone, and placed in a poorly lit part of the hall. In addition, Adèle's defective sight did not allow her to see anything of the play, and reduced her to merely hearing it, so it did not matter that her face was covered by a veil. Alas, my friend, I have surprised her many a time in the innocent coquetry of a young woman, deceiving my vigilance and lifting her veil in order to display her beauty.

In one more year, Adèle's reason would have be strong enough, and the scars on her face would have so nearly disappeared, for her to be able to receive without danger the confession of my salutary rise. A single moment has destroyed everything. Yesterday, an officer in the hussars introduced himself into our box by force and lifted my daughter's veil with an unexampled impudence. You know the rest.

So, in the case that I succumb—and that is only to likely, alas—Adèle, poor Adèle will remain without support, without help and without bread, for many days will pass before you receive this letter, if you receive it; many days will pass before the debris of my fortune, which is contested by a lawsuit on Germany, can be restored to my daughter. In order to complete the misfortune, she will learn, with the death or her father and the poverty in which she falls, that she has been the dupe of a error, and that her recovered beauty was only a lie. How can her head, already so weak, resist so many blows at once? May God take pity on her.

As soon as the reception of this letter—and, it is necessary for me to add with doubt and despair, if you receive it—come and collect my daughter, whom I bequeath to you, and may you have something other than a poor madwoman to take away!

Adieu, my friend. May Heaven recompense you!

Georges Cambernis

Our souls are never more susceptible to romantic dispositions, and never receive a more imperious need for tenderness, than during the melancholy collapse produced by a violent and dolorous shock. Romantic dispositions take possession of the imagination, turn away evil thoughts, and by their noble sensation reveal a man discontented with himself to his own eyes. The need for tenderness is nothing but the need for consolation; now, only women are able to console, and we are informed by one of those vague nameless instincts that often arise is the human heart that it is from women that it is necessary to seek compassion and the alleviation of our pains.

In addition, chagrin purifies the soul and renders it better; chagrin almost always produces repentance. During a crisis of expiation. One feels a more complete fervor for good, and one yields without resistance to exaltation and the sentiments evoked; in brief, the heart, generous by nature and accidentally rid of its habitual shackles, beats at ease and with generosity.

Thus, Paul, at the bedside of a man that he had killed, seized urgently the first means that was offered to him to render less sensible the remorse that was overwhelming him, and he took pleasure in reporting all the activity of his imagination to the orphan of his victim. The imagination works rapidly and believes even more rapidly in its own fictions. During the reading of the Conventional's letter and after having finished that reading, Paul delivered himself completely to a thousand plans that might diminish, if they could not repair, the damage that his culpable imprudence had done to poor Adèle.

He wanted to keep, and to keep religiously, the promise that he had sworn at the dying man's bed; he would consecrate his entire life to the unfortunate young woman he had deprived of a father. The beneficent error that made her believe in her beauty he would continue to maintain, and when Adèle hears Paul say, while kneeling at her feet and holding her hands in his, that he loves her, that he wants to devote his life to her, that he wants to call her his wife, she will believe even more firmly that the ravages of the fire have disappeared completely from her face. In any case, have those ravages not almost disappeared? No furrows and scars disfigure the young face with ineffaceable traces. All that now remains is an uneven redness, whose colored patches will soon disappear under the reparative influence of time. Even if time does not cure her, what does it matter? Will she not be as beautiful, that young woman, with her blonde hair, her ingenuous smile, her elegant figure and her suave voice, a voice that stirs the soul? Yes, to her, all of life's life, all of his fortune, all of his amour; to her and to him, a placid and unalloyed happiness…!

But the invalid has moaned; he makes a sign to Paul to advance; he extends his arms toward him; his lips murmur with anguish an unintelligible accent…he tries to repeat it…

"My daughter!"

He falls back—dead.

V. Another Woman

A week after the death of Georges Cambernis, a carriage quit the small town if Hazebrouck and took away two ladies. The one clad in black was Adèle; the other, who was lavishing on her traveling companion the most affectionate and the most tender care, was Baronne de Boistrancourt. Paul had written to her to confess his duel, the death of the old man and the sad situation of Adèle, and to explain to her the projects that he had formed in order to repair as much as possible the harm that he had done to the orphan.

Madame de Boistrancourt, whose soul had been sickened by the unworthy conduct of her son, experienced a sweet consolation in learning about his generous projects; she approved of them strongly, promised Paul to hasten their execution and departed with Adèle for the Château de Boussu. A letter sent the day before had conveyed the order to remove all the mirrors, a precaution all the more indispensable because her father's death seemed to threaten Adèle with a relapse into insanity.

Madame de Boistrancourt soon felt a sincere affection for Adèle; one becomes attached quickly to those whose suffering and weakness puts them under our protection. The young woman's candor, her melancholy resignation, and the love she felt for Paul—a love betrayed by a thousand indications, which she had not admitted to herself—completed winning her the heart of the baronne and made her love as her own child the young woman that her son wanted to call his wife.

Adèle's education had solidity and extent, but it was a woman's education directed by a man, and it lacked certain things that a man would neither know nor comprehend. Madame de Boistrancourt hastened to repair that lacuna; thanks to ongoing conversations, continual cares and frequent reading aloud—for the weakness of Adèle's eyes did not permit her to read herself—the baronne's pupil, who seconded the efforts of her benefactress marvelously, soon left nothing more to desire. She had acquired, in addition, the chaste sentiment of restraint of which the distancing of persons of her own sex and the slightly harsh rectitude of the old Conventional had left her somewhat deprived. As a result, Mademoiselle Cambernis lost her eccentricity and resembled other women more in the best ways; for eccentricity only exists, most of the time, at the expense of the most suave aspect of their character: modesty.

Six months passed thus, during which Paul wrote tender letters every week to his mother and his fiancée, in which he never ceased to express the desire to see the epoch of his marriage arrive. But for that it was necessary to wait for the end of the young woman's mourning, for in the situation in which she found herself relative to

Paul, decency demanded of her even more imperiously than of anyone else that she defer marrying her lover until the end of the year of rigor.

That marriage, the hope and desire of Paul, his other and Adèle, caused a great chagrin to Mademoiselle Aldegonde. The dowager could not contain her indignation when mention was made of it in her presence. As soon as the baronne had told her about Paul's plans, the old spinster had rushed to address remonstrations to her nephew and sister-in-law. Their extravagance was inconceivable! The heir of the sires de Boussu, the unique scion of the ancient family of the Boistrancourts, to marry a plebeian devoid of name and fortune! What would be said at court of such a misalliance? It would be necessary to support gibes for at least a month.

But it was far worse some time thereafter, when she discovered the even more horrible secret of Adèle's birth, when she knew that the orphan owed the light of day to a member of the Convention, to an infamous regicide who had demanded the death of the martyr king. What! Such a creature would enter a family that had only consented to end its emigration with the return of its legitimate princes! The son of a hero who had died in the Vendée for his monarch would give his name to the daughter of the assassin of that same monarch! Nothing of the sort! No, she swore it, and rather than see such an infamy accomplished, she would disinherit her nephew. At the slightest hint of that marriage, there would be nothing for her to do but flee the court, renounce her immense credit, take refuge in some cloister and bury herself there forever. At whatever price, it was necessary—she wished it—that Paul and his mother renounce a marriage that they could never have projected seriously.

The anger of Mademoiselle the dowager, her laments, her reproaches and her supplications, did not obtain anything against the calm and assured resolution of the baronne. Paul was no less indocile, and in an initial moment of despair the noble lady made a testament in which she bequeathed her immense fortune to a convent of nuns of the Sacred Heart. Once the initial effervescence had passed, however, she understood that mildness and cunning might achieve more than violence; she retracted the testament, feigned a frank reconciliation with the baronne and with Paul, and even ended up testifying benevolence to the orphan.

A month before the mourning of Mademoiselle Cambernis was due to end, two post-chaises came into the courtyard of the Château de Boussu almost at the same time. In the first of those vehicles was Paul, in the other Mademoiselle Aldegonde, accompanied by Vicomtesse Marie de Bergues, whom she introduced as her intimate fried to the baronne and the baronne's ward.

It is understandable that the presence of a stranger initially brought coldness and constraint into the Boistrancourt family, and the lovers were afflicted by that presence more than anyone else. Nevertheless, the vicomtesse was so undisruptive, and gained everyone's amity so rapidly, that the initial embarrassment and reserve soon gave way to an amiable intimacy. An excellent musician, the vicomtesse charmed the long autumnal evenings by means of the talent with which she played on the piano the music of Weber, then unknown and misunderstood in France,[38] which the baronne had brought from Germany. The three ladies came together

---

[38] Carl von Weber (1786-1826) was an important pioneer of the Romantic school of German music.

to sing the arias of the German poet; Adèle mingled her voice, devoid of art and method but accurate in spite of its lack of range, with those choruses, which ectasized Paul, still a enthusiast, although less naïve.

For a year in garrison forms a man rapidly; it does not take long to lose the chaste and pure ideas that one obtains from the education of a mother. Paul had rid himself of them as of his feminine restraint. Instead of remaining a timid and slightly gauche young man he had become a handsome officer, elegant and self-confident, whose manners attested an aplomb difficult to describe. At present he smiled at his old prejudices, the ridiculous produce of a solitary life, and in spite of his love for Adèle he had not recoiled before many garrison successes. Paul was the pride and envy of his comrades, at table, on horseback, with regard to women, and on the terrain.

Paul still retained a keen affection for his mother and his fiancée, but that affection had changed its character; he still cherished the former but she no longer inspired in him, as before, a veneration that tended toward worship, which had been a form of worship, and he no longer adopted her counsels exclusively, the ingenuousness of which sometimes even made him smile.

As for the young woman, he allowed himself to love her with all the complaisance in the world, and thought with pleasure of the three months that he would spend with her in the country every year during his leave, but he no longer retained traces of the exaltation that had dictated the first letters written to the orphan, which had filled his heart beside the death-bed of the old man. He carried out loyally and willingly the sacred promises he had made; it had never entered his mind to break those promises; but how Adèle would have suffered if the charms of the amour with which she surrounded Paul had not prevented her from remarking a a thousand nuances of change, none of with escaped the eye of Madame de Boistrancourt.

They were not, moreover, the only motives for anxiety and chagrin that Paul's mother experienced. By habitude and lack of occupation, for Paul—how he had changed!—experienced lack of occupation even in the presence of his mother and Adèle, the lieutenant had begun to pay court to the Vicomtesse de Bergues. The latter received without attaching ay importance to them the homages of the orphan's fiancé, and, as often happens in such cases, was soon surprised to find in her own heart a amour that frightened her. She resolved to depart immediately and return to Paris, but Mademoiselle the dowager raised innumerable obstacles to that design, and it was necessary for the young widow to remain at Boussu.

Adèle began to feel a vague dread, of which she could not define the cause, and which she attempted to rid herself without being able to do so. She ought to be happy, and yet she was suffering; her happiness was lacking something. She does not suspect Paul's constancy—oh, no, such a suspicion would be very culpable! Nevertheless, when he talks to the vicomtesse, and the vicomtesse smiles at him, it makes her feel ill. No more sweet future plans; no more present happiness: by day, sadness; by night, sleeplessness; constantly, an idea that obsesses her and is killing her: What if he loves the vicomtesse?

One night, when she was suffering more than usual, Adèle got up and, after wrapping herself in a mantle, went to walk in the park. The embalmed air, the murmur of foliage gently agitated by the wind, the soft moonlight, which cast great masses of shadow here and there in the midst of a thousand vaporous accidents, gave a certain calm to the orphan's agitated senses.

In order to understand the influence of a beautiful Flanders night on a melancholy imagination, it is necessary to have seen its blue sky resplendent with stars, its rivers whose waters shine with luminous reflections, and its marshes, which mists envelop with their transparent veils. It is necessary to have been seated under some great oak, among the branches of which troops of squirrels are bounding, uttering sharp little rises at intervals, while the distant lowing from the cowsheds mingles, grave and sonorous, with the plaints of the osprey, perched upright on some old ruined building, immobile and enveloped by the gray mantle of its wings. The air caresses and refreshes the forehead amorously; the heart dilates; a voluptuous freshness loosens the fibers and relaxes the limbs; the wellbeing of the body brings the wellbeing of the soul, and it is necessary for misfortune to have struck very cruelly for one not to discover a little hope in such sensations.

So the orphan forgot her dreads and allowed herself to relax into happy thoughts. Perhaps for the first time in a long time, she dreamed of an existence of amour, of the tenderness of Paul, her Paul, who would never quit her henceforth, of days of ecstasy that she would pass, her head leaning on her husband's shoulder and one of his hands in hers. She no longer wants to be separated from him; she will follow him in his garrisons, and if war ever breaks out, she will follow him to the war. How would she be able to support the apprehensions and uncertainties with which his absence would overwhelm her?

To know that Paul is exposed to perils, that he is ill, that he is wounded, and that he only has strange hands to bandage him, and strange voices to console him; but it would be to die to endure such suffering...what's that noise? She is afraid...someone is coming. My God, my God! Who can it be? She has recognized Paul's footsteps...where can he be going at such an hour...? Yes, it's really him. He passes close to her without seeing her. Where is he going? If she could only see him! Her feeble sight prevents her from doing so. No matter, she will know...It's necessary that she knows...!

He's retracing his steps...he has heard her.

"What are you doing here, Adèle?

"Monsieur Paul, I was suffering and agitated, and I wanted..."

"And you wanted to spy on me, isn't that true, Adèle?"

"Spy on you, Monsieur Paul, spy on you. Why would I spy on you? Heaven is my witness that I did not suspect you until this moment," she added, shedding tears. "Why do you want me to doubt your tenderness? Would it not be to die, to cease to believe in it."

"You might have thought that a few innocent assiduities toward the vicomtesse..."

"Yes, Paul, for why hide it from you? Yes, I've suffered from it. But without allowing it to be seen, but there"—she placed her hands on her breast, forcefully. "I'd like...I'm an insensate, I know...I'd like you only to have words and gazes for me. When you talk to any else, I envy the words you're saying to her; when you kiss your mother I ask myself, apprehensively: Does he love me as much as her? Judge, then, whether your continual attentions for the vicomtesse make me feel ill, judge whether I have suffered from your conversations, from your whispered words, from your walks, where I was not. Yes, I've suffered, suffered a great deal, but without saying anything, Paul, without showing it, recognizing that I had no right, that I was a madwoman led astray by her amour. I didn't fear losing your tenderness. My God, my God, what would remain to me if I lost it? Are you not the entire world to me? Have you not taken the place of everything: protector, friend, father? For I no longer have a father, Paul, I no longer have his boundless tenderness, his tenderness that had no other concern but me, no other thought but me; and if you were deceiving the poor orphan, if you abandoned her...oh, no, you wouldn't deceive me, you wouldn't abandon me, would you, my Paul?"

"Calm down, calm that agitation, Adèle..."

"Listen" she said, interrupting him, "listen, Paul; if you don't love me as much as before, for pity's sake, Paul, in the name of my father, tell me; I don't want anything from duty, I want love, a love like mine. Oh, I'd prefer it if you said so now, if you no longer love me, than when eternal bonds unite you with me and it will be your duty to love me. Your duty! Merely in that idea, there's enough to make one break one's head against a tree!"

"Adèle, my love, what can have made you believe...?"

"I believe everything, you see, for if you still loved me, you'd already have found a means of reassuring me, an inflexion of the voice, a gaze, a gesture would have sufficed. Woe! I've loved my father's murderer, and now he's deceiving me. Oh, I understand now; oh, I know where you're going; I no longer have any need for you to tell me. Where are you going? You're going to her, and she's astonished not to see you arriving; she's anxious, she's saying: 'How late he is!'"

The poor young woman was, however, mistaken. It was not an amorous rendezvous to which Paul was going. He too, agitated by anxieties, had been unable to sleep, and he had come into the park to seek a little calm for his agitated senses, a little fresh air to relieve his burning forehead. The insensate! He believed at first that he was playing with the amour of the vicomtesse, but that woman, whom he had judged frivolous, loved him as passionately as he loved Adèle.

Whatever decision he makes now, it is necessary for him to break the heart of one of two unfortunate women; for although he has, alas, deprived one young woman of a father, the other young woman has rights no less sacred, even more sacred, to his tenderness; it is because of him, for him, that she has forgotten everything; there is no hesitation; of two faults, it is the less irreparable that it is necessary to repair. Adèle will have much to lament, but what would become of the vicomtesse? And then, it is her that he loves, her alone; what he felt for Adèle was only exaltation and the ardent desire to repair the cruel wrong that he had done her.

In vain, Paul employed to reassure Adèle all the formulae of protestation; in vain he swore that he loved her more than ever, and that nothing could diminish that amour. Nothing could convince the orphan; she quit Paul shedding tears and spent the entire night leaning on the balcony, weeping, and trying to discover some sound that might reveal to her the intrigue of the vicomtesse and Paul.

Unable to support any longer such a state of doubt, she made a desperate resolution and went to find the dowager Aldegonde in her apartment. She affected at first to approach her with a calm that was far from being real, and after an appeal to the old woman's frankness, she said: "Madame, Paul no longer loves me, I know; he loves the vicomtesse, and it's you, Madame, whom my marriage with Paul offended immediately, that I have come to beg to prevent a union that will be our misfortune."

Her heart beating violently and in a horrible anxiety, she awaited the dowager's response. The latter, satisfied with the success of her projects, affected a false compassion for her victim.

"I would have liked to hide that sad truth from you, my child, but since you know the secret, which is only one for you..."

"Paul!" cried Adèle, dolorously, hiding her face in her hands. "Why doesn't he love me anymore? Why doesn't he love me anymore?"

Then, broken by despair, she fell into an armchair.

"If you displayed more calm, my child, if you delivered yourself with less weakness to the fits of your dolor..."

"Speak, Madame, speak; I'll be calm; I am. Look, I'm no longer weeping; her I am standing beside you; speak...."

The dowager, for it was necessary for her to render impossible any rapprochement between Adèle and Paul, did not recoil before striking the last and rudest blows.

"What I have to tell you, Adèle, is very painful to hear, but is it not better to have a great dolor today than despair for the rest of your life, for you and Paul?"

"Oh, yes, that is better, Madame."

"Well, my child, Paul had the misfortune of depriving you of a father, and in order to repair the harm that he had done you, in order to share with you the fortune that you would have refused under any other title, he feigned, out of generosity, a love that he did not have."

"That he did not have?"

"And the vicomtesse, young, noble, rich and beautiful..."

There was something satanic in the manner in which the dowager pronounced the last word in her list: *beautiful*.

Adèle shivered at it. "Noble and rich," repeated the orphan. I'm not, "but young, but beautiful! Young, I'll soon be sixteen; beautiful, I've been told many times that I am, it was repeated to me with complaisance, but my father especially...and I have memories of...oh, is it possible?"

So saying, she ran to a mirror that was in the dowager's apartment, and that mirror reproduced a face swollen by tears, oppressed by a sleepless night, in which fatigue rendered the scars apparent in a more pronounced manner than usual.

She remained motionless.

"Ugly!" she cried. "Ugly!

"They've deceived me! They've deceived me for entire years!

"Ugly! Ugly!

"So much the better, for I shall go mad, as before. And when one is mad, you see, Madame Dowager, one suffers less; one does not think.

"Mad! Yes, let my reason go astray, let me no longer remember anything, let me forget! Oh, let me forget! Let me forget...or I shall die!"

VI. The Actors

Two years later, on the fifteenth of August, on a Friday, three fiacres pulled by pitiful poorly-harnessed nags, each conducted by a coachman in a blouse, emerged from Valenciennes at four o'clock in the morning and took the road to the Château de Boussu.

Each of those vehicles contained six persons, not counting children, and in the accoutrement of those individuals there was something characteristic that contained both poverty and refinement. The women, in spite of the stifling heat threatened by a cloudless sky, were clad in their mantles, and were making use of them to hide the negligence of their faded garments put on carelessly. As for the men, the strange aspect of their battered hats, their threadbare clothes and their unkempt hair was a marvel. Some, to the great indignation of the ladies, were finishing smoking cigars; others were curling up as best they could in the narrow vehicle in order to resume their slumber, interrupted by such an early departure.

After traveling for two hours, cries were suddenly heard; the first two fiacres stopped and the passengers that filled them descended, with great emotion. The axle of the following carriage had broken on the edge of a muddy pond, and to compound the misfortune, its heavy box, lacking support, had tipped its left-side door into the muddy water of the pond. It was necessary to begin pulling the victims of the catastrophe out of the situation, not very dangerous but unpleasant, in which they found themselves.

They set to work courageously, and succeeded in pulling three women, three men and two dogs on to the highway, their heads, hands and garment covered in mud. They took the thing philosophically; the exclamations of anger quite natural in such a circumstance were soon succeeded by jokes and bursts of laughter. The men offered to complete the journey on foot and to leave the two vehicles to the women; the latter accepted, and three-quarters of an hour after the accident, a customs-officer established at the Boussu post stopped the fiacres, which had arrived at their destination, and asked to inspect them.

Cries of "No, don't open it?" and bursts a laughter departing from the vehicles responded to the customs officer, who nevertheless turned the brass handle of the door and found himself confronted by three young women, almost naked. To repair the damage inflicted on their costume, they had found nothing better, since they had no spare garments, than to rid themselves of the wet and muddy garments and to remain in the vehicle in their underclothes. The customs officer—a brave and courageous customs officer!—turned his eyes away modesty, ran his searching hands over the heap of damp dresses and mantles that encumbered the vehicles and closed the doors again, saying to the coachmen: "You can go."

In the meantime his colleagues had brought down from the imperials of the fiacres, the enormous crates with which they were laden, and they commenced to search them in the presence of one of the travelers who arrived on foot a few minutes later.

The inventory of one of those crates will give an idea of the contents of the others, That white wood crate, with the label of Mademoiselle Zerbine, poorly closed by an iron padlock and a cord extended by two or three pieces of string of another, thinner sort, offered to the gaze once rid of a large sheet that was extended over the exterior surface:

Item 1: a full-length crimson velvet dress with a large golden embroidery, somewhat faded, dappled with stains.

2: a knight's tunic, pink with silver braid.

3: knitted trousers, holed at the knees and the ends of the feet.

4: a pair of red deerskin ankle-boots, soft and spurred.

5: white satin shoes, slightly ragged.

6: two tresses of blonde hair, with little combs to attach them to the head.

7: a sword of small dimension.

8: a sausage wrapped in Joseph paper.

9: a bread roll with hairbrushes.

10: a comb.

11: a pot of rouge.

12: two flat cardboard boxes containing artificial flowers.

13: four belt ribbons.

14. two muslin pocket handkerchiefs, closely imitative of batiste

15. and finally, in a corner, carefully packaged in three napkins, a partially-consumed bottle of wine.

After that crate and a dozen others, the inventory of which was very similar, had been inspected, the old man to whom surveillance of that inspection had been delegated had them loaded on to a cart and came to join the rest of the society at the Château de Boussu.

The remaining members of the society were swearing and storming, finding themselves in great embarrassment at the Château.

Monsieur le Baron de Boistrancourt had written the week before to the associated artistes of the opera troupe exploiting the town of Valenciennes; he desired them to come on the fifteenth of August to perform in the pretty theater of his château a play that he had chosen. He had offered in exchange for that representation a sum well beyond the demands that the theatrical company could have made. Such a favorable bargain has therefore been rapidly concluded, and on the designated day, they had set forth joyfully, for the baron's thousand francs arrived all the more conveniently because for a week, the receipts had barely covered the expenses. The entire week's subsistence therefore reposed on those blessed thousand francs. In all the troupe, I am sure, there was not a single valid écu, not to mention, alas, that the innkeepers of Valenciennes were already holding, by way of security, half the effects of the artistes, who had not been able to pay to drink, to eat, for laundry, for lodgings, the barber, the tailor, the boot-maker or anyone else.

But—O cruel disappointment!—having arrived at the Château de Boussu, they had found the gate closed, seeing the preparations for the fête abandoned, and learned that the baron had departed in a post-chaise the day before, after having fought a duel with an officer in his regiment; with the result that, instead of the good dinner they had been eating in imagination during the journey, instead of the thousand francs on which they had been counting with such great covetousness, they found themselves confronted with a cadaver that was being buried, busy individuals and men of law.

The stage-manger finally reached the steward, and the steward replied to him: "Monsieur, you will be paid as if you had performed, but not today, for Monsieur le Baron's abrupt departure has left me without money. In a week at the latest, you'll receive yours."

"But Monsieur..."

"But Monsieur, it's impossible today..."

The stage-manager came back, his head bowed, to tell the troupe about the cruel disappointment. After having held council, they decided that it was necessary to return to Valenciennes, and told the coachmen to turn around.

The coachmen demanded their money.

"We'll pay you in a week."

"No money, no carriage. Hard cash or feet on the ground."

"How can we give you what we don't have?"

"Feet on the ground! You still owe us for the last trip to Condé; you were to pay for that one with this one; we don't want to travel for nothing, so, feet on the ground!"

"And we'll keep the crates as a pledge until we're paid in full," added another.

Feet on the ground! Feet on the ground!" said the coachmen, opening the carriage doors.

That quarrel amused the whole village, and in spite of the fine promises that the actors tried to give the coachmen, it was necessary to get down and go into an inn, the three poor women in their underclothes along with the others, except that they wrapped themselves in their shawls and carried the rest of their wet clothing in their arms, which they came to hang in front of the hearth, where a large fire of carnation stems was burning, under a pot-hook from which an enormous stewpot was hanging.

Although it was in a poor village inn, the theatrical troupe was no longer sure of its shelter and its supper. The innkeeper, who had witnessed the quarrel with the coachmen, declared that he would not furnish anything on credit. It was necessary at any price that they get out of that painful situation; Mademoiselle Zerbine made the sacrifice. She detached from her ears a magnificent pair of earrings, the last debris of her former opulence. The offer of that pledge, which was worth a hundred francs, mollified the conductors, who finally consented to take the troupe back to Valenciennes.

That important negotiation concluded, everyone sat down at table, relatives and enemies, artistes and coachmen, and they had a joyful meal, in which Mademoiselle Zerbine's sausage and bottle of wine, combined with a few other comestibles brought by the actors, were the most exquisite dishes. Dairy produce, eggs and a few slices carved from enormous six-livre loaves completed the frugal collation. Before departing, everyone emptied his purse and put everything that it contained together; it was found that they were rich enough to pay the bill; that good news finished dissipating the worries caused by the disappointments of the day, and everyone climbed back into the fiacres with beaming faces and laughter on their lips. O poverty, poverty, what good joys and insouciant happiness you have!

The fifteenth of August was both Madame la Baronne's feast day and the anniversary of her birth. Paul had resolved to celebrate that day with a ball that would bring together the elite of the society of Valenciennes and its environs. In addition to the pleasures of dancing, he wanted to provide a magnificent meal, fireworks and a spectacle. Everything was ready the day before, except for an important crate of comestibles ordered from Paris, which had not arrived. Doubtless it had been stopped in Valenciennes by some accident. Paul departed in the evening in a calèche in order to go and claim it himself, promising his wife to return early the next morning.

A league from the château he met the messenger who as bringing him the crate about which he was worried; Paul turned around joyfully.

His first concern, on arriving, was to show himself in his wife's apartment; the latter was in the arms of the Vicomte de Niergnies. The vicomte and the baron went out; two pistol shots were exchanged; the vicomte fell and the baron returned to his wife's bedroom.

"Everything between us is finished, Madame; I shall return your dowry to you and I forbid you to bear my name; on those conditions, if you refrain from infringing them, you are free."

Post horses took him away five minutes later on the road to Paris, where he arrived the next day in a state of extreme agitation and despair.

Deceived by her! By the person he loved so tenderly! By the person he had surrounded by so much happiness! Deceived in a cowardly fashion, and for a brazen libertine! The ingrate! He had sacrificed everything for her! He had preferred her deceptive tenderness to the devoted tenderness of poor Adèle. Oh, it was not Adèle who would have deceived him thus!

Into what abyss does he not find himself cast by that treason! No more repose, no more happiness, nothing, except dishonor and ridicule, Ridicule! Malediction upon her! He has not chastised her sufficiently; he should have killed her as he had killed her accomplice.

Who will love him, now that his mother is dead? Who will console him…? Nothing, nothing any longer, except dishonor and ridicule!

For an entire month, that was his obsession.

Time bought him scant consolation, for Paul was obstinate in living in solitude, and solitude further augments melancholy. Another might have sought to distract himself in society, and doubtless would have succeeded in doing so, but, as we have said, Paul had preserved from his first education a residue of candor and tenderness that had his new mores had not been able to destroy, and which returned to seize him when he found himself under the weight of a chagrin. Instead of shaking off his dolors like a man of experience, he collapsed under those dolors with the deception of a naïve soul.

Soon, Paul fell ill.

Whatever suffering it causes one to experience, illness has nothing frightful when one has a mother, a sister, a wife of a mistress watching by one's beside, ready to console and soothe at the first plant. But to be lying on a bed of pain in the midst of indifferent mercenaries, to think that one is paying for the hand that advances to sustain one's burning head, to seek in vain a compassionate gaze, not to hear an encouraging voice, oh, that is horrible, more horrible than the fever that makes one tremble, more horrible than the blood that spread from the breast over the pale lips. No woman was stationed beside Paul's bed, no woman! For it would be a blasphemy to name thus the ignoble and stunted creature who sold him, for five francs a day, care calculated with the same avarice that a merchant puts into weighting his goods.

She gave him five francs' worth, conscientiously, but not a centime more. When he was thirsty, she gave him something to drink; when he had thrown off his blankets from his burning sides, she readjusted them. Of the rest, alas, nothing; none, my good sister, of the affection that you put into watching over your dying brother, you, a frail young woman, who became strong because I was weak!

How could one forget the gentle inflections of your voice, which roused such good courage? Your ingenious deceptions gave hope, and you made efforts to prevent your tears from flowing, your large tears, which flowed so abundantly when you turned your head away. To believe you, the next day would bring the cure, and without adding faith to it, I was glad to hear those promises. Before I had asked for it, the cup brought the salutary beverage to my lips; and when drowsiness closed my eyes, you let your hand fall on to your knees and you wept freely. My sister, my good sister, what charms I experience in those sad, sweet memories, in tracing the lines that I am writing, and which will fill your eyes with tears when you read them, as my eyes are filling with tears as I write them. For we are far from one another now, my poor sister, and if your brother falls ill, he too will have to buy cares and compassion from those whose métier is to sell it!

Paul suffered greatly, therefore, from his isolation, suffering for the first time without having is mother, his good and saintly mother, beside him. One day, one of his friends came to visit him and found him in one of those fits of despair to which the weakness of the organs and the irritation of the fibers render invalids so susceptible. The friend counseled him to summon to his bedside a "chariotte" sister. Paul rejected such an idea; he did not want beside him a young nun crammed with orisons who would have given him prayers instead of tisane. He finally yielded, but more out of fatigue than conviction, and the chariotte was requested.

The chariottes are pious young women devoted to caring for the sick in exchange for a retribution that serves them to lavish good works upon the poor; in the religious hierarchy they are the humblest of all the orders; like the Sisters of Charity, they do not make vows and can quit the veil and the black robe whenever they wish in order to recover a secular costume and way of life. There are, however, few examples of such renunciations, and although permitted and in the spirit of their institution, the holy women regard it nevertheless as an apostasy.

A sister arrived, therefore, at the home of the Baron de Boistrancourt, established herself at his bedside, and lavished cares on him as tender as they were devoted

Certainly, it was a great consolation for the young man to have that woman by his side, that woman whom he called by the name of sister, whom nothing discouraged, and who rendered him, with a celestial modesty, the most repulsive cares; yes, certainly, it was a great consolation to him, and when he became less ill, when the transports of fever were succeeded by the mild languor of convalescence, he could not help shedding tears, for misfortune and suffering purify the soul and render it more sensible; he could not, I say, prevent himself from shedding tears, on learning that Sister Ambroisine was to be replaced beside him by another nun.

Hazard dictated that the other nun in question was Sister Adèle Cambernis.

After her fatal conversation with the dowager Aldegonde she had quit the Château de Boussu immediately, and in an insensate crisis of despair, having arrived in Valenciennes, she had written to the baronne, her benefactress; she had said that Paul loved the vicomtesse and that she did not want to become an obstacle to his happiness. She indicated her retreat to the baronne, and begged her to give her he means to enter a convent. The baronne came to see Adèle but her tears and supplications could do nothing against the young woman's resolution; it was necessary for Madame de Boistrancourt to take her to Paris and enter her in a seminary of chariottes, Adèle also obtained from her benefactress that she would keep the most complete mystery regarding the decision she had made. The marriage of Paul with Vicomtesse Marie de Bergues had followed not long after the flight of Mademoiselle Cambernis.

One can imagine the emotion that they both experienced in finding one another again in such an unexpected manner.

Paul recounted his misfortune to the woman whom he had rendered so unhappy himself; she listened in silence.

"So, I am isolated, without amour, without affection, for the rest of my life; no one in the world to love me, for my mother is dead, and you, Adèle, can no longer love me, alas. And yet Heaven is my witness that I would pay for your amour at the price of the rest of my life; that that amour alone could render me repose and happiness!"

"You could be happy, Paul? Happy with my amour? Oh, don't say such things to me, don't deceive me thus!"

"You're mistaken, Adèle. Tell me, do you believe that a man who has only found lies in the holiest affections, a man who nearly died from the loss of those affections, could not be rendered happy by a true love?"

"Shut up, shut up," she said, "in the name of Heaven, shut up, for you don't know to what such culpable temptations you're exposing me."

"Adèle, my Adèle!"

"Lord, have pity on me. My God, my God, come to my aid!"

The next day, the chariottes learned that Sister Adèle was going to depart for London with Baron de Boistrancourt. That day, there were solemn prayers to ask God not to abandon the culpable sister to a fatal impenitence, and that he would deign to touch her heart with repentance.

VII. A Conversation

One winter morning in the year 1830, the young and pretty Marquise de Senançay, the wife of the old lieutenant-general commanding the third military division, was drawing up the list of people that she ought to invite to a great ball, the preparations for which had preoccupied her for a week. Sitting familiarly by Madame de Senançay's side, a young aide-de-camp with a very black moustache and a conceited smile was amusing himself turning each of the invitees to ridicule as the marquise named them. She arrived at the name of Baronne de Boistrancourt.

"If you want to invite all her lovers, your drawing room will be full, Louise."

"We'll only invite the present one, and we'll leave the past behind," the marquise replied.

"If you invited the past, the present and the future, you might as well open your drawing room to all comers."

"Tell me, Casimir, I was assured yesterday that her husband's regiment is to be garrisoned in this town."

"That's true, my friend."

"It will be a curious thing to put them in one another's presence; I'm impatient to see what a face they'll put on."

"It will be all the funnier because the Baron doesn't know that his wife has made the choice of this town for her residence."

"The choice of his wife! You mean the choice of Major Saint-Vincent."

"Of Major Saint-Vincent or Captain Bournonval."

"Naughty!"

239

"And Baron de Boistrancourt's mistress, will you invite her?"

"Fie! Me, receive such a creature?"

"That woman is an entire romance. Can you imagine that during the war in Spain, she followed the colonel even into battle, dressed as a man? Without her, it's said, he'd be dead."

"How's that?"

At that time, as you know, I was General Aubencourt's aide-de-camp; the Baron was only a lieutenant-colonel, but he was in command of his regiment because the colonel was gravely ill—a malady from which, in parenthesis, the old Chouan died."

"The old Chouan! There's a word worthy of a liberal of your species. Why do you defer thus to manners that reek of the parvenu, which make one nauseous?"

"That doesn't happen to me anymore, pretty ultra." And he opened the marquise's peignoir and gave her beautiful shoulders a tender and familiar kiss. The marquise put her arm around Casimir's neck and returned his kiss on the lips.

"And the end, or rather the beginning, of your story, Monsieur?" demanded Madame de Senançay, nestling on the sofa in such a way as to repose her head on the aide-de-camp's shoulder.

"I was sent by my general to Lieutenant-Colonel Boistrancourt to give him the order to occupy, with his regiment, a very important military position, which was defended by a numerous party of Spaniards. The colonel had his mistress with him. 'Adèle,' he said, 'return to the tent.' She hesitated, 'Do as I ask,' he repeated. His mistress didn't listen, and transported her gaze to a bush fifty or sixty paces away. Suddenly, she threw herself in front of the colonel, shoved him forcefully, and fell, her

240

chest pierced by a bullet. She had seen a Spaniard hiding behind the bush, and when he took aim at the colonel she had immediately thrown herself in front of him."

"That's a veritable chapter of a romance."

"Isn't it my angel?"

"Is it true, Casimir, that the woman was a nun?"

"So it's said, but I don't know anything positive in that regard."

"And the colonel drags that everywhere with him?"

"Everywhere."

"He loves her very much, then?"

"He loves her, he loves her—I don't know to what point; I believe he holds on to her above all out of habit and human respect."

"Human respect! But human respect demands, rather, that he put an end to such a scandal and doesn't attach himself in that fashion."

Casmir stood up and picked up his hat in order to leave.

"Already?" said the marquise, with a delightful little moue.

"Its two o'clock, Louise, and you know that the general is going to come back."

"Go, then, since it's necessary, but come to the prefecture this evening."

"I'll be there early."

And try not to spend entire hours again with Madame de Trancy, whom I detest."

"Jealous!"

"Would you prefer it if I wasn't, Casimir?"

"Oh no, my darling."

"By the way, my God, I forgot to tell you some good news. I hope that the general will soon be leaving to carry out an inspection in the department, a week-long inspection. That's lucky, because Monsieur de Saint-Ans, my husband's other aide-de-camp, will accompany him on the voyage, and you'll stay here, unless you prefer..."

The aide-de-camp came to kiss the marquise tenderly, and left; a few minutes later, the general came in, and in the same way as the aide-de-camp, he kissed the marquise.

"Well, my friend, I hope that wretched inspection won't be necessary, and that you won't be making it."

"I hardly dare tell you, Louise, but it's necessary that I go, and that I leave tomorrow."

"That's very annoying," said the marquise. She had joy in her heart.

VIII. What is necessary to make an end

Time had gradually tendered heavy to Colonel Paul de Boistrancourt the bonds that united him with the daughter of Monsieur Cambernis. Young and unhappy, he had accepted the love of that woman with enthusiasm; but experience had come to temper his imagination and harden his heart. Now that age had altered Adèle's beauty and habit had destroyed the prestige and charm of a romantic union, the colonel was, to use the aide-de-camp Casimir's expression, regretfully dragging the poor woman everywhere, who fatigued him with an exaggerated tenderness. Certainly, he no longer loved her, so he did not hesitate to offend a tender and devoted soul, not by ill-treatment, of which he was incapable, but by insouciance, by neglecting her, believing that he was fulfilling all his duties toward her provided that, to use the common expression, he conducted himself well in her regard.

Adèle was suffering greatly, but no complaint ever emerged from her mouth; she wept in secret; in secret she deplored such a fatal change; as for her conduct in the colonel's regard, it was still the same: incessantly benevolent, attentive, obliging—perhaps too obliging—trembling under his gaze, ready to obey the most unjust orders, resigning herself to his demands and his caprices, whatever they might be.

The colonel had become a man of good fortune, and did not take the trouble to hide those he obtained. Adèle, poor Adèle, knew them all: let the women reading these pages judge the despair that those infidelities caused her. The women—for it is nor given to men to understand it; they are prevented by their manner of seeing in that subject, by their liberal education and above all by their less exquisite delicacy. The infidelity that he commits seems insignificant or trivial to a man; he cannot conceive the dolorous blow with which he is striking the person who has invested in him her dreams of happiness, her amour her entire life, her future.

If the colonel did not pride himself on fidelity, he was, on the other hand, very jealous. It is a sad thing that jealousy can exist without amour. By virtue of a contortion, we reject on to the woman who cherishes us the lack of esteem that we have four ourselves, for in general, it is by ourselves that we judge others; hence the ignoble suspicion that outrages and profanes, the insult to a loving heart of a heart that no longer understands love. The colonel was jealous, pettily jealous, jealous with espionage and without delicacy; Adèle had to live in solitude; the most innocent visits, a smile or a word angered the colonel, made him proffer the most humiliating reproaches or take precautions that were even more humiliating.

And yet, Adèle still loved him, Adèle would still have given her life for him, and if he did not have tender words for her, confidential conversations, tender gazes, at least she could hear him, find herself close to him. For that soul broken by misfortune to which nothing remained but its amour, there was still joy in that.

A passion that had taken possession energetically of the colonel's soul had contributed more than satiety to destroying Paul's amour for Adèle. The passion in question deprives all others of their prestige, presents objects and sensations from a clear, dry and cold viewpoint; it absorbs the faculties entirely, invades the mind and kills the heart; it displays a goal, and as soon as it is attained, it displays another more attractive; it has no remedy, and like Greek fire it burns inextinguishably.

The colonel was ambitious.

Ambitious! Not with a paltry and vulgar ambition but an ardent and unbridled ambition. Ambition occupies all the activity of his energetic imagination; it is scornful of obstacles; the more rapidly he has progressed in his career of honors, a colonel at thirty-three, the more he experiences the need to progress more rapidly still. Nothing can impede him; nothing can prevent him; he wants to be a peer of France.

Peers are to be created in a month's time; he wants to be in that number; it is necessary. Once a peer, he can offer to the ministry a deadly opposition or a faithful alliance. Young, with courage, talent and perseverance, it does not matter which of the two paths will open; his future is certain; if the power refuses to elevate him, he will elevate himself over the ruins of the power

To think that all that depends on his nomination to the peerage, to think that within two months that nomination can take place, and to doubt, to wait…it will not be long before he knows the result of the steps taken by his aunt, the dowager so powerful in the court, who was at odds with him, badly, for such a long time. It is not without difficulty that he has been able to bring about a reconciliation; only the hope of seeing her nephew become a peer of France has softened her. Finally, she has promised to write to tell him the result of her maneuvers; he will doubtless find a letter from her today, arriving from Beaugency. That is why he is thinking in such a somber manner about Mademoiselle Cambernis.

"The post. Has any post arrived for me?"

"Yes, Colonel, it's waiting for you, charged with dispatches that are for your eyes only."

He opens the letter and reads it avidly.

My nephew, I obtained a formal promise from His Majesty yesterday of your nomination to the peerage. These evening, when I renewed my thanks to the king, he said to me: "Madame dowager de Boistrancourt, I regret that I am obliged to retract the promise that I made yesterday, but it has been made known to me that your son is living publicly with a nun who fled her convent, and that he had quit his wife for that wretch. Now I make you the judge yourself, would it not be to authorize such conduct, would it not be to share the complicity, to nominate your nephew to the peerage?"

To deny it was impossible. "Sire," I replied, "the scandal of which you speak no longer exists. My nephew has broken off culpable and scandalous relations; he is reconciled with his wife, and the first step made for that reconciliation was a complete rupture with his mistress."

"Give me proof," replied the king, "and on my faith as a knight and a Christian, I swear to you that your nephew will be a peer of France."

It is up to you, my nephew, to know what it remains for you to do; think that time is pressing and that you have enemies interested in dooming you.

Your aunt,

Baronne Aldegonde,
Dowager de Boistrancourt.

The colonel remained pensive for a few moments. And then, his head burning, not knowing on what projects to settle, but resolved to become a peer of France, he went into the apartment where Adèle was waiting; the latter read in Paul's face that a great misfortune threatened her, and became pale and tremulous.

The colonel threw himself into an armchair without pronouncing a word, still absorbed by his thoughts.

"Are you suffering, Colonel? Why this sadness?"

"Listen Adèle, you know how much I loved you."

"You don't love me any longer?" she asked

"Let's not argue about words, for time is pressing. Answer me: do you love me?"

"Paul, do you have to ask me that?"

"Do you still love me with that love worthy of the greatest sacrifices? Nothing would make you recoil before any proof of devotion whatsoever?"

"Nothing, Paul."

"Not even..." He hesitated, for he understood how cowardly he was at that moment.

"Speak, speak, in the name of Heaven," said Adèle, with the sang-froid of a horrible despair. "You're going to announce frightful news to me, but no matter, it will be less frightful than such uncertainty."

"If it were necessary for us to separate?"

"Separate! My God, have I heard correctly? Separate, Paul! But I only have you in the world for support, for affection, nothing but you alone."

"Have no fear, Adèle; a brilliant fate..."

"Oh, Monsieur!"

"It's a dolorous sacrifice, for me as for you, but necessity demands it."

She folded her arms and looked at the colonel in silence; then she suddenly burst into tears and threw herself t Paul's feet.

"Never! Never! Oh, don't demand it!"

"I have duties to fulfill with you, Madame; I'll fulfill them; I'll hand in my resignation, since the king demands it; we'll depart tomorrow for the Château de Boussu."

"Your resignation! You, renounce your career! You, lose your future for me!"

"Read this letter, Madame, if you doubt it."

She took the dowager's letter and read it slowly; her tears flowed one by one over her pale and burning cheeks.

In the end she said, with a strange smile and a hollow and scarcely intelligible voice: "You'll be a peer of France."

IX. Conclusion

"I'm curious, Casimir," said the Marquise de Senançay two days later to her husband's aide-de-camp, after the third quadrille of her ball, "I'm very curious to know what figure the colonel will cut when he finds himself in the presence of his wife."

At the same time, a domestic announced: "Monsieur le Baron and Madame la Baronne de Boistrancourt."

The baronne was leaning with grace and almost tenderly on her husband's arm.

"What are these stupid stories you've told me, then, about a duel, a separation and a nun?"

"They're true, Madame," replied the aide-de-camp, "they're true but they're finished."

"Why and how?"

"Because Monsieur le Colonel is a peer of France."

At that moment the orchestra started to play a quadrille, and Casimir went to find his dancing partner, Madame la Baronne, who received with an amiable ease the congratulations of the officer on the return of her husband and the high office that he had just been awarded.

In the meantime, two women climbed into the diligence to Paris.

One of them was named Zerbine. Hissed at the Théâtre de Beaugency, she was returning to Paris, where she hoped to contract another engagement for the province. A lady in tears, whom no one conducted to the vehicle, took her place beside the actress. On an overnight bag that bore the address of the lady and which she placed under her feet, Zerbine read: *Mad. Cambernis, to Tarbes (département des Pyrénées)*.

But the lady did not go to her destination, for she fell ill on the way and it was necessary for her to stop in Paris. Zerbine, who gave her care throughout the journey, the good Zerbine, received this response from the physician she had summoned on arrival in Paris:

"She won't last the night."

ALSO FROM BLACK COAT PRESS